Head Hunters

Published by Honno
'Ailsa Craig', Heol y Cawl, Dinas Powys
South Glamorgan, Wales, CF64 4AH

1 2 3 4 5 6 7 8 9 10

A catalogue record for this book is available from the British Library.

ISBN 978 1 906784 02 7

Published with the financial assistance of the Welsh Books Council

Cover image: Giselle Burns
Cover design: Giselle Burns

Printed in Wales by Gomer

Head Hunters

by

Claire Peate

HONNO MODERN FICTION

For Lesley, for the emails

With thanks to Richard Neave and Denise Richards for introducing me to the world of facial reconstruction. Thanks also to Dr John Crook, Winchester Cathedral's archaeologist, for sharing his knowledge of what lies beneath. And finally thanks to Jane and Hugh for their help on matters of religion, and their literary support over the years.

One

Caer Caradoc rose sharply out of the Carmarthenshire landscape, a gloomy mass against a darkening November afternoon sky. At its foot sat an old farmhouse, only the strings of fairy lights in the windows giving any indication that there was life in this remote landscape.

Professor Hilary De Lacey gamely mounted the slopes, her three-inch lilac stilettos sinking holes into the hardened earth. With one hand she pressed an enormous lilac hat to her head, the gales whipping at it, scattering its lilac silk flowers in all directions. With the other hand she clutched her mobile phone.

"MUM!"

Hilary turned. At the foot of the hill her daughter was attempting to follow her, grasping at the mounds of white voile and satin of her wedding dress, her veil lifted straight towards the heavens. "Mum what the *bloody hell* are you doing?" she shouted over the howling wind.

"Don't worry dear, Hilary called back, steadying herself on a ledge of rock. "Just want some signal to make a phone call. We've been out of signal all weekend. You go back in – I'll be back in a—"

"No. I'm sorry," the bride snapped, scraping her white silk shoes against the rocks as she stomped towards her mother, "I meant what the *bloody hell are you doing*?"

"Isobel! There's no need for—"

"It's. My. Wedding."

"I know darling—" Hilary put her hand on the bride's bare shoulders. "You must be frozen. Go back in and—"

"No! You bloody come back in! You put that bloody phone down and come in. It's getting dark! And I'm *sick* of your work getting in the way of everything. We're going to cut the cake!"

"Look darling, it's starting to rain. And it's freezing. Go in and I'll be with you in two minutes. Just let me make a quick phone call."

"What about the cake?"

But Hilary had already turned and continued her ascent.

Wild with anger the bride pounded down the hill, skirts and veil and expletives flying as she stormed back to her wedding reception.

Reaching the summit Hilary couldn't help but walk around the remains of what she immediately recognised as an early iron-age hill-fort.

"Oh superb! Superb!" She clambered the mounds. "Ditch here, good oval shape to it of...about two acres. Counterscarp bank over there. And hut circles, possibly. So magnificent..."

Her phone beeped. And beeped again. And again.

She held it up and scrolled the menu.

It beeped again.

She had had four missed calls.

It beeped again.

Five missed calls.

She checked the numbers. They were from her Site Manager, the very man she had wanted to call all weekend.

Being in charge of the Kings Cross Archaeological dig was the single most important role Hilary had been given in what was already a distinguished thirty-year career in archaeology. The Kings Cross Dig had come completely out of the blue, starting when a routine health and safety check of the overground station sensationally revealed that the whole western section of the station was subsiding.

The Museum of London Archaeology Service had taken the call early on and was instructed from on high to excavate *pretty bloody quickly do you understand* to minimise disruption on the rail network. The contractors needed to begin rebuilding the station within three weeks of it being closed to the public. Hilary knew that the mayor's office had made significant efforts to find a way around legislation that stated archaeological excavations must be allowed to take place before any new building work occurred; but eventually they relented. Under extreme pressure the Museum of London Archaeology Service, with Hilary put in charge, was forced to agree to spend just three weeks conducting what would be a token archaeological investigation under platforms eight through to eleven. Teams of archaeologists would work shifts, twenty-four hours a day, every day. They would unearth a section, record it, clear it, and then move on to the next section, with the construction teams moving in. And so it would go on, archaeologists and builders, moving side by side across the site.

Hilary had complained bitterly, after all it would be near impossible and certainly very unpleasant to work shoulder to shoulder with the construction people with their heavy machinery and noxious building materials. She was winning the argument to buy more time for the dig when a man from a government office had pulled up at the dig site in a black Daimler. He gave a succinct presentation to the archaeologists and to the builders on the impact of closing Kings Cross station. He put the situation into a context that no-one could argue with. No-one knew his name, no-one knew which department he represented, but everyone agreed he had a very nice car and that his suit would have cost more than their individual monthly salaries.

Three weeks it was, then.

"William? It's Hilary De Lacey!"

"Hilary! Jesus, Prof, I can hardly hear you. Where are you?"

"I'm in an early iron-age hill-fort would you believe." She sank below a high ditch, out of the worst of the squalls. She checked the display: still two bars of signal. "But never mind that – has it turned up?" Her heart was pounding in her chest.

The Site Manager gave a laugh which sounded tinny and hollow up on the darkening summit of Caer Caradoc. "At eleven yesterday morning we finally cleared Brill Farm and all of its Late Medieval outbuildings from beneath platforms ten and eleven..."

"Yes..."

"And below the outbuildings were earlier layers of crops: wheat, corn. Evidence of flooding several times. All as

4

predicted..."

"And The Brill William! What about The Brill? Did you find any evidence of Caesar's camp there?"

There was a pause. "No. We didn't find any Roman camp."

"What?" Hilary snapped. The hand that had been pinning her hat to her head dropped to her side and in an instant the hat was snatched away in a gust of icy wind and tossed down the slope, disappearing into a gloomy copse at the foot of the hill. "But Brill Farm — the name! The location! Everything pointed to it..."

"Oh no. It's better than finding the Roman Camp."

"No...?"

"Yes." The Site Manager paused. "We found *bodies*."

"Bodies? You've found bodies?" Hilary held her breath. "And absolutely no indication of the Roman fort? Not even evidence of post holes?"

"No postholes. No fort. But we did find bodies."

"What layer? From when? Are they connected to the medieval farmhouse in any way? How many bodies are there?"

"Can't you get here; I think you should get here." The voice on the phone, however tinny and distant was unmistakably tense with excitement.

"Dammit, I'm stuck at my daughter's wedding in Wales, you know that. I'm back tomorrow. Tell me!"

"OK then, we found more than nine hundred bodies..."

"*Nine hundred*!"

The Site Manager was laughing now. "That's twenty-four hour archaeology for you."

"But…"

"The bodies are in mass pits," the Site Manager was saying, "many pits, eight to twelve feet deep and thirty feet wide, extending from the station concourse out towards the tracks. There's more; we haven't even begun to dig the west side of the site yet but we already know the pits extend out that way." He paused. "And they're deep down. *Deep down.*"

For the first time that day Hilary felt her throat tighten and tears of joy prick behind her eyes. "You're saying the bodies are pre-medieval?"

"Unquestionably." The Site Manager was unable to conceal his excitement. "Once the Home Office pathologists gave us the all-clear we were free to examine the pits…and it appears your initial theory could well be right."

Hilary took a deep breath. "Have all the archaeology teams been briefed? Have you issued everyone with a confidentiality contract?"

"Done and signed." She could hear the grin in his voice. "Looks like we found her, Prof."

She looked down at the lights in the farmhouse.

"I'm on my way."

Two

In a squeal of brakes the scarlet Alfa Romeo mounted the stone curb and skidded into the Close. Deftly the Very Reverend Archie Cartwright, Dean of Winchester, slammed on the brakes, yanked the wheel and the car shuddered into the ancient covered passageway that ran between the Cathedral's south transept and the Chapter House.

He pulled to a halt half way down, beside an unimposing door marked *staff entrance* tucked in to an alcove. He cut the engine and slowly sank down on to the red leather steering wheel.

He was numb from the chin down. How long had he been driving? He peered sideways at the clock display. 12.17am.

Five and a half hours. Five and a half hours he'd been on the road! And it wasn't even over yet. Now he had a boot full of Winchester Treasures Through the Ages that he had to deposit in the Cathedral safe before he could finally get some sleep. He ran his hands through his messed-up blonde hair and rubbed his eyes so hard he could see little pricks of light against his eyelids. Sleep...the thought of it made him dizzy. He hadn't had any sleep since Thursday.

Aah, Angela.

The exhibition of Church Treasures Through the Ages had been a rip-roaring success: plenty of cover in the media, a good opportunity to network, and in particular to network with the very lovely Reverend Angela Jackson from Truro (who had been so very warm and welcoming).

Above all, love each other deeply, because love covers over a multitude of sins. Offer hospitality to one another without grumbling Peter 4: 8.

Archie had two weeks holiday coming up and he could hardly wait for the moment when he would be free and could bomb it down to Truro and offer up a bit more of that hospitality without grumbling that the Reverend Jackson had so enjoyed. It was rare that he ever wanted to see a woman again, but Angela...well, maybe Angela was something different? From the time he had spent with her, he sensed something of the kindred spirit in her. Another lost soul...

Archie sighed and raised himself up off the wheel.

For a very brief moment he contemplated leaving the WTTtA in the boot of his car. After all, his pride and joy was kitted out with the best alarm system money could buy.

Tempting...

But no – he couldn't leave it overnight. There had been a spate of joyriding incidents in the city recently and suppose his car was taken and the Winchester treasure stolen? Bishop MacNeath would kill him. Literally *kill him*. Come at him in the Presbytery and cut him down like a modern day Thomas A'Becket. Never mind that Archie was a broad-built six foot three and MacNeath's pie-filled middle-aged bulk barely came up to his chest. Men like the Bishop of Wessex were the type one had to watch; they waddled and wheezed and panted red-faced around the place, lulling you into a false sense of security, and then one day, fuelled by anger and revenge, performed amazing feats of agility.

Archie shivered.

He definitely ought to get the treasure from the boot.

Uncurling himself from his sports seat and feeling the blood flow back to his legs he hobbled his way to the back of the car. Odd…

He paused by the boot and looked about. It was unusually dark tonight. It took him a moment to realise that the only light to find its way down the Slype was coming from the far-off orange lanterns in the Close. There were three old lanterns that should be illuminating the covered passageway but none was working.

It was the Archdeacon: the man must have forgotten to leave the lights on. Nevermind – there was just enough light with which to navigate between the boot and the Cathedral door, treasures in hand.

Grabbing a few of the smaller platters and the vulgar Chalice of St Aidan, Archie left the still full boot open and, squeezing past the car, stepped up to the unassuming, narrow door He punched the door code into the security panel.

He paused.

There was no familiar beep; no click of the mechanism.

Squinting in the dark he could see, now, that the door was already ajar.

Tentatively, Archie pushed it further open. It creaked. Groping around to his left he found the light switch and in a blaze of white light the South Transept was illuminated.

"What the—" He was thrown to the ground by a figure

who had darted out from the direction of the Chapter Room and raced past him through the half-opened door. The treasures he'd been carrying clattered to the floor.

Scrambling to his feet he bolted back into the Slype. He could see someone running down the lane. He chased after them, his Converse All-Stars slipping on the wet path.

"Damn it!" He drew to a halt, panting, as the lane opened up on to Colebrook Street. Which way did he go now? The intruder had probably turned right, away from the Cathedral, but he couldn't see anyone: it would be hopeless to even attempt to find them.

He caught his breath and, slowly, made his way back towards the Cathedral and the open car boot of Winchester treasures. Now accustomed to the dark he could see that the lanterns in the Slype had all been smashed, the shards of glass crunching beneath his feet.

The Bish was going to have his head for this.

And Kwik Fit was going to have the contents of his wallet for four new tyres.

Back at his car he locked the rest of the treasures in the boot and, entering the Cathedral, picked up the remaining dented treasures and began the long walk down the darkened transept towards the vaults.

It was strange, he thought, that he wasn't more on edge. After all, he *had* just witnessed a break-in. He *had* been thrown to the floor. The Bishop *would* be wild with rage. His tyres were going to cost him a *packet.* But actually he felt quite calm about it all.

In a half-daze he unlocked the door to the vaults and like an automaton he walked up to the safe, fishing the heavy old key out from his pocket and inserting it into the correspondingly ancient lock.

Perhaps he felt so calm because, from the very brief glimpse he'd had of the intruder, he'd seen that it had been an extraordinarily beautiful woman running away from him. He regularly spent time with the Hampshire criminal underclass, bending their ears to the word of God, but never had he met one of them he would consider taking out to dinner.

Three

Kate put the phone down and looked at the neat and orderly notes listed on her old notepad. The daily call to the police station was always disappointing; the standard medley of provincial city-centre brawls and unimaginative arson attacks. Last night was a variation but no more stimulating. There had been two events: a break-in at the Cathedral but nothing had been taken, and a joyrider had been caught on the bypass doing a hundred-and-three in a Fiesta. She tapped her pencil on the pad as she contemplated the two leads. The joyrider was eleven, so the story did have legs. And he was from a family of known trouble makers. Was there a spin-off feature on the state of British families? The breakdown of parent power? Society in decline? Possibly.

Neither was going to be headline news though.

Her nemesis Lynn Paget had, once again, been given the big story of the day. It hadn't come as a surprise to Kate: Lynn always got the big stories, despite having absolutely no journalistic talent whatsoever. She did, however, have other skills which she put to full use. At thirty-eight she was ten years Kate's senior but the age gap between them was blurred by Kate's sober-suited drabness and Lynn's short-skirted tight-bloused wardrobe. Lynn was always made-up, hair perfect, immaculately presented and dressed for a cocktail lounge rather than the shabby beige offices of the *Winchester Echo*. Pouting by the water cooler, bending over her desk, crossing her long slim legs in a meeting, Lynn Paget had a way of getting exactly what she wanted by exerting her own brand of power over the male senior management. Their boss, Dr Evil, had actually acknowledged at last year's Christmas party that Lynn had only made it to the senior position she was in because she was one of life's *graspers.* Kate had choked on her luxury mince pie but then Dr Evil, realising his mistake, had gone on to explain that it was meant in a purely professional sense, that Lynn got her teeth into a story and, going for it, she bled it dry.

And *that* was why Lynn had been put on the breaking story: the triple murders down at Pit Close Farm, despite having a prior appointment with a local celebrity she'd been setting up for weeks.

It was always the same, and Kate had always accepted it. But not this time.

"I can cover the story. Lynn shouldn't have to postpone her celebrity interview, she's been trying to arrange it for weeks. And anyway, I used to live near Pit Close Farm." She'd marched straight to Dr Evil's office and practically begged him for the story. He'd sat there as he always did, squinting and leering slightly, stroking the edge of his desk like a Bond villain.

"It's quite a nasty situation up there on the farm. It's not for you Kate, my girl. Bits of people all over the place. Half the wife was stuffed into the washing machine and put on a wool cycle. Not for my little Jane Austen in the making, eh?" *Stroke, stroke, stroke.*

Like a church funds appeal Kate could feel the red bar rising.

"But one of the murdered party was a child! Don't you think Lynn might react badly if she got involved: her sister has just had a baby."

"Lynn can handle herself just fine. She's a big girl. She has a passion for this kind of story and she has the professional detachment needed to stand back from the story and report it objectively."

Kate snorted.

"Now you stop fretting about other people and run along and chase up those two stories I gave you earlier." Her boss winked at her with his one good eye. "Both great leads Kate – both great opportunities for you to do us all proud, eh?"

Stroke, stroke, stroke.

She'd been shocked at herself, storming out of his office and fighting an overwhelming urge to stick two fingers up at him.

Where did this anger come from? Partly it was directed at Lynn. It sickened her the way Dr Evil and all the men in the office fawned over her, falling over in a bid to please her: everyone knew that when Lynn Paget worked late it wasn't because of a heavy workload.

She sighed and savagely tied the thin mousey hair back off her face with an elastic band and, flicking back a page in her notebook, chewed her already well-gnawed nails while she read her notes on the other story. Break-in. Female. Possibly something in that? Nothing taken, nothing disturbed. Cathedral door left open. Surely the woman, attractive apparently, was just an opportunist wanting to have an empty Cathedral to herself? Hardly headline stuff. OK there was two million in silver Church treasures in an open car boot outside, but not even that had been touched. What kind of a story was it: *door left open, burglar walks in, man returns, burglar leaves empty handed.*

Kicking off her plastic shoes she leant back in the chair and deliberated who would be the subject of the second page of the *Winchester Echo* that evening. Would it be the luckless young joyrider from a broken home or the beautiful trespasser who missed an opportunity to get rich quick?

Which story would allow her to stretch those journalistic legs and show them just what she was capable of; to demonstrate that there was a deeper journalistic talent at the *Winchester Echo* than just Ms Paget's sensationalistic, thin reporting? Which story could she mine to get to the real issues underneath that the people wanted to read about…

The Cathedral intruder or the joyrider?

She turned to her contacts book and started to leaf through the pages.

She'd contact his school first.

Four

Edgar Thompson sat rigid on the grey plastic chair, clammy hands balled in his lap. He could feel the prickle of a bead of sweat as it ran from between his shoulders down to the small of his back; thank goodness he was wearing his suit jacket and wasn't going to have to endure all these new colleagues getting an eyeful of his wet-shirted back. Still – looking at everyone else filing in to the Board Room he was painfully high-profile, being so over dressed. Not even the managers wore suits. For a moment he felt, in the pit of his stomach, a feeling he had not felt since he had been at school; turning up at the school gates in an oversize blazer with *no one else* wearing any sort of jacket: he'd always got it wrong. He might as well be sporting full James-Bond attire.

Surreptitiously Edgar ran a finger around the edge of his shirt collar; the shop-fresh starchiness of it was irritating his skin, the unfamiliar feel of a tie was unpleasantly tight, the new shoes were rubbing blisters on his heels. His was a slow and painful death by tailoring.

"Hello Ed-gar!" the department secretary Erika Jönsson flopped into the chair beside him, running a hand through her long white-blonde hair. Momentarily Edgar forgot his wardrobe anguish and perked up. From the moment he had set eyes on Erika, yesterday, he thought she was one of the most beautiful women he had ever seen. More than beautiful. And totally and utterly out of his league.

"I like your suit Ed-gar. I think you look very smart! Charming!" She patted his lapels.

"Yeah. Thanks Erika." *Look everyone! Tomo's wearing a blazer! Ooh can I be Head Boy please sir, please sir?*

"Well this is exciting!" Erika abandoned his lapels and craned her neck to see the other occupants in the room. "You see over there Ed-gar? That is Camilla from PR, and next to her is Jacques also from PR. He is very nice, well, I must introduce you to them. And behind them are Maggie and Chloë from Marketing, Peter who is Marketing Manager and Steve from Advertising..." She pointed out his new colleagues, some of who caught her pointing them out and gave a tentative wave.

It was his second day at his new job. At his *first* job.

Edgar Thompson knew that he was not completely suitable for the cut and thrust of the media world he was newly having to inhabit. The trouble was Edgar's father had been very high up in archaeology. A brilliant man who was fascinated by all things Roman and, following thirty years at the Museum of London Archaeology Service, was now living out his retirement in Italy, walking round nigh-on complete Roman buildings and, he endlessly griped to Edgar, wondering why the bloody hell he'd devoted the best years of his life to crouching knee deep in mud hacking out shards of pottery and boot rivets when all this was here for the taking.

But before his father had left the London suburbs he'd had a long and meaningful conversation with Edgar which went something along the lines of:

"You're not working in textiles my lad. There's no money in it and it's for *women*."

"But Dad it's what I want to do. It's what I did my degree in!"

"That's as maybe but who makes good money in wool these days? Five hundred years ago of course it was a different story – plenty of money to be made in wool, you only have to look at places like Lavenham to see the wealth that was generated here in England..."

Edgar, with much experience, had tuned out of what, he knew, was yet another conversation in which his history-fanatic father would shoe-horn in some useless historical facts in a bid to surreptitiously educate his son and break him in to becoming an archaeologist.

"It's the real world Eddie," his father had moved back into the present as Edgar tuned in again, "you've got to make a living, earn some money. Plenty of time for your women's hobbies later on. I've asked at the Museum of London and there's a position in the press office going and your name's on the desk already."

"But I—"

"Lot of people wanted it Eddie. But you've got it. You start next week."

"But I—"

"It's a good salary, son; I negotiated it for you. And it's a very exciting time to be at the Museum of London my boy, what with this unprecedented Kings Cross archaeological dig. What a time to be there when it's all happening! Biggest thing to take place in London since, well, since I can remember… I wanted to stay in London myself and get involved in it. But you know your mother…sun, sun, sun!"

"No I—"

"Well, you have a choice of course. But the sale completes on the house next Thursday and you'll be homeless unless you have a particularly kind friend whose floor you can sleep on. But if you were to take this job then I'm sure I could arrange for you to have the Bloomsbury flat rent free, at least until you get established. The tenant moved out two weeks ago, so it's yours if you want it."

"But—"

"Come on lad. Textiles are for night classes and the sort of old women who've never been married. Or *those* men. You're not a puff are you lad? Come on Eddie! Rally round! You'll enjoy it. You'll love it. Living in the capital, flat in Bloomsbury to yourself, working at the Museum during this exciting time. What can go wrong?"

After two days Edgar had ascertained that a lot could go wrong.

All of it, in fact.

"Well thank you all for coming to this department meeting at such very short notice." A portly red-faced man stood before them in an outsized purple velvet jacket, straining to cover a stomach that suggested a career spent enjoying good lunches. He was part Father Christmas, part Oscar Wilde.

"For those of you who don't know," the man shot a look to the back of the room, straight at Edgar, "I am Aubrey Tomsin-Bowen, Head of Marketing and Communications here at the glorious Museum of London, which means, amongst other things, that I am responsible for you rabble."

There was polite laughter while he reached for a water glass.

"Now then folks, there are three points I'd like to cover in this department meeting, the first of which is to welcome our newest recruit Edgar Thompson to our team."

There was polite applause and everyone turned to look at him, smiling politely. Edgar looked round with a rictus grin on his face, trying to look composed yet happy, digging his tightly-clasped hands into his lap.

Erika leant over and patted him on the knee. Blushing a furious scarlet like a school boy, his mortification was complete.

"Edgar joins the Press Office team as a junior executive and we wish him well. Which brings me on to the second point I want to mention; the three *other* members of the Press Office..."

Laughter erupted.

Erika had already told Edgar about the rest of the Press Office team and the recent team-building day. It turned out that his would-be colleagues had spent the last two years nurturing a substantial store of hatred towards Richard, the boss of the Press Office. Forced late nights, unreasonable and unrelenting pressure, a bullying management style and meagre salary reviews had come to a head when the paint guns were placed in to their trembling, grateful hands and the pair had, according to Erika, tracked down their boss like crazed animals hunting prey, sniffed him out as he cowered in a darkened clearing, shot him in the chest, the groin, the arm and when all the paint was spilt then they came at him with the butts of their rifles, stabbing and beating him into a whimpering bloody pulp.

Erika had blithely gone on to say that the owners of Paintballing Krazy Kingdom had claimed they'd never seen anything like it, and the police took a very dim view of the whole episode. Richard was hospitalised and the two Press Officers, shocked at their own capacity for violence, were put on gardening leave pending an employment hearing.

So from his first day – yesterday – Edgar had been the sole man in charge of the Museum of London Press Office; the words of his father ringing portentously in his ears, *Come on Eddie...what could go wrong?* Richard's vacant office and his would-be colleague's empty chairs and desks were his only companions, keeping him company as he was besieged by phone, email and in person by members of the media every minute of every hour of the day with no break for lunch or a cup of tea or anything.

"...and of course we wish Richard all the best with his upcoming operations," the Head of Marcoms was continuing while Edgar momentarily stopped listening, "and we should hopefully be seeing him around the office in two to three months time. And my third point, which you will no doubt *all* be wanting to hear – the Kings Cross Dig." The Head of Marketing and Communications raised his hands in the air as the room burst into life.

"Now I know it's been a difficult time for most of you." More jeering. "But I do appreciate your situations, and the senior team in charge of managing the dig at the Museum is trying to keep everyone in the loop but there are some things we aren't able to share with you at this time..."

"For bubonic reasons?" came a voice from a corner of the room, at which point there was more laughter.

"*Not* bubonic reasons Simon, thank you for bringing that up; our good friends in the media still haven't quite grasped that we haven't unearthed the bubonic plague have they? Well – the status of the Kings Cross Dig is this: we started the dig twelve days ago following clearance of surface buildings and debris. The archaeology teams dug down through the modern layers, found the remains of a late medieval farm on the site and having cleared that five days ago we have begun to uncover what we strongly believe to be early medieval mass graves. Yes, Robert, you want to ask something?"

"I'm sorry, sir," a man from the front cut in, "but why were mass graves dug in medieval times if not for a plague or some other disease? Are you talking early medieval or late medieval? And if it's late medieval could we have the Great Plague which was so much more virulent a strain?"

"Is it true that if the plague were uncovered it would still be live? I was reading in the papers that it has a half-life of—"

"Enough! Enough. Come on Brian, we've had the Home Office pathologists crawling around the dig and there's not one hint of the plague virus to be had. Or any other viruses for that matter. We covered this in the press release last week. Nevertheless until we've cleared the site we can't be absolutely sure what we have there."

"So why are mass graves under there if not because of

disease? There's no record of a religious building or hospital on that site…"

"That's what we're trying to find out. Obviously as soon as we know why they're there then we'll let you know. Until then… Yes Sandra?"

"What about the rumour that it's not medieval at all and that it's a cover-up for something else altogether? I've had enquiries on the phone from some universities who are saying that they've heard some of the finds taken from the site aren't corresponding with the period you're suggesting. That it's pre-medieval."

The Head of Marcoms laughed a deep laugh. "Sandra – all I can tell you is that we strongly suspect the site to contain the mass burials of medieval Londoners. There is no risk to public health from the site being uncovered and you can bet we're monitoring public health constantly as we're revealing more and more. And as to the rumours of a cover-up and that it's not medieval – all I can think is that there is a chance some of the archaeological layers have become mixed up as a result of the hasty nature of the dig and we have some non-medieval finds in the medieval layer. But I'm no expert and that's just my educated guess. As soon as we feel confident we know exactly what we have on site then we'll share it with you all and together we can break it to the world but until we reach that point, then all we can do is reassure everyone that there is *no risk whatsoever* to public health."

"Edgar! One moment!" the Head of Marcoms called him back from the doorway as he made to follow the others at the lively close of the meeting. "I just wanted a quiet word. Pull up a chair my boy. Now then, how are you settling in?"

"Oh fine. Fine..." Edgar balled his hands in his lap.

"Good stuff. Well it's one hell of a time to be introduced to the Museum what with this dig kicking off and your colleagues out of action. But rest assured we're doing all we can to shield you from the worst of the media interest. You don't need to write any press releases concerning the dig; the senior team in charge of the dig will do all that. I'll be feeding you, and your colleagues in other departments, press releases for general distribution every couple of days or when we have an update. So you just hold tight and we'll get through these difficult few weeks. Take the calls, reel off our approved press releases and if any member of the press abuses you then you report it to me and I'll be on their case. I won't tolerate bullying in any shape or form."

Edgar nodded.

"Good man!" The Head of Marcoms slapped him on the back. "Nice suit, by the by. Don't see enough smartness around here lately – it's all got a bit sloppy; Marketing looks like Starbucks on a Saturday afternoon and the chaps in Advertising look like they're off out to the pub. But this I like – keep up the good work young man and you'll go far."

Edgar smiled politely and walked out of the room with the Head of Marcoms. He had never, in his life, wanted to go *far*.

Five

Rain was rattling against the leaded panes of the old manor house and Archie, seated on the stone window seat with a gin and tonic in one hand and a Marlborough Light in the other, felt enormously content with the world. He was full of paté and confit and mousse and to top it all, the black-haired Spanish beauty who was one of the hired-in waiting staff had been giving him the glad-eye all evening.

Sir Wragby's pile was a very fine red-brick Queen Anne mansion. And the drawing room in which Archie was lounging with its vast chandeliers and roaring fire was a very fine drawing room. In it were assembled the finest human beings local to Winchester, hand-picked for the table and served with the very best wines. Lord and Lady Wragby beside the fireplace talking earnestly to the Chief Constable and his wife. A selection of overfed heads of commerce, jovial bankers, po-faced barristers, a surgeon, the Vice Chancellor of a nearby university and his young girlfriend, and even a well-known playwright who had annoyed everyone by talking loudly and wearing yellow trousers.

"Hello you." The wife of the mayor sidled up to Archie in the bay window. "Mind if I join you?"

"Not at all." Archie slid further towards the leaded panes to make room for the vampish woman with the scarlet lipstick. "Cigarette?"

"Love one darling!" She took one from the packet and, holding his gaze, lit the cigarette from his *Genesis 1:3* lighter.

"So how are you?" She shot a brief look across the room at her red-faced husband but he was absorbed in conversation with one of the bankers. "You never called me."

"Believe me I wanted to," Archie whispered. "It's just… you know…my profession."

She gave a soft laugh and, crossing her legs, she let her high-heeled foot come to rest against his calf. "You know," she whispered huskily, leaning close to him, her breast brushing his arm, "I was—"

"Smokers corner is it, what?" A well-fed commerce type had appeared from nowhere and plonked himself down on the opposite window seat. Despite the pin-striped self-satisfied swagger of the man, Archie was relieved to see him. The Mayor's wife surreptitiously moved away to a more respectable distance. The new arrival puffed at his cigar and it filled the window bay with a fug.

"Can't be doing with all these bloody smoking laws can you? Bloody illegal, that's what they are, taking away a man's liberty to do as he pleases. My God – sorry Dean – but you wouldn't have got those Victorians acting like the flimsy politicians do these days. Back then there were smoking rooms Goddamn it – sorry Dean – and those who didn't like it damn well went elsewhere. Tush!" He worked up another fug.

Archie was poised to say something because he felt he ought to, possibly about the catering staff's French-maid outfits, when he was cut short.

"Terrible to-do at your cathedral, Dean." The University Vice Chancellor had joined them. "Read about it in the local rag. Breaking into a cathedral – I ask you! Is nothing sacred?"

"Apparently not," said Archie.

"Are you absolutely sure nothing was taken?"

"Our lads did a sweep of the place," the disembodied voice of the Chief Constable wafted through the smoke from the other side of the bay window and, as the clouds parted momentarily, Archie caught a glimpse of the man puffing away on a newly-lit panatella, "and didn't find anything. We reckon she was interrupted before any mischief could take place."

"I did my best," Archie said.

"So is it true you actually tackled the female intruder to the ground?" the commerce type asked.

"Well I..."

"Oh come on Peter, you know what these journalists are like." The Mayor's wife stepped in to save Archie.

"Was that what they printed in the *Echo*?" the Chief Constable asked, mildly irritated. "That the Dean tackled the woman to the ground?"

"No. The *Hampshire Gazette*," Archie said. He'd kept all the press releases including that particular one, and had only felt the smallest smattering of guilt when the journalist had got a slightly wrong take on the story. "But the *Winchester Echo* seemed to have got the story right."

"My God you lot are going to stain my William Morris wallpaper with all your smoking." Sir Wragby had wandered over to the group now filling the bay window. "Archie! There you are. Didn't have a chance to speak to you over supper. I was going to ask you – what the bloody hell are you doing associating with the clipboard brigade?"

"Pardon?" Archie leant back, amused.

"I was stopped in the street on Saturday by one of those market researchers. Asked how *satisfied* I was with the provision for my religious needs in the area!" There was a rumble of laughter in the bay window and Sir Wragby ploughed on. "Never heard anything like it in my life! And then the stupid woman gave me these damnable showcards to read and went on to ask me about my opinions on your cathedral and whether I'd *used its entertainment facilities* in the last six months! Was that anything to do with you?"

"Oh that!" Archie caught the eye of the Spanish waitress and handed her his empty glass, indicating he wanted the same again. "Yes, I commissioned a market research company to do a survey for me."

"*What*?"

"Market research – you know – everyone uses the stuff." There was a pause and Archie saw the need to explain. "Well I'm a service provider aren't I? How can I deliver what my customers want if I don't know what my customers want in the first place?"

"*Customers*?" the bank manager choked on his sherry. "*Service?*"

"Oh come on Malcolm, we're all customers now." The commerce type patted his choking friend on the back. "It's the service age isn't it? The times for dictating how things should be is gone."

"Well you could ask us what the public wants." The mayor had sauntered over to the group and joined his wife who had by now slid several more respectable inches further from Archie. "We could tell you what the public wants. I represent them, after all."

"Aah well, you couldn't really tell me exactly what the public wants could you? You could only tell me what your opinion is of what the public wants. And that's all well and good but what I was after was the man on the street—"

"I'm *damned* if I am a man on the street!" Sir Wragby purpled.

"Well you were on the street when they interviewed you, weren't you Wragby? And you are a man," the mayor's wife quipped, "so technically..."

"I think the Dean is doing a fine job," the young girlfriend of the Vice Chancellor said softly, and caught everyone's attention. Sensing everyone turn to her she blushed and added, "the Cathedral has really taken off since you joined, Dean. I love the restaurant there. And I went to the jazz evening last month with friends and we really enjoyed it. It's a beautiful place to be at night-time and there are no tourists about so you can enjoy it all the more."

"Well I'm afraid I'm rather old school when it comes to the Cathedral," the mayor weighed in, "what I want are the good old fashioned Services, the hymns, the hard pews. I'm not into any of this bistro business or music evenings."

Archie shrugged. "That's all well and good but I haven't ever seen you at a service."

"Ah, you've got me there!" the mayor said. "Well, good luck to you my boy. There probably does need to be a shake-up doesn't there? I just thought the Church was exempt from all this mania for modernising but there you go. I was wrong. You seem to be doing a good job. What does the Bishop of Wessex have to say about what you're doing?"

"Not a lot," Archie said, blithely. He kept his superior at arms length as much as he could. Mostly the Bishop found out about Archie's activities when it was too late for him to do anything. He'd only told him the barest details about the break-in, conveniently forgetting to mention about the treasures in the unlocked boot of his car. No point in giving the man ammunition to use against him...

"So what's next then Dean," the Vice Chancellor broke in to his thoughts. "What else can we expect from your new and improved Church of England?"

Archie twirled the ice in his glass. "One idea I'm considering is the drive-thru service. Tarmac over the grassed area in front of the West Doors, hook up the service to a screen outside and cars could pull up and people join in without the inconvenience of leaving their vehicles. And maybe give out those handheld voting controls so that the congregation can have a vote on what hymns are sung. Get a bit of audience participation going."

He leant back and sipped his fresh gin and tonic.

The expression on their faces would amuse him for many days to come.

Six

Eight days into his new job, something in Edgar snapped. At the point when the phones had been ringing for three unrelenting hours, the emails from that morning alone had reached the seventy-five mark and the fax machine had finally run out of paper, Edgar decided that now was a good time to go for a nice long walk. He had to escape and get some air. Think things through. He would go mad if he had to sit in the lonely office and get shouted at by journalists any more.

Slipping out unnoticed when Erika was making tea, he willingly gave himself up to the hectic, anonymous press of pedestrians on London Wall; one more suit in the continuous stream of suits, busy dashing from A to B and minimising the time away from their desks. Time was money and the brisker the walk the greater their value; even walking was a marker of status in the City.

Ten minutes later and he was disappointed that whatever it was he had been searching for – some clue as to how he should handle those voracious journalists, or even manage his workload – it had not come to him. No matter how far he walked he still had no idea how best he could deal with the incessant inquiries.

Could he confirm what had been dug up at Kings Cross: was it a plague pit? No, it was a mass burial from around

31

the early fifteenth century... *A plague pit then.* No, there was no evidence of disease and the Home Office... *Is this all a cover-up?* No. *What have they really found down there?* Mass graves. *Mass graves from the fifteenth century that contain no plague or disease of any kind? Are you having a laugh?* That's what we're saying at the Museum of London and it's backed up by... *Is it true that the Mayor actually smashed his water glass against his office wall when he heard that those four platforms at Kings Cross station were going to be out of action for a further few months?* He couldn't possibly say...

Instead of finding answers Edgar continued to pound the pavements, working off his anxiety with the exercise, and, for the first time, finding some measure of perspective on his situation.

He was, after all, just two weeks in to his first job: who would expect him to be coping with what was a very unusual and demanding situation?

His father.

His father would expect him to cope.

The very thought of his father made Edgar's shoulders tense so he stepped up his walking, beating a path through the City boys around Liverpool Street Station.

His father would never tolerate the idea of a son of his not coping with some flimsy non-job like Junior Press Officer whether it was for the Museum of London or not. Edgar's father expected him to be just as strong and just as single minded as he was; he would never accept that Edgar was a separate being with different interests and skills and abilities.

And, likewise, Edgar had difficulties in coming to terms with his being a separate person from his father. He had been so influenced by his father that he had at one point thought of himself as nothing more than a diminutive orbiting moon of his father's planet; another being wholly dependent on the greater being for ideas, opinions and, of course, money.

But, recently, Edgar had started to inch towards becoming his own person; pulling away from his father's force field. He began, privately, to hold views that were not entirely those of his father, taking a path that his father did not wholeheartedly endorse, or indeed set up for him in the first place. The real coup had come when he had intentionally failed to get the required A-levels to study archaeology at university, which had sent his father to the phone – *let me call Malcolm, he's the head of the department at Sheffield, Malcolm will let you in* – but it had all been a cleverly thought-out plan: to achieve sufficiently poor grades to preclude the study of archaeology, but to gain entrance at the University of Derby to study what he really wanted, and to take his life in the direction he wanted it to go. To get his own way it had meant he had set himself up to fail, but if that was what it took to get his own way, then he was prepared to do it. In the case of the degree subject, his father, naturally, had been devastated, but had eventually relented and agreed that he would rather his son actually did a degree – *even a crap one like textiles, for God's sake Brenda what's it come to* – than do none at all and spend a lifetime scanning shopping at Tesco.

His father had won in the end though.

Inevitably.

Here he was working at the Museum of London, knee deep in archaeology and his father's world. His exertion of free will had only got him so far. He was living in his parent's pied-à-terre and working in a role his father had set up for him, in a field his father was master of.

The moon was orbiting the planet again.

Edgar continued, pounding the wide grey streets of Moorgate; eyes down, deep in thought, distracted only briefly by the soft stone foundations of the Roman wall and the red-brick medieval ruins decaying gently between the hard glass office blocks: archaeology was in his genes, he couldn't deny it completely.

More streets, brisker walking, dashing and darting through the crowds and, eventually, somewhere near Finsbury Circus, beside a Books Etc, just before a Sushi bar, it was enough. Edgar reached the state where he had worked off his nervous energy. He stopped in his tracks and, turning to point in the opposite direction, he headed back to work.

A quarter of an hour later, back at the Museum of London, Edgar was walking through the vast new atrium towards the staff-only entrance. He was forced to skirt around a group of suits milling around one man in a particularly sharp black suit and red tie standing by the leather sofas. Not the typical Museum of London visitors, especially not so early on a weekday. The man in the black suit was standing still, looking around calmly while the others buzzed around him, talking in to mobile phones and flicking through documents pulled from leather-bound wallets. The calm, solitary man caught Edgar's gaze and smiled at him. Edgar raised a hand in a half-wave back. It was one of the managers from his induction at the museum, but he couldn't remember who it was. A director of some department or other – there had been quite a few of them and his first few days at the Museum had been a blur. Edgar walked on, through the double doors, past the security guard and into the press rooms.

He froze.

He slapped his hand on his forehead.

"Welcome back Ed-gar." Erika was perched at her desk sipping lemon tea and rifling through a set of black and white photos.

"Erika..." Edgar walked over, slowly, in a daze. He reached Erika's desk and, leaning on it he looked her straight in the eye and said in a calm, quiet voice, "I just waved at the Prime Minister."

"You did *what* Ed-gar?" Her beautiful blue eyes sparkled and he took a moment to break free from her spell and pull himself back into the real world.

"The Prime Minister. I just waved at the Prime Minister."

Erika giggled and put the photos down on the table. "It is like you are a little boy Ed-gar! Waving at the Prime Minister!"

Edgar frowned. "What is the Prime Minister doing in Reception downstairs?"

"Waving back at you?"

"Erika be serious. What is going on around here? Why are the Prime Minister and his entourage standing downstairs by the staff entrance to the Museum of London?" He stared at her, wild-eyed. "It's connected with the Kings Cross Dig isn't it? I knew it! It's all connected to what they've found at Kings Cross. That's why nobody's mentioned the Prime Minister's visit. Do you know anything about it? Anything at all?"

"Well I do know..." She leant forward to him, speaking barely above a whisper.

"Go on..." Edgar crouched down to her level. She smelt good. "What is it? What do you know Erika?"

"I know that the Head of Marketing and Communications is sleeping with the receptionist on the front desk."

"What? Just...just...don't be so daft! Anyway, the receptionist is male."

"I know that."

"Yes but... Oh. Oh. Goodness. Really? REALLY! But isn't the Head of Marcoms married?"

"And he has four children."

"Crikey!" Edgar stood unmoving for a moment. "Well, it takes all sorts doesn't it? I thought there was something of the Oscar Wilde about him. Anyway..." He pulled himself together. "What I meant was what's really going on with this Kings Cross Dig?"

"How should I know? I am very, very low here."

"Mmmm." Edgar frowned, pondering the question himself.

"But see, here, I have photos of my weekend!" Erika spread the prints out on her desk turned towards him. Photos of her friends, of London scenes, all beautifully captured although he wasn't in the mood to look at them.

"What do you think? I want your opinion."

"They're good. Very good."

"Yes. I like this one." She pushed forward a picture of a reflection of Buckingham Palace in a puddle. "I will try and sell this photo to the newspapers I think."

"Good. Good." Edgar nodded and giving her the photo back he went into his office, absorbed in his thoughts.

He checked his email. It was now mid-morning and besides the many emails from the media there was the daily email briefing from the Head of Marcoms to his team.

To: all marketing staff
From: Aubrey Tomsin-Bowen, Head of Marketing and Communications, Museum of London
Subject: Kings Cross Archaeological Excavation Update
Prime Minister in for meeting this morning – permission to confirm to press/public. Reason for meeting is Kings Cross Dig – plans to go forward. No further detail of meeting to be given out. Press release 8.4 (4ᵗʰ November) still stands. Expect new release end of Wednesday (9ᵗʰ November).

Christ, the press were going to have a field day knowing the Prime Minister was now personally involved in the Kings Cross Dig.

Edgar stared out of the window towards the towers of Moorgate. Was it true? Was the portly and somewhat elderly Head of Marcoms really having it away with the black-eyed French boy on reception?

Focus!

Already the phones were ringing and now he had

composed himself and worked off his anxiety he needed to do his best to fight the fires once more.

At two o'clock Edgar panicked and put a call in to his old boss in hospital. He needed help – there was no way he could do this on his own. The walk around the City had done nothing but help wear out his shoe leather.

"Richard! Richard, it's Edgar from the Museum Press Office. We met at my interview a few weeks ago. You have to help me. This Kings Cross Dig is getting out of control!"

"Eddie? Eddie! Nice to hear from you. Hey, I've been reading about the dig in the papers. Got a lot of time on my hands! Sounds like... Oh shit, hold on a minute Eddie..." There was a rustle of a mobile phone being stuffed under bedclothes and Edgar, holding on desperately, could just make out the grating voice of a nurse, "What the...Mr Davidson...*MR DAVIDSON WILL YOU KINDLY TURN OFF YOUR MOBILE PHONE THIS INSTANT. DO YOU HEAR,*" followed by a beep and the line going dead.

Edgar was well and truly alone with this.

Sighing he put his head on the table, enjoying the coolness of the wood-effect plastic against his forehead. The prospect of remaining pinned to his desk by a continually ringing phone lay ahead of him. Call after call after call of questions he couldn't answer from people he didn't want to speak to who mistook downright rudeness for dedication in pursuing the truth.

He needed help. Regardless of what the Head of Marcoms had told him, he was still under enormous pressure with no knowledge of what was going on other than what little information was given in the vague emails that he was expected to peddle out and satisfy the slavering press. It was an impossible situation.

Perhaps he should swallow his pride and call his father? His father would be able to help him.

Edgar's heart sank.

Seven

Kate padded silently down the nave in her rubber-soled shoes, clutching her Primark handbag nervously. She never felt comfortable in churches, with their private rituals and language. It was a club she had been excluded from all her life, her parents preferring to spend Sundays worshipping at the tills of Marks and Spencer in the vast American-style shopping mall off the motorway. Kate wasn't even sure what she was, religion-wise, presuming that she *was* actually something.

She didn't like not knowing, not being 'in' on the same thing that most people seemed to be 'in' on. Still, there didn't seem much point in knowing about it all now anyway. It wasn't as if she was going to get married or produce children for baptism any time soon; her long-term boyfriend Mike stopped any talk of marriage the minute she brought the subject up.

Mike I've been thinking about us *lately and—*

And we're fine! Come here and shut up you silly girl.

"Hello, can I help you?"

Kate snapped back to the present, coming to an abrupt halt and almost dropping her handbag. Clutching it tightly to her chest she looked up at her affable assailant.

She recognised him in an instant.

It was Archie Cartwright, the new Dean of Winchester,

it had to be, the man Lynn Paget referred to as the *Holy Poster Boy* after an article she had run on him when he first usurped the position. The man standing before her with the shaggy hair had seemingly appeared out of nowhere, his noiseless arrival disturbing her. There was something striking about his appearance, something ethereal and fragile, his blonde mop divinely lit by a shaft of light from the stained glass window so that he looked, for a moment, as though he wore a halo. Kate made an attempt to pull herself together, here was the twenty-nine-year-old man the Church of England had appointed to lead it into the 21st century. The saviour of the Church in flesh and blood standing before her.

"Dean Cartwright?" she managed.

"Archie. Please." He held out a hand and she shook it. "You must be Karen is that right?"

"It's Kate actually. Kate Grey." She fumbled with her bag and a file, dropping the file on the floor as she made to shake his hand.

"Sorry, cold hands..."

"...but warm heart." He half-bowed, and for Kate, disliking the cliché and the over-theatrical bow, the spell was broken. It hadn't lasted long. "This way to my office, if you will. Is it the *Echo* you're with?"

"That's right." She padded after him, caught in his slipstream, moving quickly down the nave and past the cleaning women lurking in the shadows, eyes narrowed behind thick glasses, mops stilled in plump hands, watching the young woman suspiciously as she dared to walk along with their boy, the virile young man who ruled the roost.

Was it Kate's imagination or could she hear low whispers echoing off the walls as she passed them: *He's mine. Mine. Leave him alone. Mine. All mine. Leave him alone. He's mine...*

Picking up her pace she focused on following Archie through the Cathedral; it was as much as she could do to keep up with him as he swept along, robes flying. Were robes supposed to look like his? They were broad across his shoulders, tailored in at his waist and then they cascaded out in folds of heavy black fabric billowing down to the floor where they swept the tiles as he strode silently before her. There was, she thought, something of the vampire about him.

He half-turned back to Kate as they walked.

"I think I met one of your colleagues a few weeks ago – Lynn Paget?"

"Yes, Lynn works with me."

The Dean had an odd expression on his face. "Good looking woman. And so...energetic." He gave a short laugh and turned back.

Slapper. Kate frowned and dug her nails in to the palms of her hands. *Energetic,* indeed. Were no men exempt from Lynn's attentions?

Within another minute they had reached the Dean's office, tucked away beside an elaborately carved tomb. He gallantly held open the door for her and she walked in.

"Well I must say it's nice to have you here, I do like the press taking an interest in the Cathedral. Tea?" Kate nodded and sat down on an old leather chair facing his cluttered desk. After the vast columned grandeur of the nave and transepts it was a relief to be in a room that was designed on a human scale. It was plain and cosy, lit only by an old window at the far end and standard lamps. The crumbly walls were painted a deep red, which, together with the shag pile rug and enormous leather sofa in front of the vast brick fireplace gave the room the look of a Victorian gentleman's retreat more than an annexe within a Cathedral. Archie went over to a sink beneath the leaded window and filled a kettle as Kate took out her file and arranged it on the only small space that was free on the cluttered desk in front of her, noticing, amongst other things, a bottle of designer nail polish. She leant in closer to read the tiny gold label. Lust Red.

"Oh. Not mine!" Archie strode over and picking it up he threw it into a drawer. "Anyway, like I said, thanks for coming. And thanks for that article on my new Cathedral branding. You like it then?"

"Yes?" Kate wasn't sure whether she liked the branding or not and her very confusion had formed the basis for her original article, which had not been printed. Why, she had argued, was the Church adopting brand logos and mission statements and behaving like a marketing company? And did the Church really need additional logos and mission statements since it was one of the first organisations to have these things; wasn't, she had argued, the crucifix the original Nike swoosh, and what was the Bible except a rather lengthy mission statement? Even Kate with her scanty knowledge of the Church knew these things. But she also knew that she was pushing it, and it was just one more time when her journalistic creativity was forcibly stifled and she was reined in to write the bare facts and no more. Just like Lynn did. Good old predictable, unimaginative, transparent-blouse-wearing Lynn.

Kate's branding article had been another sign that something was changing within her. She had gone ahead and written the controversial article and submitted it with the knowledge that it was going to ruffle feathers; but that hadn't stopped her. She felt that she owed it to herself to at least *try* and push the journalistic boundaries a little. Who knows, maybe it would strike a chord with Dr Evil. And it did just that. Discord. A few minutes after it was submitted an email came through from Dr Evil. *Could you pop in to my office Kate?* And she had sat down opposite him and he, stroking the table top, had explained to her that it wasn't their job to go upsetting the Church now was it? Think of the readership. Seventy per cent of *Echo* readers were over the age of sixty, or was it sixty per cent over seventy? He couldn't quite remember but it didn't matter because *the main point was* we're talking *old* and we're talking *conservative*. Near-blasphemous articles about the Church would not go down very well with their readership would they? *Stroke, stroke.* It was all very well for your *Guardian*s and *Telegraph*s to go lambasting the Church, it was practically expected of them, but not the *Winchester Echo*. There would be letters. There would be complaints. A fall in circulation. A reduction in advertising spend. Re-dun-dan-cies. You can sex up your articles as much as you like, they love a bit of sensationalism, but you leave criticising the Church and the Conservative party well alone. Look what Lynn does...

Archie mashed a tea bag in Kate's cup and then flung it into the sink. The woman sitting at his desk was certainly not how he had imagined her from the phone call yesterday, and she was nothing like her extrovert and attractive colleague of a few weeks before. Straight brown hair, no make-up, saggy baggy clothes. Not his cup of tea.

"There you go." He placed the cup before her and she took a polite sip.

"Well what do you want to know for your article?" He sat down in a whirl of robes and leant forward on his desk, smiling, his hands clasped together and resting in front of him in what he hoped was a confident and relaxed attitude. Journalists recorded everything these days...

"Let's start with the details," Kate began, staying firmly within her comfort zone of details, lists and plans. "Can I confirm it was twenty past midnight that you arrived at the Cathedral on the night of the break-in?"

She ran through each question methodically, making a note of the response before moving on to the next. Exactly how she had always played it in the past. And without an angle: no controversy. Just facts. The way Dr Evil wanted it.

"And, can I just check, is the staff entrance normally locked."

Archie gritted his teeth. "Yes. It was a mistake OK? Can you say something like *the door that was always carefully locked just happened to be open that night.*" He leant towards to her, "And can you just spell out that it was in fact *not me* who left the door open that night because I was, as you know, on my way back from the Treasures

Through the Ages exhibition, which had been a complete success I might add. In fact if I could tell you more about that exhibition..."

"So which of your team would you like me to publicly pin the blame on for leaving the door open?" Kate asked, her voice tight with rising anger. The man had the audacity to tell her what she should be writing, giving it to her verbatim, in fact, as though she wasn't even capable of putting it into the appropriate language herself. He was, she realised, just another version of Dr Evil.

"Well, why not just say it wasn't me." The Dean said, "*Dean Cartwright was alarmed to learn that a member of the cathedral staff had forgotten to lock up that evening.* That should be enough, don't you think?"

Kate looked up from her list of pre-prepared questions. A thought struck her. "So...you'd just returned from the exhibition?"

"Yes it was—"

"With the treasures?" She put the question as innocently as she could. "It must have been quite a fright to have so many valuables in the car and be confronted by a burglar. It must have made the situation all the more terrifying for you."

"You have no idea," Archie said, glad for the opportunity to add yet more drama to his story. "I'd left the boot unlocked when I chased after her, so if she'd had an accomplice – well! At least Winchester has so much treasure the theft of the pieces would only have made a blip in its coffers."

"Really?" Kate was wide-eyed.

"Oh yes. It probably wouldn't have been noticed if it had

been stolen."

Kate smiled to herself and jotted down on her pad. "Going back to the exhibition if I may, how did Winchester compare to the other cathedrals? Was our treasure up there with the best?"

"Oh absolutely." Archie was delighted at the opportunity to promote his good work at the conference as well as his role in defending the cathedral. "We had just over two and a half million pounds worth of treasure in the exhibition... some exceptional pieces of national importance, which I put a lot of thought in to. York Minster only managed half of that value. It was a very poor show by York. Can you put that in your article, about York?"

"Oh I'll try." Kate nodded, lips pursed. "Well, I think I've got everything I need." She stood up and slipped her pad and pens into her bag.

"Great." Archie escorted her out. "Will you be writing this up in two separate articles, one on the exhibition and another on the break-in?" He paused at the West Door exit.

"Oh no. I'll be combining them in one." Kate shook his hand and left him, frowning, watching her walk in the direction of town. He'd managed to give her two stories of two separate good works he had done, great publicity for him, great publicity for the Church. So why did he have a nagging doubt that he ought to be worried about something.

Eight

Bishop MacNeath was livid.

The man was full, purple-faced, spittle-jowled livid and it was all directed at Archie.

It was down to the way in which the press had broken the story of the cathedral break-in. The *Winchester Echo* had run a photograph of Archie standing in front of the choir, sunglasses on his head, arms crossed and looking straight into the camera with a *'Pour Homme'* expression on his face.

To Bishop MacNeath, reading the paper with fat trembling hands, the photograph epitomised the cocky, vulgar and irreligious man he took Archie to be.

To Archie, reading the paper with his morning coffee, the photograph had been a pleasant surprise. It made him look dignified and resolute and smouldering. It was even possible to see that he'd had his robes illicitly tailored. Very flattering.

Such a shame then that the dowdy female journalist who had interviewed him had then slapped the rather profane 'CATHEDRAL'S SAVIOUR' headline above the picture. Even Archie acknowledged that it was going a tad far. And was there a hint of irony in it? Certainly there had been something about the journalist's attitude that he hadn't been able to put his finger on, an irreverence, a suppressed sort of devil-may-care way about her, however unremarkable and conformist she appeared to be.

The article had started out very promisingly. It was thanks to local hero (local hero!) the newly appointed Dean of Winchester Archie Cartwright that the would-be burglar had been interrupted and nothing had been stolen. The new and dynamic Dean, the article went on, had confronted the petite female burglar without any regard for personal safety (more irony? he wondered) and had then bravely chased her off the premises before anything was stolen.

The Bish had not taken the time to mention this detail when he'd called up to discuss his views with Archie.

It was fortunate nothing had been stolen, the article had continued, because the Dean had been carrying a cargo valued at more than £2.6 million in the *unlocked* boot of his car – a significant haul in anyone's eyes. And then, in a bold font, *"Winchester has so much treasure," the new Dean quipped, "it would only have made a blip in the coffers. It probably wouldn't have been noticed at all if it had been stolen."*

The Bish *had* taken the time to discuss this in detail with him. Archie was kicking himself for revealing the fact that the treasure had been in his unlocked boot. His desire to milk the media for all it was worth had blinded his reason. He'd need to be more cautious in future, that was certain.

By and large, not the best of articles for the Church to be associated with perhaps. The instant it had been published MacNeath had been on the phone, dishing out fire and brimstone over the line and promising that *this will all go much higher than me, my boy, you just rest assured about that.*

Righto, he'd said and put the phone down.

Right from the start the Bishop of Wessex had despised him. Loathed him. The dark, lurking hatred had come to the surface when Archie made the mistake of pulling up in the wrong parking space. Bishop MacNeath, with his trembling girth and his quivering jowls, had strode out of his office, taken one look at Archie's new car and pronounced it *Quite shamefully unsuitable for a man of the Church of England.*

"Unsuitable? But it—"

"It is a Catholic car, Dean!" The spittle went flying.

"It's what?"

"It is a Catholic car my boy, and what's more it is *red.*"

"That's ridiculous," Archie began but seeing as the Bish was obviously gathering himself together to blast him with the F and B evils that the old-boys of the Church did so well he relented. "Just because it's made in Italy doesn't mean it's Catholic…Your Grace."

Bishop MacNeath looked to heaven and said quietly, "My boy, I suggest your next car is something more suited the Church of England. Like a Rover."

Archie had wrinkled up his nose. "What about a Morgan?"

He knew very well that he could afford to be flippant. It came with being so young. But it also came with being so damned successful at what he did. Real rock-and-roll preaching; packing them in at the pews and giving the Church of England a good kick up the backside. *Cartwright,* wrote the *Guardian* at the time of his appointment at

Winchester, *is the Mick Jagger of the Pulpit.* Initially Archie had been enormously offended by that comment but had learnt that it was in fact positively meant. Mick Jagger, Archie had been reliably informed, had at some point around the Second World War been mildly handsome and popular and this was the context of the compliment. It was not, it seemed, likening him to a haggard, wrinkled poser who spent his time divorcing women and denying love-children: a real career-stopper in the Church of England if ever there was one.

Archibald Cartwright was what the Church had wanted. After a fashion. The Archbishop of Canterbury had made it clear that there needed to be a change in direction, a bringing closer together of the Church and youth and some felt that Archie was the man for the job. Yes he was controversial, yes he was potentially a liability, yes Winchester was an established and mature community but with falling congregations across the UK something needed to happen. And something significant.

But there had been many, many, *many* people who opposed the appointment: old Church and new Church never mixed smoothly in the cocktail of religion.

Amongst Archie's fiercest critics was the previous Dean of Winchester, for whom the new appointment had come out of the blue. And of course Bishop Alfred Gregory StJohn Brian MacNeath.

According to a friend in the know, Bishop MacNeath had been on tablets for his blood pressure since the ordination of women priests back in 1992. In 2006 when the first steps towards making women bishops were underway,

MacNeath had advanced to a stronger dosage, and any hint of new developments in that field sent him to his sick bed for days on end. In moments of quiet reflection Archie allowed himself the thought that he, too, might hope to have a similar pharmaceutical effect on the obnoxious old man over the coming months.

Aside from the purple-faced Bishop, life after the break-in had become very exciting, in the manner of a TV detective series. Two days after the break-in the police had installed themselves temporarily in the Visitors' Centre, and with the help of the Archdeacon, who understood Latin, had worked their way through the vast and complex Cathedral inventories that went back nearly a thousand years, eventually concluding that everything was as it should be, give or take the odd irregularity that could well be put down to a millennia of accounting practice irregularities. It was doubtful whether Winchester had ever held the cup of St Joan in the first place and even if they had the Archdeacon declared that he'd never been aware of it in the fifty-four years he'd been at the Cathedral. But that was neither here nor there. The Archdeacon seemed to live in his own private world and wouldn't have noticed if the Cathedral was turned into a mosque or the choristers replaced with naked dancing girls.

It was nearly a fortnight after the break-in. Following a surprise visit from the Bish himself, rapidly followed by several swift G&Ts in the King's Head, Archie began to get the feeling that perhaps all was not entirely as it should be in the Cathedral. Something was different. There was a change; an anomaly only visible out of the corner of an eye. Small enough not to grab his attention but it was there nevertheless, lurking on the periphery. What *was* it?

It was when he started to search for the tall wooden ladder that it became obvious that things were *definitely* different since the break-in. The ladder wasn't to be found in its usual place. He'd been searching for it in the north transept where it should have been, along with the concert lighting and the stage platforms, but he had finally located it leaning up against a wall in the presbytery. Puzzled he'd gone to his office to hunt for the newspaper article and there, sure enough, in the newly framed photograph on his wall he could see the ladder poking out behind him; the photograph that had been taken the morning after the break-in. He took the framed photograph straight to the Archdeacon, who said that he had told the police it had been him who had left the ladder in that position. But now, thinking about it, he wasn't quite sure that it *had* been him leaving the ladder there...

Archie reassured the Archdeacon that he wouldn't be arrested for wasting police time and then spent the afternoon pacing the Cathedral, eyes raised to heaven, deep in thought. Invisible to him the hordes of cleaning ladies looked on their lost little boy, their collective maternal instincts resonating throughout the building.

Nine

You can record your message after the beep. If you want to re-record your message press one at any time.

"Angela? Hi. Angela, it's Archie here. From Winchester. Well, crikey, er, oh damn it."

BEEP

You can record your message after the beep. If you want to re-record your message press one at any time.

"Angela? Hi it's Archie here. How are you? It's been mad here for the past few days and that's why I haven't called you. There's been a break-in at my Cathedral would you believe, and I was the one who rumbled her. I say *her* because it was a woman! It happened when I came back that night from the TTtA. Anyway, nothing was taken but the media have actually given me bad press… Oh why am I even telling you all this stuff damn it."

BEEP

You can record your message after the beep. If you want to re-record your message press one at any time.

"Angela, it's Archie here. Call me! Sorry I haven't called you but we've had a break-in. Nothing taken but, well, anyway, police everywhere. I've been dying to call you and I've thought about you every day and… argh no too desperate."

BEEP

You can record your message after the beep. If you want to re-record your message press one at any time.

"Hey Angela! It's Archie. I've been thinking about you babe. Call me."

Ten

Kate carefully placed her carrier bags by the front door and made her way to the kitchen, stepping around the debris of filthy exhaust manifolds, carburettors, windscreen wipers and a shredded fan belt; it looked as though a car had made its last dying attempt to reach the kitchen before it finally expired on the threshhold. Inside the kitchen the scene was no better – on the counter was a pile of engine related junk and even though Mike had been in all day he hadn't touched the washing up, which was still piled in the sink, a large fly walking along the rim of his breakfast bowl.

Mike was upstairs, she could hear the TV on, something sporty.

Kate loved order and cleanliness and the state of the house got under her skin. How could Mike tolerate this filthy mess? Why couldn't he keep the car bits in the garage and not have them messing up the hallway? OK it was his house and he could do what he wanted, but even so...

She placed her coat neatly on the only free chair and rolled up her shirt sleeves. Back from the drudgery of work and she was straight into the drudgery of being a charlady, just like every other day. She turned on the stereo and the first chords of her newly acquired album *Strong Woman* came on.

Clearing a path on the floor she made her way to the

counter beside the sink and methodically arranged the washing up in the order in which she would tackle it: cutlery, glasses, bowls, plates, saucepans. She picked up the sponge, rinsed it, rinsed it again, and then placed it in the bowl with the hot water running.

Calmed by the familiarity of her daily routine she reached into the cupboard to get the washing-up liquid.

Oooh is it hot in here?

Or is it just me?

Yeah it's me!

It's me bay-beh!

I'm so h- h- h- h- hot!

She loved this album; it was so uplifting and so positive. She played it all the time when she was doing her domestic chores; she had memorised most of the lyrics and could belt out the songs, especially; *My Life (Not Yours babe)* and her particular favourite *Woman on Top (of the World)*.

But, over the last few days, Kate had been getting an inkling that something sinister was afoot with *Strong Woman*.

It had first reared its head in relation to Mike. Suddenly she was finding herself angry at him: angry that he left the washing up to her, angry that he left the cooking and cleaning to her, and angry that he expected her to rejoice in this domestic bliss.

And when she wasn't frustrated and angry with Mike she was frustrated and angry with Dr Evil, infuriated with the metaphorical patting of her head and the "my little Jane Austen" in the making" comments.

Yeah baby 'cause you can't do that to me no more.

I ain't gonna take it oh no baby.
No man gonna do that to me no more yeah.

It was beginning to worry Kate that, quite possibly, the album *Strong Woman* was turning her against men. Was she subconsciously being manipulated into hating all things male because she was consuming all these lyrics at a deep level and they were actually reprogramming her brain? Was it fuelling the anger she felt at the disinterested boyfriend who never talked of love, and the fury at the sexist boss who would never give her a break and over-promoted the office tart. And might it be causing her to fail to respond to the advertised charms of the Dean of Winchester? In her eyes he was nothing but a cock-sure City-boy in the wrong job. But to most people at the offices of the *Winchester Echo* he was a divinely blessed Brad Pitt.

Was she anti-men?

Were there no men she could look up to and admire in the world?

Give me back my keys and leave oh leave yeah go on right now baby, right now, right now oh yeah.

The raw bitten skin around her fingernails stung when she immersed them in the water. Her hands looked more like builder's hands than a woman's hands. Maybe she should get a manicure and perhaps that would help her take pride in her nails. She glanced down at her baggy black trousers and the greying supermarket blouse. The nails were only the very start of it. Maybe she needed to take pride in more than her nails. What she needed, she decided as she dunked the first plate violently into the water, was a lot more than a manicure.

But a manicure would be a good place to start. She'd never given much thought to her appearance other than *does this look nice, does this fit*. But perhaps the time was right to think a little deeper. But then, if she were to abandon this comfortable but unremarkable look, what would she abandon it *for*? What did she aspire to? Who could she emulate? To get on and empower herself in this job she would need to follow the style cues of Lynn Paget because it was obviously working for her. Could she even wear skirts that short?

Because baby I'm strong. Stronger than you'll ever know. Oh yeah. Ain't no man gonna hold me back yeah.

She dunked the sponge into the beer glass, and, without giving it the usual two full turns to clean it thoroughly, she slammed the glass on the drainer. With a loud snap it broke into shards.

She froze.

The sight of the glass broke her reverie. She stood motionless, hands submerged in the soapy water, staring at the damage beside her on the drainer. Where was this coming from? It was totally unlike her. Completely unlike her. She was usually so calm and so quiet…

But then why not be furious? Why not have had enough of the men in her life? The boyfriend who had turned her into his mother, the boss who was keeping her down, and the arrogant Dean who had made her feel grey and dowdy with his comments about Lynn and the *Lust Red* reminder of his presumably racy private life. Why did men treat her this way? Why was this shaping up to be her lot in life?

She violently dunked Mike's breakfast bowl into the

soapy water.

Because, she was coming to realise, *she* was making it her lot in life. The problem was that obediently washing Mike's dishes and subserviently writing Dr Evil's column inches and dressing like a frump was all of her own choosing. And all of it she could change, really, if she wanted to. If she dared to. No-one was making her do these things. Only her: these were all her choices.

Kate Grey was putting Kate Grey down.

And, if Lynn wanted to get ahead in her career then why should she not do it in the way she had chosen? It was her game. And Lynn was in control. *That* was the difference. Lynn had taken control of her life and Kate had not.

There was a crack.

Kate drew her soapy hands from the water. The bowl was broken. She'd actually broken Mike's breakfast bowl. Fishing the sudsy pieces from the water she dropped them on the drainer alongside the shattered glass.

She began to smile.

Slowly she reached for a dinner plate.

Eleven

Alone in the darkened stationery cupboard, pressed up against the boxes of coloured paper, Edgar was coming to terms with the need to admit defeat and call his father to ask for advice. After all, his father had got him into this mess by urging him, if not forcing him, to take up the position in the Press Office. Anyway, calling him would be a completely logical thing to do, and not an admission of failure, because wasn't he the leading authority on archaeology after that bloke in Durham who found the Viking longship burial? Surely, if anyone, his father would have learnt a few stock phrases that Edgar could impress the journalists with. So all in all, calling his father was a very positive thing for him to do.

But then, did he really want his father holding his hand all his life?

He stared blankly into the stationery-filled blackness.

Yes. Yes he did.

This was not the time to be fretting unnecessarily about standing on his own two feet. Let that come later, preferably when all hell wasn't breaking loose beneath Kings Cross station.

Fishing out his mobile he dialled his father's number, illuminating the small cupboard he'd climbed in to with the spooky green glow of his phone screen.

The mobile phone you are calling is switched off. Please try again later.

"Damn it." His father was probably out of signal. Wasn't he in the south of France or something walking Roman aqueducts or viaducts? He dimly recalled the postcard that had arrived yesterday at the flat. Another plaintive cry from a man who'd spent his life studying the vagaries of post holes and soil markings in Britain.

The light on his mobile dimmed and went out. He was back in complete darkness again.

The phone call that had sent Edgar over the edge and into the cupboard had come from no less than the Mayor's Office and the efficient-sounding man on the other end of the line had fired some frighteningly intelligent questions at him.

"The Mayor is concerned about the Kings Cross Dig. Very concerned."

"Of course, of course."

"We understood, in fact the *Government* understood, that *your* archaeological dig would be scheduled for no more than three weeks and due to complete tomorrow but there appears to be no sign of your archaeologists moving off site. And the Mayor's Office has a trusted source at the construction firm who has insinuated that there may well be a delay to the start of the construction of the new platforms..."

"Right..."

The Government? *His* dig? Edgar was right back in the playground of Bromley School but this time the bullies were *really* big boys and he had the feeling that they would grab more than his bag of sherbet lemons.

During the call Edgar had scrabbled on his desk for the latest version of the authorised press release that would tell him what to say. Where was it? What had he done with it? He tore at an invoice, an old memo, a scheduling meeting note. But no press memo.

"The Mayor, personally, wants a full report. And wants to know why there's been so little information on your dig throughout its duration when we were assured at the beginning that we would be kept fully updated at every stage."

"Right."

"And he also wants you to know, and for you to diss-em-in-ate," the man continued, "throughout the Museum of London the fact that for every day platforms eight through to eleven of Kings Cross overground station are out of action the UK loses approximately two hundred thousand pounds in revenue. That it impacts workers, tourists and most of all *British business*. Do you know what this is doing for the image of the rail network?"

"No?" Edgar squeaked.

"Four o'clock."

"Pardon?"

"Four o'clock."

"Oh. Right." Edgar paused in his scrabbling. Had he missed something? "Sorry I..."

"The Mayor needs your update on his desk by four o'clock today to discuss with his management team. Or should I tell him you're not able to do this?"

"'s fine."

"Thank you. I look forward to reading it." He rattled off his email address which Edgar hastily scribbled down between the greasy mayonnaise smears on his Prêt à Manger sandwich box and then the line went dead.

Edgar shivered at the memory of the call.

He hit a button on his mobile phone and lit up the cupboard again. Right – that was it. He'd try to speak to his boss again. Maybe Richard was now well enough to hobble out of bed and take a call in the grounds of the hospital or something?

He called his boss's number.

Hey there! You've reached Richard Smedley's voicemail. Shoot!

Shoot. How very apt.

Edgar hung up. "Damn."

Alone in the dark again he could hear the sound of his breathing coming in quick gasps. He was panicking but, on the plus side, the adrenaline coursing through him had gone some way to clearing his head. He stroked his chin and examined the courses of action open to him. He could speak to his boss, but he was temporarily out of contact. He could speak to his father but he too was out of contact. Or he could speak to a senior member of staff at MOL.

Or, of course, he had the option of walking away.

He could get up from his desk – or rather out of the cupboard – collect his jacket and walk out of the doors a free man. Yes, he'd lose his flat. And his income. And the pleasure of seeing Erika every day. So he'd lose pretty much everything. And he had nothing to go to. But he could do it, if he really wanted to.

But Edgar knew that walking away was not an option: he was no quitter. No-one made it through three years at Derby University only to come out a quitter; it took great courage and strength of character to live in Derby city centre for three years; it had toughened him up and made a man of him, even if he had come away with a degree in Contemporary Woven Fabric Design.

The only sensible course of action left open to him was to speak to a senior member of the dig team and ask for help. To find out what was *really* going on at Kings Cross. The Head of Marcoms for instance. He would be able to help. If his boss Richard was out of the equation then his boss's boss would have to do. He had seemed a nice enough chap at the department meeting. Friendly. Accessible. And he liked Edgar's suit: surely that would stand him in good stead.

Resolve strengthened and a plan of action decided upon, Edgar uncrumpled himself and emerged from the cupboard, smoothing down his trousers and running a hand through his hair. Walking out of the press office he bounded up the back stairs, two at a time, to the top floor where he headed over to the office of the Head of Marcoms.

The secretary to the Head of Marcoms was over by the fax machine, preoccupied by her task, so he hovered politely by her desk, gnawing his nails, resolve weakening in the high-powered gloss of the senior offices. He could hear the rumble of conversation coming from the boardroom opposite: the Head of Marcoms must be in a meeting. Should he stay? Maybe he should go?

While he stood in a quandary he scanned the clutter on

the secretary's desk. Amongst the debris of stationery he spied a copy of the official Museum of London press release – the same one that he had been trying to find when the journalist called a few minutes earlier. Glancing over to the secretary at the fax machine Edgar tentatively reached over and picked it up. If nothing else it would help.

The paper had been resting on a pile of glossy red files, stacked up beside an enormous plate of sandwiches, all no doubt destined for the boardroom. Shooting another quick glance in the direction of the fax machine Edgar picked up the top copy. *Project Rebel site analysis, timetable, financial control, risk analysis. Issue 5. Copy Twelve of Twenty Three. STRICTLY CONFIDENTIAL.*

"He's in a board meeting!" The secretary was beside him, beak nose wrinkled in distaste, eyes flashing behind her half-moon framed glasses. She snatched the copy of the report from his hands, opened her desk drawer and threw it in, along with the other twenty-two copies, never taking her eyes off Edgar who stood fixed to the spot, sweating. "And these aren't here for you! Strictly confidential!"

"Yes, but… I…"

"Yes?"

"Well, the thing is, I need to see the Head of Marcoms. I had the Mayor's Office on the phone…" He petered out when he saw her expression, which was somewhere between haughty and disdainful. Not one for wedding day photos.

She leant forward until her face was just centimetres from his, and, breathing tea-and-biscuit-breath on him she said, "The Prime Minister, the Head of English Heritage, the Secretary for the Environment and the Head of the British Museum are holding what I can only describe as an emergency meeting specially convened for this morning. They all had very *very* important prior engagements that they cancelled in order to sit in that room just there. Do you want me to interrupt them to ask if they'll speak to you? Just say the word and I'll go and inform them that a Junior Executive is demanding their time. Would you like me to?" She stepped in the direction of the boardroom.

Edgar stared at the egg sandwiches. "No."

"Right then. You'd better be off. Here," she conceded and held out the platter, "take a sandwich."

He picked up a sandwich, mumbled some thanks and slunk out of the Director's offices, crept down the back stairs and returned to safety.

Crouched in the stationery cupboard with the lights off, eating his egg sandwich, Edgar could still hear his phone ringing and the gentle *ping* as email after email entered his inbox.

Erika had pretended not to notice when Edgar had shut himself in the stationery cupboard that morning. Twice. It was a hard time for him, she knew that. Having worked in the Press Office for nearly a year she had a fairly good idea of what constituted a normal workload and she knew that this was crazy. The phone didn't stop ringing and there was just the poor new boy in the office – since all the others had been shot or cautioned.

She briefly toyed with the idea of involving the Head of Human Resources and asking him about work-related stress. Edgar was not looking well. He had been slightly podgy and rosy-cheeked when he started and barely a fortnight later he was thinner, paler, with dark circles under his eyes and a nervous, hunted look about him. He was suffering, she could see that.

But at least he had returned to his desk now.

Edgar stared blankly at his PC screen. He read the words over and over and over again, swallowing hard.

To: all staff
From: Aubrey Tomsin-Bowen, Head of Marketing and Communications, Museum of London
Subject: Kings Cross Archaeological Excavation
It has been decided to extend the period of the archaeological dig by a further three weeks (to 11th December) with a possible extension thereafter depending on the success of the dig at that point. For this much welcomed stay of execution the Museum of London is indebted to the excellent work of Professor Hilary De Lacey and her team, to whom I extend my warmest thanks.
As you will all be aware this dig is attracting some media attention

Edgar looked longingly at the stationery cupboard.

and this extension will no doubt further ruffle some media feathers. We appreciate the efforts all staff are making in order to maintain confidentiality on this matter and we recognise that for some of you this is a very difficult time.

Nevertheless we are making good progress at the dig site and intend to launch a comprehensive press event day on-site in three weeks time. All departments and staff members are likely to be involved to some extent in the planning and execution of our Press Event Day and individuals will be briefed in the coming week by their line managers. In the meantime please continue to apply press release 8.7 (12th November) with the addition that all members of the media are invited to the event at midday on 1st December when all will be revealed. The PR department will publish the full details of the event on our website by 2pm this afternoon so please direct any enquiries to our site.

Edgar took several deep breaths.

Maybe he should try again to have a word with the Head of Marcoms. See if there was anything he could be involved with: ask how he should be handling the press, handling all the enquiries about the plague pit...

"There is a man holding on the phone from the *Evening Standard*." Erika padded in to the press office and put a hand on his shoulder. "Can I put him through?"

Edgar continued to stare at the PC screen, the memo from the Head of Marcoms. An idea was starting to form; perhaps there was another avenue down which he could go.

"Yes. No. No – Erika I have to go out now."

"But he was really quite insistent that he talk to you."

"Tell him I'll call him back."

"He will not like it."

Edgar faltered. "Well I..." Involuntarily his hand flicked

down to his phone. He jerked it away. "No. Tough. I'm going." He stood up and reached over for his jacket.

"But Ed-gar he—"

"Sorry Erika. I'm going out."

"Where to? Your appointment it is not in the office diary."

Edgar flung his jacket on. "That's because it's on the hoof."

"The hoof?"

"You know, the spur of the moment. Spontaneous. Unplanned."

"Here, let me help you with that." She pulled out the sleeve of his jacket which was tangled up.

"Thanks." He looked at her sheepishly. "Look, I'll be back later. Not long."

"But where are you going? I need to write it in the office diary."

"Urgh!" Edgar grabbed his staff ID card, his pad, pen and the press office's camera and headed out, pausing only to yank open the office diary, scribble a note in it and snap it shut. "Back at midday, Erika," he called as he pushed through the double doors.

"Are you contactable by mobile?"

"No." And he was gone.

Huffing she walked out of the press office and went back to her desk, opening up the desk diary and reading Edgar's note.

@ kings cross dig

Twelve

Archie could see one of the Cathedral's cleaning women was approaching him. He looked for a hiding place but, unless he could dive into the five inches of space behind the organ, it was too late. He fixed a placid smile: inwardly fractious, outwardly holy.

Margery Down was one of the necessities of any house of God. Small, plump and elderly she headed up the lavender-scented *cleaning ensemble* made up entirely of small, plump, Scholl-clad ladies who turned up at 9am every Tuesday and Friday to clean God's house for him: wide bottoms in the air, Marigolds on, dusting, sweeping, polishing and, most of all, gossiping their way to a spotless cathedral.

They frightened him.

They frightened him because he assumed at some point in their lives they would have been young, svelte but buxom, attractive women. They would have enveloped men with their perfume, enticed them with mischievous eyes, dressed in stockings and stilettos.

So just *what* happened to a woman to mutate her in to this? When were mischievous eyes hidden behind thick brown-rimmed glasses, when did shoulders slump and heels get substituted for lace-up brogues? If he were to make a go of it with Angela – because she was something special and he couldn't get her out of his head since their time at Lichfield – then would he wake up one morning nuzzling a woman like this with his morning glory? These were thoughts he had privately in moments of calm when there weren't more pressing things to occupy his mind. He would watch them as, in a huddle by the crypt, they would don their blue nylon aprons with the same pride as an RAF officer dons a uniform; the Winchester Cathedral logo worn as proudly as a ribbon of medals across their vast and terrifying bosoms.

Usually he exchanged a few words with them as they pottered around the cathedral: quite a *dusty* day today isn't it Mrs Simons, terrible weather eh Mrs Robey, goodness what a full Hoover bag Mrs Jackson. That sort of thing. It kept them happy.

Today, however, he really didn't have time for Margery Down and the Winchester Cleaning Ensemble.

The Bishop of Wessex had just been on the phone, and *sotto voce,* in between discussing the various cathedral affairs he poked his port-swollen nose into, the man had dropped the bombshell that, oh by the way, before I forget, terrible memory these days, the Bishops of Sussex, Hertfordshire and Somerset would be paying a visit to Winchester next week, *next week,* to discuss Archie's plans for the direction of Winchester Cathedral and then apologised for having sat on that nugget of information for well over two months *but haven't things been busy lately*.

"Excuse me, Dean..." Margery Down shuffled closer.

"Margery! Hey! How's it going with the mops? Everything all right is it?" He caught her look of anxiety and his smile froze.

"Oh yes, Father. Well, you see, I was giving the presbytery a good clean in preparation for the Bach concert this weekend and, well, I was right underneath one of the seats and I found…well I found this." She opened up her fist. In the palm of her hand lay a dark wooden carving of an animal's head: snarling, teeth-bared and eyes bulging.

"Golly." He took the ugly wooden gargoyle off her and went through the motions of examining it.

A snapped bit of carving. Great. Just great. MacNeath's ecclesiastical heavies would be rocking up in six days' time and she had a snapped bit of wood to distract him from coming up with just what he was going to do. "Well, my goodness me… Well, thank you Margery."

He went to hand it back to her.

But then a thought struck him. He looked at it again.

He turned it round and round examining it closely, running his fingers over the tiny fangs of the ugly beast and along the rough edge where it had snapped from its original position. "Where, exactly, did you find it Margery?"

He followed her down the aisle to the area she'd been cleaning, the mop temporarily abandoned beside the wall.

"Here. Just here." she bent down as quickly as her bad back would allow and pointed underneath a seat.

Archie crouched down and checked there were no more pieces, running his hand across the newly cleaned stone floor. "Well, let me see…" He stood up and Margery watched adoringly as he raised his eyes upwards.

The Bishop's Throne loomed before him, its wood as dark as pitch and carved in tight leaf scrolls and animal heads just like the piece he had in his hands. Behind it stood the rood screen, on which was mounted three mortuary chests containing the remains of former kings of ancient England.

Archie stared at the dark wood throne. Towards the top he could make out a lighter patch of wood from which the animal head he was clutching had broken off.

"There you go! Look up there." He pointed its position out to Margery. "Now, that is strange!"

"What's strange Dean?"

"Well, it's clearly broken off quite recently. You guys would have spotted it during the last cleaning session wouldn't you? And it's come from the presbytery, which is where the long ladder was found after the break-in. It's rather a coincidence isn't it? Our female intruder must have climbed up the rood screen and broken this off the throne in the process. But why, Margery? Why would someone break in to the Cathedral and climb up the rood screen?"

"There's some funny folk about and no mistaking."

But Archie barely heard her response. His attention had been caught by one of the mortuary chests mounted on the rood screen, the one nearest to the Bishop's Throne. The chest was one of the great treasures of the Cathedral with its winged cherubs holding up a scroll proclaiming the object to be the resting place of the remains of Canute, King of England 1016 to 1035. On top of it was a large lid and what had particularly caught his attention was the angle of this in relation to the chest itself.

Archie felt a heavy dread descend upon him.

"Margery would you be so good as to fetch the Archdeacon? And tell him to bring the long ladder."

*

"You want me..." Cedric Cooper, the Archdeacon of Winchester Cathedral faltered.

"Yes..." Archie stared wide-eyed, waiting to hear what the Archdeacon had taken in from the last ten minutes of conversation.

"...to go up there?"

"Yes!"

The Archdeacon looked up to the top of the rood screen.

"I'm sorry, Dean, run it past me one more time. Why can't *you* go up there?" At thirty years Archie's senior the Archdeacon had a good point. Enthusiastic, keen to the point of mania and scattier than all the Winchester Cleaning Ensemble put together, the Archdeacon was nevertheless not physically fit or active. Yes, he did cycle to the cathedral every day but then he only lived three and a half minutes from the building and spent longer meticulously applying his trouser clips and helmet than he did in the actual saddle.

"Cedric, you know I'd do it myself if I could, old chap, but I have this irrational fear of ladders. I get the urge to throw myself off them. Comes in waves all of a sudden and I'd happily start climbing and then *bang!*" He slammed his hand down against the rood screen making old Mrs Peters who had been polishing the brass leap into the air and then hurriedly rush in the direction of the toilets.

"Bang?"

"Yes bang! I'd be on the floor. Pancaked. I'd get disorientated you see Cedric. No, all I need you to do, and it's quite simple, is to climb up this *short ladder* and peer into Canute's tomb."

"But this is the *long* ladder..."

Archie gritted his teeth. "Please, Cedric, go up the ladder!"

"Because..."

God give me strength! Archie was perpetually amazed at the low-level awareness of the Archdeacon. Sometimes even the fact that he kept remembering to breathe was a miracle in itself. "Because you can see quite clearly from here that the lid of the tomb is at an angle."

The Archdeacon peered up. "You're right, Dean."

"So if you could just peer in, check everything's as it should be, and put the lid back on then I'd be really very grateful."

"Best not have the place a mess when all the Bishops come round, eh?"

Archie's left eye went into spasm. *Six days.*

The Archdeacon began to climb, Archie holding the ladder steady.

"You know..." The Archdeacon paused two steps up.

"What?"

"Well couldn't one of the choir boys do this? After all they're agile and light."

"Are you insinuating they're expendable, Cedric?"

"Oh, good heavens, no. It's just—"

"Their parents would go nuts if they found out I'd got them climbing ladders. And besides, I need someone with the strength to close the tomb lid. The thing's bound to weigh a bit and one of those pipsqueaks just wouldn't be able to close it would they? Like as not they'd get their sticky mitts caught in the lid and then there'd be lawsuits flying…"

"Good point!" Happy now, the Archdeacon recommenced his climb.

"That's it, Cedric! You're doing fine! Halfway now!"

The Archdeacon pursed his lips together and continued to climb, the dry old ladder creaking beneath his feet. He was near to the bottom of the tomb now, level with the top of the rood screen.

"OK, Cedric!" came the voice from Archie many, many feet below him. "You're there. Can you climb onto the rood screen itself?"

The Archdeacon slowly reached the top of the ladder. It wobbled violently as Archie, whistling softly, had stood aside and with his thumb nail was attempting to tighten the screw on his sunglasses, which had come loose. Didn't want to lose it in the cathedral – he'd never find it and then his three hundred pound glasses would be unusable.

"ER DEAN…!"

"Oh! Sorry. Marvellous! Oh well done, Cedric! Now what can you see?"

The Archdeacon wiped off the sweat that was running down his face. His hands were sticky and wet. Pausing to get his breath back he looked down at the cathedral spread out below him, newly disturbed clouds of dust shimmering in the sunlight that flooded in through the window and illuminated the tiled floor thirty feet below with the Dean standing looking up at him, replacing the sunglasses on his head and mussing up his crop of blonde hair, a gaggle of cleaning ladies behind watching the action. The Archdeacon felt a wave of nausea and he gripped the narrow stone plinth for all he was worth. There was a long, long way to fall to those hard floor tiles.

Concentrating hard on the stone directly in front of him the Archdeacon pulled himself into a seated position and turned to face Canute's tomb. From this position he could see quite clearly that there had been someone up there recently. The thick layers of grey dust had settled around the base of the tomb but around one corner it had been scraped away by feet or hands. Mindful of what the police had said about evidence he manoeuvred as carefully as he could so as not to disturb the marks. Although how the police could tell anything on such scant evidence as dust scrapings he would never know. Unless they found a set of very dusty clothes somewhere.

"There's definitely been someone up here!" he called down to Archie below, his voice wobbling and indistinct.

"I knew it! And what about the tomb?"

"Well..." The Archdeacon cautiously raised himself up and peered into the mortuary chest through the gap. It was dark inside and it took a few seconds for his eyes to adjust. "Well I can't be sure about the bodies because the bones are all jumbled up..."

"Well what can you see?" Archie had one foot on the ladder. It would have been easier to have done it himself.

"Bones. Lots of bones. And a black box with a Latin label on it. Do you want me to read it? It says that these are the remains of Canute, King of England, and his wife Emma."

"Anything else?"

"No. Just bones. A skull."

"A skull?"

"Yes."

"One skull?"

"Yes."

"Not two?"

"No, Dean. Just the one."

"Oh, pissing hell!"

The crowd of cleaners gathered silently behind Archie dispersed quickly, scandalised to their cores.

Thirteen

Edgar made the decision to walk to Kings Cross rather than take the underground; he needed to work off some of the nervous energy that was making his heart race and his hands shake. With the stress of the past week Edgar had shaken and sweated his way through nearly a stone in weight and now half his clothes no longer fitted him, his trousers hung gathered around his waist, bound in place by a belt that was on a tighter setting than he'd had since before university. It wasn't all bad though. Standing in front of the mirror in his tiny bathroom last night, self conscious but curious, he'd noticed how his stomach, usually softly rounded was now flattening and even a trace of muscle was showing. And his face was losing its baby-like roundness about the cheeks and jaws; he was looking sleeker. Not, it had to be said, enough to propel him into the world of male modelling and a career cavorting bare-chested on deserted beaches for aftershave commercials, but it was a step in the right direction. Yes he might be putting his body through immense physical strain but at least he was gaining cheekbones.

He set off, pushing open the glass doors of the Museum of London and heading down Montague Place and up Little Britain. A light breeze was rattling the branches of the vast London planes, picking up the cigarette packets and blowing them down the streets. The traffic thundered down the busy road while clueless half-terrified tourists and tense-looking businessmen did battle on the pavements.

In under half an hour he'd arrived at Kings Cross, slowing his pace as he weaved in through the crowds milling around the station entrance.

Cutting a path through the torrent of focused travellers Edgar managed to navigate his way towards the back of Kings Cross overground station, its plain sandstone façade rising up before him. Checking his progress was a wooden screen, over seven feet high, that stretched around the perimeter of the building. It was topped with springy loops of razor wire. And security cameras. And alarms. Emblazoned on the wooden screen was the Museum of London logo, along with signs for Pentonville Security Ltd complete with a picture of a large toothy dog and *I patrol here* emblazoned across it.

Edgar was reminded of a particular interview with a journalist from the *Telegraph* earlier that week: "Why is it," the man had asked, "that the dig site at Kings Cross has so much security when Number Two Poultry in the City had virtually no security for the two years it was being excavated?"

Edgar, as much in the dark as the journalist, nevertheless felt it was his duty to come up with some plausible explanation to fob the man off. He had said it was because the Kings Cross Dig was situated in a *deprived area* and there were *large volumes of pedestrian traffic making it difficult to secure*. The journalist didn't buy any of it.

"Why, for that matter, was a medieval pit given such tight

security?" he had continued. "Surely a pit with rumours of plague and disease, whether they were true or not, would be its own security?"

Edgar had assured him that there was no risk of infection, that was made clear in the press release dated…

"And presumably the dead bodies, be they infected or not, were thrown into mass graves and not buried with their belongings? What would there be to steal from a medieval mass grave but bones? The site must surely be of no value to anyone but archaeologists?"

"Yes but—"

"Going back to Number Two Poultry, the archaeologists there uncovered a key area of Roman London with Roman shops and houses containing coin hoards and jewellery and other items of great value and yet security had been low-rise fencing and two security guards. So why are there guards, dogs, fencing, razor wire, cameras and alarms at Kings Cross? Why aren't the media allowed inside? Why aren't we being told anything? *What have you found beneath the platforms?*"

Later, in the dark beside the boxes of manila envelopes, Edgar had replayed the conversation and had concluded that perhaps the journalist had had a good point. A mass grave with the rumour of plague in such a deprived area as Kings Cross should be its own security.

Edgar had reached the back of Kings Cross Station. He walked over to a guarded wooden door with the sign *Site Entrance Strictly No Admittance to Non-Authorised Personnel* above it.

"Nah mate. This is a restricted area innit?" A wardrobe of

a security guard stuffed into a pseudo-police type uniform barred his way. "There ain't *no* public in 'ere at the moment. If you want the mainline station it's round there on the left mate." There was something of pure violence about the man who, although slightly shorter than Edgar, was broad and heavy and incredibly, prehistorically, hairy with a black wiry mane and thick bushy brows that met in the middle and then began to run down the length of his nose.

"Ah yes but…" Edgar couldn't help but smirk as he fished in his jacket pocket and produced his new pass. "I *am* staff." The guard took the pass off him, suspiciously examining it, studying his face and the face on the photograph in his hands.

"Shiny pass this. Just 'ad it done?" He was suspicious.

"I've only been at the Museum a couple of weeks."

The security guard leered. "Do I look like a bleedin' lemon, mate?"

"What?"

"You don't look nuffin like the bloke on the pass."

"Well neither would you if you'd lived the last fortnight I'd lived. Can I go through now?"

"Wot? Are you like saying you've aged ten years in a fortnight?"

"Yes."

"Phnerr. You ain't." The guard thrust the pass back at Edgar and assumed his position, legs apart, arms crossed across his chest. Resolute and hairy.

"Look!" Edgar whipped out his driving licence and the security guard bent over to examine it. He looked from museum pass to driving licence to Edgar.

He raised his eyebrow.

"Jesus mate. You must 'ave had one 'ell of a shit few days."

"I have."

The security guard shrugged and stepped back, arms crossed again.

"So can I go through now?" Edgar made to walk past the guard and into the doorway.

"No." The security guard blocked his path. "You ain't never comin' in here not even if you've aged ten years or more. No public, no employees, and absolutely no press. Is that a camera?" He pointed to the camera sticking out of Edgar's satchel.

"Erm…" Edgar thought quickly. "Yes. Look – I could leave it with you. Now can I come in? I'm staff for goodness sake. This is the organisation I work for. I work in the Museum press office and I have spent the last two weeks answering bloody questions about this bloody place and I have no idea what I'm doing, so I have to see it for myself."

"That's as maybe but you ain't getting past me, mate."

"Oh for God's sake!" Edgar turned and walked away, kicking at the litter. This was ludicrous! Why was he not allowed in to his own company's dig? How the hell was he supposed to peddle the press releases when he had no idea what was going on in there? He turned and walked back to the security guard who was picking the skin round his nail, looking up at him, waiting for the next move.

"I'm sorry but you've got to let me in!"

The guard continued to look at him from under his eyebrow, biting the hard skin around his nail and spitting it out.

Edgar clenched his fists. He was not going to leave. He had to find out what was going on. To know more than these smart-arsed journalists purported to know. How could he do his job if he didn't know what was going on here?

"I know!" He dived into his satchel and pulled out his mobile phone. He would get the Head of Marcoms on the phone. The Head of Marcoms would let him through. He dialled the receptionist's number at the Museum.

"Henri, its Edgar Thompson. Can you put me through to the Head of Marketing and Communications please?"

Your gay lover.

"Hold please."

The familiar holding music played as Henri put the call through. A pianist belted out Brahms' Sonata No. 1 *allegro appassionato.* Holding the line patiently Edgar watched as, across the Euston Road from him, a grey-looking woman slouched in a derelict shop doorway passed something surreptitiously to another younger grey-looking woman who handed the older one some money. The sordid event was rendered poignant by the building crescendo of the music, like some modern urban opera. All it wanted was one of the two to fall to her knees and sing plaintively of the abuse she suffered at the hands of her crack-addict pimp boyfriend. But they didn't. The seller walked away, wiping her nose on her sleeve while the music died down. In the slow melodic aftermath the young grey woman leant against the dirty boarded up doorway, watching the passers by, briefly catching Edgar's eye across the street.

He turned back to the Museum of London boards beside

him. 'We apologise...' the posters read. They ran the length of the boards and were full of the usual stuff, hackneyed phrases much the same as the ones he was required to use in his press releases. There was *important work in progress*, and it was *helping to shape our understanding of the past*, the Museum of London was *working to minimise disruption*, blah blah blah.

The pianist started banging the keys again and Edgar held the phone away from his ear.

Which department was responsible for these notices? Edgar peered closely at the bottom right of the poster nearest to him. In small print he could make out "Reb 11-11-07 AT-B version 2".

AT-B? That was Aubrey Tomsin-Bowen, the very man he was hoping to be put through to on the phone. Eventually. When Liberace gave it a rest.

The date and version number in the small print were self explanatory but 'Reb'? What did *Reb* signify?

"I'm sorry he's not answering. Do you want his assistant James Sanderson?"

Do you? "No. Thanks, Henri."

"No problem, Edgar. I am getting *a lot* of calls for you by the way. Do you want me to give them your mobile number?"

"No! No – I'll be back in the office in an hour or so."

He hung up and stared at the small print on the poster, still watched by the hairy security guard.

Reb... Reb...

Images filled his head. Aubrey Tomsin-Bowen and the board meeting with the PM...the plate of egg sandwiches...

the tall pile of glossy red reports waiting to go into the emergency meeting in the board room... Project Rebel Site Analysis...

"Rebel!" Edgar strode up to the guard.

"Wot choo say mate?"

"Rebel!" He walked closer. "I'm here for Project Rebel." The security guard winked and stepped aside. "Well why din'choo say so? Come right in, sir." And he stepped aside, holding open the narrow red door.

Trying to play it cool, but failing, a beaming Edgar eased himself past the guard and into the gloom of the station sheds.

"You ain't comin' in 'ere." He could hear the guard with the next lot of people at the gate.

Inside the sealed-off section of Kings Cross station a muffled dampness enveloped Edgar. The silence was the biggest shock after the roar of traffic and people and road works outside on the Euston Road. Now the only sound was his breathing and the faint *bing bong* of station announcements wafting from further on in the building where the platforms were still functioning. To his right was a dimly lit staircase winding upwards and to his left the corridor stretched out several metres before turning a corner. A sheet of A4 paper was taped to the tiled wall in front of him, "Project Rebel ☞ this way".

Edgar stood for a moment allowing his senses to adjust to the place, his eyes growing accustomed to the poor light and his ears attuned to the silence. Gradually he began to pick up new sounds, the faint drone of voices and machinery coming from his left.

"Right then," he said into the silence and, feeling rather foolish for having done it, walked in the direction of the voices, tense with the anticipation that at any minute a security guard would jump out and grab him for being somewhere that he shouldn't be.

As he inched toward the voices a sense of foreboding grew.

What if there really was a danger to human health with this dig?

Generating media attention was something the Museum of London constantly strived for. It boosted visitor numbers, increased the likelihood of funding, and was generally an indication of the museum doing the *right thing*. So why was this dig being kept from the media and the public when everyone was desperate to know what was going on?

Because they had found a plague virus.

A live plague virus.

That would explain why this dig was under such tight security. Maybe at that moment, somewhere in a top security hospital, there were wards full of shaggy-haired archaeologists writhing and screaming in agony having dug up the polluted bodies and themselves become infected. Perhaps the noise coming from around the corner was the sound of machines hurriedly infilling the putrid pits that had been exposed, confining the plague and its original victims to the ground once more. And after a light-hearted *nothing much found here folks* press release, the new platforms would seal the top of the site and everything would go on much as it had done. Except for the shaggy-haired archaeology teams whose losses whilst digging in action would be hushed up with substantial payouts.

Edgar took a shaky breath. Possibly his last if the Black Death was stalking Kings Cross.

Oh God. He didn't want to die. He'd hardly done anything yet. If this was going to be his last week on earth then he should have plucked up the courage to ask Erika out on a date. Or at least put more effort in to having a conversation with her without blushing and feeling as awkward as a teenager.

Edging forward he fished in his pockets for a handkerchief – perhaps if he held it up to his face…

There had been an awful lot of plague speculation in the papers and what did they say about no smoke without fire?

On his first couple of days in the press office the pettiness of the argument between the two opposing sides of the Kings Cross Dig had amused him, even when the concept of plague was bandied around. The Mayor's Office had attempted to use the threat of Black Death as a political weapon in order to get the site closed down and the building works started. The Mayor's Office had told *The Times* in an interview that they were concerned that there could well be a *significant health risk* in exposing plague pits so near to the general public. They felt the Museum should let the dead alone.

With little comfort Edgar now endeavoured to recall the Museum of London's response to the Mayor's allegations as he neared the turn in the corridor and on into a possible bubo-festering, blood-coughing death.

The Museum had teamed up with St Bartholomew's Hospital, and in a three page exclusive given to the *Daily Mail*, but also leaked to every paper and TV and radio station known to man, had wholly denied any risk to public health.

But then there was Nigel Partner.

Nigel Partner was a computer programmer from Hemel Hempstead who used Kings Cross daily on his commute to work. Five days into Edgar's job, the man called Nigel Partner had developed swollen glands and the whole of Kings Cross overground station was sealed off for twenty-four hours. One of the tabloids had succinctly summarised the situation when it ran the headline "PLAGUE!" In an article spanning the first three pages it had conjectured that the computer programmer was one of many who had caught the still-live plague virus from the medieval plague pits beneath Kings Cross Station; the secrecy of the dig being evidence itself that the dig was "not in the public's best interest." Subsequent articles further into the paper had gone on to examine the various plagues since the fourteenth century, their probable causes, effects and, in detail, the symptoms of the diseases. It had even run a centre-page spread of what the top ten British celebrities would look like with the plague virus.

Meanwhile, at Kings Cross, there had been no trains, no archaeologists, no developers.

The Government had swiftly intervened and the Health Secretary reiterated that there was *no risk whatsoever to human health* from the dig and that Nigel Partner's illness was simply influenza and in no way connected with the archaeological dig at Kings Cross. The man with the shiny black Daimler paid a visit to the Mayor's offices one evening and the story died a death.

As did Nigel Partner.

No-one, not press, Mayor or Museum dared comment on his passing.

Edgar had reached the end of the corridor. He turned the corner and entered the dig site.

"Oh dear Lord..." He put his handkerchief up to his mouth.

Fourteen

"Hello there young Kate." Pasty-faced Sean from BBC Radio Hampshire News eased himself down beside her and wiped the sweat from his forehead. The media briefing room in Winchester police station was a hot, airless annexe of the basement *not even fit for criminals* as Dr Evil had once quipped. Something about the quality of the circulated air. Sitting next to Sean, with his sweaty bulk and nylon shirt, she experienced the full effect of non-circulating air.

"Getting here early?" Kate looked at her watch. "This must be a first for you Sean."

"Well I'm intrigued." He leant close to her on the pretext of pulling a crumpled pad from his back pocket. "Sorry Kate, didn't mean to do that. What a lovely blouse by the way. Anyway, of course I'm here on time. Body snatching ancient kings? Who'd miss this one? Beautiful story. I see our friend from the *Southampton Evening Telegraph* even managed to get here on time." He nodded over to the sullen man sitting in the corner. "Hello, hello." Sean shuffled forward in his chair and Kate looked up. Two men were striding in to the briefing room, loud shirts and the glint of cufflinks, bellowing with laughter at something one of them had said. Each had a laptop bag slung over his shoulder. Following them a third member of the media walked into the room: a woman in a white wool coat, an oversized turquoise suede bag slung over her arm. It was enormous. Kate marvelled at it. What on earth could a woman need such a large bag for?

"London train's come in then," said Sean, leaning closer to Kate, brushing her breast again with his shoulder. She smiled tightly and leaning away from him she shot a quick glance at the three journalists. The woman had perched daintily on the edge of a chair, unbuttoning the expensive coat to reveal a fitted blouse and pencil skirt. Frighteningly sharp. Self-consciously Kate kicked her cheap bag under her chair and smoothed down her baggy M&S trousers.

"Do you know them?" she whispered to Sean.

"Not the woman. Or the first man with the pink shirt, but the other man with the stripy shirt, that's Geoff Lentward from the *Telegraph*. Met him at a dinner a couple of years ago. Thinks he's God's gift, but then you can tell that from his choice of glasses, can't you. Ponce."

"He's from the *Telegraph*?"

This must be a significant briefing if the big London journalists were present. Kate regretted not having asked Dr Evil for more details of the story beforehand, so she was more prepared than this: more prepared to ask an intelligent question and make the woman with the gigantic turquoise bag look over in her direction. She wanted her to look over and nod in a *yes, sister journalist, what a good question* sort of a way; to be worth at the very least a moment of the smart woman's attention.

"Still slogging for that Roger Effel then?" Sean leant over again.

"Something like that." Kate feigned disinterest, flicking

through her scrawled and doodled upon pad.

"Bloody slave-driver that man. Has he made you a senior reporter yet?"

"Still not, Sean." Kate bit her lip.

"You know BBC Radio are always on the lookout for talented reporters." Sean looked at her meaningfully.

"Mmm."

The door swung open and in marched the police officer in charge of the operation. Kate recognised Sergeant Swain and he acknowledged her, nodding in her direction. She bristled with pride, hastily regaining her composure and shooting a glance in the direction of the female journalist with the enormous statement bag. She hadn't noticed.

"Thank you all for coming." Sergeant Swain pulled up a chair and began the press briefing. A second policeman scuttled into the room, arms laden with press packs. Wishing she had a Dictaphone like the female journalist Kate scratched her notes on the paper as fast as she could.

Details of break-in as before. Midnight. Female into staff side door (door left open). Ladder (see prev photo) rood screen – Canute skull!!!

Police – witnesses, appeal (publish tel no – tbc).

No leads.

Photofit produced (source: Dean's description) female, long red hair, 5'2"?, green bag (bought fr Hobbs – this season's stock). Age…late 30's???

Head taken. Confirmed Canute. Wife Emma also in grave – remains untouched. Scrape of gold from shoe taken from Rood Screen. Under analysis.

The sergeant leant back and watched the faces of the

journalists assembled before him. "So, ladies and gentlemen, any questions?"

One of the two London journalists leant forward, "Excuse me, Sergeant Swine—"

The female journalist kicked his chair with her turquoise shoe, hiding the smirk on her perfectly red lips.

"Swain."

"Oh, I beg your pardon. Swain. Can you be sure it was Canute's skull in there?"

"A good question. To which the answer is a tentative *yes*. The Winchester Archaeological Unit say that they're *reasonably confident* it was Canute's skull that was taken. The only skull now remaining in the tomb is that of a woman whom we believe to be Emma, Canute's wife. Obviously it's been a thousand years since the man died and that means we rely on early record-keeping. We know there have been mix-ups between this and the other five mortuary chests over the centuries but the bones in this particular chest were carbon-dated around five years ago and found to be from the right period to indicate that we have Canute. There were even samples of tooth also taken at that time which, when analysed, indicated that the person in the tomb had originated from a Scandinavian country. So, to go back to your question I think it's fair to assume we had Canute's skull in the casket. And, most importantly, our woman believed she was taking Canute's skull when she selected the male skull that evening."

Kate desperately searched for a question. Something clever. Something witty. Let the London journalists turn round and look at *her* ask the key question; *that was a clever question, would you like a job at the* Telegraph*?* Had they already said anything about the possibility of more thefts of skulls around the country? She couldn't remember.

The man from the *Telegraph*, with the pretentious glasses, shot his hand up. "Sergeant *Swain*, have any more skulls been taken from around Winchester? Or indeed anywhere recently?"

Kate gritted her teeth. Dammit. That was her question.

"Not from Winchester they haven't. As I've said we checked all the other accessible tombs and they were untouched. But I can't speak for those residing in other Church properties around the UK. It's something we're obviously going to look at but our priority at the moment is locating the woman in the description and returning Canute's skull to its mortuary chest."

"What if there were more skulls taken, but new ones substituted?" Kate piped up from the back of the briefing room. "If the Dean interrupted the thief then maybe the thief didn't have time to substitute a skull in place of the one she had taken? If the Archdeacon had seen there were two skulls in the chest when he checked then the theft wouldn't have come to light would it? He wouldn't have thought to have it checked out whether the bones in there were the original ones?"

"A good point."

Kate pursed her lips together to suppress a smile, noticing out of the corner of her eye that the other journalists were looking in her direction.

"But in answer to your question we have no idea if a substitution has taken place elsewhere in the cathedral with other tombs. We don't have the resources to check that all the bodies match their skulls but what we have done is examine the containers and immediate environments around those containers for signs of forced intrusion and so far we haven't seen any more signs of tampering. At this point we believe Canute to be the only victim."

Kate flicked through the press-pack the young policeman had just handed to her, pausing when she came to the photofit. She was beautiful, this intruder, if the photofit was anything to go by. A rough artist's sketch in pencil of a woman who reminded Kate of the film stars from the silent movies, a veritable Clara Bow with her doe-eyes and cupid-bow lips, wearing a slightly startled expression. A missing king and a beautiful woman. This was Kate's story and she was going to make it work for her. For once Kate Grey would have the opportunity to make something of herself.

She walked out of the briefing and back to her car, half-heartedly waving farewell to Sean who was easing himself into his old Volvo. The three London journalists had a cab waiting, probably to take them on to the Cathedral for a quick scout around before heading back to the capital in their business-class carriage: thundering through the Wiltshire countryside tap-tapping up their articles on laptops, discussing the story, name dropping, networking over a glass of wine.

Kate spun her little Metro round in the car park and headed back to the office via the town centre. There were a couple of things she needed to buy.

There is no way but up for me, baby, yeah.

Fifteen

"Dear boy, dear boy!" Edgar shook Professor Hilary De Lacey's soil-covered hand as she peered at him over her glasses. Edgar distantly remembered her as one of his father's friends, dropping round for supper, discussions of archaeology that lasted all evening. She had worn in those days, and wore now, a tailored wool suit and smart heeled shoes – so unlike the other archaeologists in their scruffy jeans and t-shirts. For her it had obviously been a matter of pride to remain presentable, regardless of the nature of her job. "You've grown up young Edgar! How's your father?"

"Fine."

"Yes? Enjoying his retirement out in Italy eh? Can't be bad. Still, wouldn't want to miss out on this I should think. Tell me Edgar, why have you got that handkerchief over your mouth?"

"No reason..."

"Well! Terribly exciting moment isn't it for the Museum? So when were you drafted in on Project Rebel? I missed the last meeting because of the visit from our friends at the Home Office. Good job too as it happens, they granted us permission to move some of the bodies so we can get tests done up at the University of North East London. But I'm wandering aren't I? Were you brought in to Project Rebel at the last meeting?"

"Oh, well, just this week." Flustered, Edgar tried to affect a casual air, ramming his hands in his jacket pockets. "They think that there should be someone from the press office in the know. You know… So here I am. Come to learn about it."

"But of course we're not going to the press with this yet are we?" Hilary looked concerned.

"Oh no. No. Not at all. No. I just need to get a better idea of what I'm *not* telling them to help me do my job properly. And of course it will help me prepare for when we do go public."

"Well marvellous. So then, are you suitably impressed by our dig?" She stood back and let Edgar have full view of the excavation that was going on around her.

It was hard to imagine how this space had looked when there had been platforms and trains. The vast area boarded-off from the public was now stripped back to soil levels many feet in front of and below the old concourse where they stood. There were hundreds of pits and trenches dug into the earth with archaeologists in white boiler suits everywhere. Some were in groups, others alone, crouched over the ground, scraping away surrounded by their sieves and trowels, bags for the finds and clipboards and drawing boards. But the biggest shock was that everywhere in the ground there were bones. Thousands and thousands of bones heaped together in a mess of limbs and skulls and spinal columns. And above it all hung the now redundant platform numbers and fire exit signs, remnants of the station that had sat on top of it all for one hundred and fifty years.

"Good stuff, eh?" Hilary linked her arm through his, smiling at the incredulous expression on his face. "We run teams twenty-four hours a day: the pressure is on I can tell you. We need to get this place stripped back, recorded and the key materials removed and preserved before the public finds out what's really here; every day is another day when we could have a leak. And if what they found out..."

"But would it be *so* bad if the public did have more of an idea what you are doing?" Edgar began, cautiously.

Professor De Lacey looked horrified at his suggestion. "Well of course it would! If we told them the truth then we'd be required to have those devils from the newspapers prowling all over the place, and the security that would need to be set up – well, we're just not ready for it yet. Not at all. We couldn't cope with the public interest so we have to fob them off until we're ready."

"Of course." Edgar nodded rapidly.

Professor De Lacey patted him on the arm. "Well, let's not stand here like a couple of turkeys. Let me take you a bit further into the dig and you'll see what we've uncovered." Her twinkly eyes narrowed for a moment and she laid a hand on Edgar's arm. "I have no problem in you knowing what we've got here, young Edgar, but I must make it absolutely clear that this must go no further. Not to the press, not to friends and family, and not to your colleagues at the Museum of London. Most of them are entirely unaware of what we have here. They all buy in to the medieval mass grave story we put out."

Edgar nodded sagely.

"And not one word to your father either. I'm sorry to say

it, but if he found out then the entire British archaeology network would be in on the secret in a few hours. Now, follow me, and if you can, try to put your feet where I've put mine."

In on the secret. Edgar considered her words as he attempted to follow her across the site.

For a woman of her age Professor De Lacey was surprisingly agile. Despite her unsuitable footwear she hopped like a vivacious mountain goat from wooden walkway to wooden walkway between the vast and deep pits of jumbled bones. Edgar lurched after her. He was terrified of losing his footing and plummeting into the bone pits where he would be pressed into the spines and ribs of the dead like a child in some grotesque ball-pool. What must it be like to work here at night, he wondered shivering, to be silently hollowing out eye-sockets in a darkened pit with mangled bodies on all sides, kneeling amongst them, their finger bones stretched to your knees, their arm bones brushing your shins…

"Come on then my boy, over here, round past the head of the large trench there. That's it! Onto that planking, walk round. Good, good. Well done!"

"Sorry, I think I may have trodden on a bone back there. I heard a snapping."

"Not to worry." Hilary patted him on the shoulder. "You did well. The first time your boss Aubrey visited the site he fell headlong into one of our main trenches and disrupted the entire excavation there. We hadn't recorded a single thing in that trench. But there you go; accidents happen. Now then, take a look here then my boy. This is where we first came to realise just what we had here."

Edgar peered cautiously into the pit: another tangle of bones that, when he stared hard, vaguely echoed the remnants of the twisted and arched bodies that had once existed.

"Look closely," Hilary prompted, sensing Edgar was at a loss. "Look at their *spines*."

"It's tremendously exciting!" the Professor pointed to a gnarled clod of orange-tinged earth going in to the middle of one of the lower bones.

Edgar shook his head. "I'm sorry I—"

"Well, it's actually a spear tip. Rusted, decomposed, covered in clag but it's a Roman spear tip all the same. Embedded in the vertebrae. Nasty."

Edgar looked at the Professor, down at the spear tip and back at the Professor again. Roman? This was all *Roman*?

Professor De Lacey stood back. "I can see you're as taken aback by it as I was. To think that what you're seeing here *right here* are the remains of the last battle between two early Briton tribes and the Roman army."

Edgar stared wild-eyed at the professor.

"To think, in the first century AD a group of Britons took on the Roman army and what you have here are the remains of those killed in battle. Hacked, stabbed, decapitated, you name it they're marked with it."

"So this is a battle scene?"

"Mmm, well not as such. Probably the mass graves dug after the battle which would have been either on this site or nearby. Very nearby. I don't know how much you've read of the Site Report but just over there is where the eastern edge of a Roman camp, known as the Brill, once stood, probably somewhere near the cigarette machine. This mass burial would no doubt have been organised from the Brill." She swept a hand across the entire excavation site. "Mass burials of bones that were interred up to a fortnight after slaughter."

"How can you tell?"

"Well one can read the signs that they weren't disposed of immediately. There are the bite marks of scavengers on the bones, picking at the flesh. And then there are very few finds associated with the dead, which means that the bodies were left in the open long enough for human scavengers to come along and take the few beads and weapons and brooches and shoes: whatever few possessions these people died with. And then lastly you've got the preserved larvae of flies, would you believe, and that indicates that the first stages of decomposition had already begun while the bodies were above-ground. I bet that's put you off your lunch, eh lad? Not so keen on tucking in to a ham sandwich now I shouldn't wonder. So…" She paused and looked at Edgar. "I expect you want to see her?"

"Yes?"

"OK. Come here then." Hilary climbed out of the pit and Edgar followed. They picked their way down narrower planks precariously balanced between pits and trenches and over to an excavation that was screened off from the others. A lone archaeologist was slowly sweeping with what looked like a make-up brush, barely moving the earth at all, absorbed in giving the top layer of soil a light dusting. He didn't acknowledge the pair of them even now as they stood beside him looking into the four metre square excavation trench. Edgar peered in at the soil. There was a body, lying straight before him, and bones on either side in a sort of symmetrical pattern. Big bones.

"Beautiful isn't it? Look closely at the edge here you can just see—" the professor pointed with her silver pen "—that's a possible shield boss or even a decorative centre to a wooden wheel, just beside the body. And we think this could be a spear tip, just here, but obviously it's got to be cleaned up and x-rayed, there's too much corrosion. But look..." She crouched lower now and tapped a large flat bone just visible at the edge of the dig. "This is really exciting."

Edgar knelt down close to the soil and stared at the jumble of bones that had been meticulously exposed. He looked back up at the Professor. "It's not a human bone. I can tell that!"

"We'll make you an archaeologist yet my boy, your father would be proud."

Edgar snorted.

"Yes, what you have here, and also—" Hilary pointed with the silver pen to the other side of the trench "—just there, are the skeletons of *two* horses."

"Horses?"

"That's right. Two horses. Beautiful large beasts they would have been, the most prized of all possessions I wouldn't doubt. Like her they were hacked to a nasty death but magnificent specimens nonetheless. And can you see that they're lying in identical positions like a mirror image, their heads looking towards one another, legs half-raised."

Edgar's mind was racing. All the informal training in archaeology from the cradle might be worth something after all. The facts, the stories his father had told him, were all swirling in his head. A Roman battle. Britons. A warrior woman buried with her horses. In London.

Edgar stared down at the skeleton at his feet. The enormity of the find hit him and he gaped. The Museum of London had found Boudica. Project Rebel was about the biggest rebel there had ever been. The Queen of the Iceni had been uncovered. Edgar felt horribly lightheaded and nauseous.

Hilary was talking and he tuned in. "She still shows signs of having been picked clean by human scavengers, and some animal activity on her lower legs, with fly larvae around her feet, so we're confident she was lying unburied with the others, but at the point when all the hundreds of bodies around you were thrown into those hastily dug pits, Boudica was given a proper burial, with her horses, away from everyone else." She pointed down to their feet. "One proper grave amid all of this.

"Now, my colleagues and I disagree on this point but, in my opinion it would have been the Romans who would have dealt with the problem of so many rotting corpses impacting directly on their camp – the Brill. So they most likely arranged for these huge pits to be dug and the bodies thrown into them; to bury the problem underground. And it is my informed guess that our friends the Romans would have used locals, most probably the few survivors from the defeated Britons, to dig the pits and throw the bodies in. I don't imagine they would have been keen to do what must have been a truly horrific job themselves, especially given the partially decomposed nature of the bodies. Nasty. So the poor old surviving Britons buried their own people. Bad business, eh?"

"And Boudica?" Edgar turned back to the solitary body lying just beneath the sign for the men's toilets. "You think the Britons buried her in a grave with her horses?"

"Yes. And, again, this is *my* hypothesis although most of my eminent colleagues who have been brought into the loop are coming round to it: those Britons digging the pits and throwing their lost comrades in, well they recognised her. They saw their leader dead among the others and they gave her a proper send off. A hero's grave, a *heroine's* grave. To be laid to rest with her horses, killed in battle and buried amongst her people, that would have been the ultimate honour for a tribal Briton."

"How can you tell it's really her?"

"Well that's a jolly good question isn't it?" Hilary said. "After all you're not going to find a marked grave with 'Boudica RIP' are you? But what I can tell you is that right here under Kings Cross Station we have the fallout from a war between Romans and Britons. From the very few finds that escaped the body-pickers after the battle we have Iceni tribespeople and first century Roman militia. From these and other facts we can date the site to around AD 60, which we know was when Boudica drove the Britons into battle with the Romans after having set fire to London and completely destroyed it. Of course, up to this point we've never known precisely where this battle took place. Most people seem to have favoured Mancetter in Warwickshire, but there was always a story that it was around here somewhere. In Kings Cross or possibly in the old druid settlement up near what we know today as Primrose Hill. The data and location of the site all add up to an Iceni and Roman battle, but as to whether this female buried here at our feet is Boudica herself, well, we have to examine the *likelihood*. What we have here is a woman of around the age Boudica would probably have been when she died – that is she's not in her early twenties and she's not in her late fifties, she's somewhere in between. The woman here was obviously physically powerful, we can tell that from looking at the bones and we see evidence of strong muscle attachments that indicate good physical strength, which she would have needed to be a leader during those times. We know Boudica had children, two daughters, and we can tell this woman went through childbirth. And above all, the nature of the burial itself suggests that this body was important to the people who buried her and they found a way to give her a proper grave, without the Roman oppressors realising what they were doing. The chances are the Romans wouldn't have been keeping too close an eye on the clean-up operation; they would have just made sure that it was completed to their satisfaction. So what escaped their notice, and what we have at our feet, is one final defiant act by a defeated people for their brave Queen."

"But I remember learning about Boudica at school," Edgar began, hesitantly, knowing that if a panel of experts had pronounced it Boudica then it was a pretty sure bet that the conflicting facts from a dog-eared school textbook may not be the best, "and we were told her daughters were raped by Roman soldiers and she took her own life with poison. So why is she dead on the battlefield?"

"A very good question. But that's Tacitus for you."

"Who's Tacitus?"

"Roman historian. He described the battle pretty much at the time it took place, well, a bit after, but it's taken as a fairly reliable source. But what you have to remember is that history has nearly always been recorded by the victors. And that means you don't necessarily get the true story. For example Tacitus told us that eighty thousand Britons were slain in the battle, and only four hundred Romans. But from what we see here, it's more likely to be around forty thousand Britons and more than four hundred Romans. It was in his interest to exaggerate the success of the Roman army..."

"Forty *thousand* Britons dead. Here? There are forty thousand dead Britons under Kings Cross station?" Edgar looked at the site, appalled.

"Yes, well we haven't got forty thousand within this limited area that you see stripped back before you. The burials extend under the platforms still operating in the other part of the station. And they also extend out under the tracks, which we haven't had permission to dig up. But yes, my guess would be around forty thousand. Still an awful lot."

"An awful lot."

"And you see the victor gets to put their own spin on the story. And a female warrior, well that would have sat rather uncomfortably with those Romans wouldn't it? They didn't like it, not at all. Terribly unfeminine for a woman to gad about with a sword and chop at people. So much better for a woman to die by poison – after all it worked for Cleopatra – than die in the middle of bloody battle with a hacked neck and stabbed breasts. But think about it, young Edgar, a good Roman death makes no sense at all for our Iceni tribeswoman. Put yourselves in the shoes of the Britons if you will. Consider the savage Briton warriors fighting for their rights in a land that, up to that point, they had pretty much considered to be their own. Boudica lived as a warrior leader and she would have died as a warrior leader. To take your own life would have been beyond cowardly, it would have been to fail her people and would go against everything she had lived for. A Briton warrior would want to die by the sword in the glory of battle. Tacitus wrote her a Roman death. Dio is another contemporary Roman chronicler who tells us that Boudica simply fell ill and died. Pathetically feeble. Boudica died in battle, fighting, with her people around her. And that, young Edgar, is the truth without the Roman gloss."

There was a silence between them. Edgar looked down at the body again.

"Do you know another thing?" Hilary looked wistfully over the site. "The Romans not only found women warriors distasteful but they were horrified that the Britons brought their families with them to battle? Women, children, babes in arms. They all came to watch, standing on the sidelines while their fathers and husbands and sons and some of the fitter women threw themselves into battle right in front of them."

"That's dreadful."

"Today, maybe. But back then what could you do? You took your family with you because if you left them unguarded back at home they would be vulnerable to attack by other tribes. Or other Roman armies. No, you brought them with you to protect them. But of course, if you lost the battle..." The words hung in the air. "One thing you have to do is stop applying today's values, or even Roman values, to the Britons. You have to think from their point of view. Difficult one that. Difficult..."

"So..." Edgar swallowed. "There are women and children here?"

Hilary nodded. "Old women, young women, babies, children, everyone. We even found the papery bones of an unborn child in the ribcage of a pregnant woman. What you have here isn't the annihilation of an army. It's the annihilation of a *people*."

Professor De Lacey fished in her pocket and pulled out her change, shuffling it around the palm of her hand before selecting a fifty pence coin and turning it, so its back was uppermost. "Here." She held up the coin. "What do you think; a good likeness of our woman here?"

Sixteen

"Give the good Dean another drink, Sam." Jackie, the landlady of the King's Head, nudged her husband and he dutifully poured out another double G&T and walked it over to Archie, sitting alone at a table by the window staring out into the darkened street.

"Tough day was it...sir?" Sam wasn't quite sure exactly how you should address a man of the cloth, especially one who didn't seem like a man of the cloth at all. Except that he was wearing the cloth now. A bit skewiff and mangled. But then he had been drinking since five o'clock and drinking with a passion at that.

"Yes, Sam. Tough day. God moves in mysterious ways."

"That he does, sir. I saw them television vans turning up this morning, sir. Big event was it?"

"Oh. You know. A coven of bishops popped round." Archie took off his sunglasses and laid them on the table in a pool of gin and tonic. He sighed and, picking them up again, pulled up his cassock and wiped them clean.

"Why were the bishops here then?"

"To see how I was treating the place. Keeping it tidy..." He waved his hands around vaguely.

"Like a landlord, sir?"

"Something like that." He took a gulp of his double G&T. "Don't think I'll be getting my rent deposit back, that's for sure."

"Really?" Sam pulled the bar towel out of his trouser waist and mopped up the table where Archie had spilt his sixth drink. "So you rent the cathedral off them, do you, sir?"

Archie looked askew at him. "No Sam."

"Right." Sam nodded and fled back to the safety of the bar.

Archie absentmindedly stirred his drink.

Had today really gone that badly? After all, it was never going to be a riproaring success having the Bish creeping round the place making thinly disguised threats about Archie's non-traditional behaviour. But at least Archie knew that he had more than risen to the challenge.

Since he had been notified of the visit, at the last minute, he had made sure in those terribly few days' notice that school kids visited by the truck load, the choir was in to practise every evening, the place was spotless, and the accounts were up to date and very positive indeed. The broken Psalter of St Andrew was hastily mended with superglue, the scaffolding holding up the rear porch was temporarily removed – at great personal risk – and the stock of *wind them up and watch them glide* plastic figurines of Jesus, Moses and St Peter were taken off sale in the cathedral shop.

He'd gone ahead with the Bach *Concert by Candlelight* and raised nearly two thousand pounds from the night. In the past few months he had been all over the papers for his good works; raising attendance levels, which were up 14.23 per cent year on year; he was out in the community, meeting the public. It was all good. He loved his job. And yet…

"Well I must say Archibald, this is a lovely cup of tea. What make is it?" The influential Bishop of Sussex had sat opposite him, serene, amiable, quiet, sipping tea and making small talk while Archie wrung his hands beneath the table, still not at all sure what the Church heavyweights were doing at Winchester and why this man was sitting opposite him in the house and sipping tea.

"Oh. Er…Sainsburys I think your honour. Yes, Sainsburys."

"Well, quite lovely. I always say it's important to have a good cup of tea, none of that cheap stuff. Leaves a bad taste in the mouth. No, this is a very good choice of tea, Archibald. So do you know why we are here today?"

"Erm. Yes?"

"Good. You don't have a biscuit do you? A custard cream would go very well with this tea."

"Erm. No, not as such."

"Such a shame. Well, anyway, let's get straight down to business then shall we?" He gently pushed the empty tea cup and saucer away and looked up at Archie, smiling politely. "To be frank we're very disappointed with you."

"*Very* disappointed," added the Bishop of Wessex. The others nodded gravely.

Archie stared.

"I'm sorry, I just don't see why," he stuttered eventually. "If you're talking about the break-in then the cathedral's possessions were safe, the door was left open but then it wasn't directly left open by me and no harm was done. I've got attendance figures up, good profiles for the cathedral, money raised by us this quarter alone—"

"Yes, yes." The Bishop of Wessex held his hands up. "Can I just stop you there, Dean. Now let me just see." He reached down into an old leather bag and pulled out a file.

"Here we go. Now if you would be so good as to take a look at this, Dean." MacNeath carefully laid a multitude of press cuttings in front of the sweating Archie, fanning them out. Wordlessly the men bent forward and read the articles, the slow tick of the venerable clock the only intrusion into the silence.

MacNeath was the first to speak, leaning back in his chair and looking Archie in the eye, *"Cathedral's saviour..."* he began.

"Yes, I know, I had a word with..."

"Sex in the Vestry: How religion just got sexy?"

"What? I haven't...who published that?"

"The *Daily Mail*. Here!" He tapped an article beside his cup. "But look at this, *It's Only a Head, We've Got More."*

With a trembling clammy hand Archie took the proffered slip of paper. It was from the *Guardian*. He remembered the journalist who'd come round to interview him; brittle and cold she'd fired short clipped questions at him, smiled once, and then gone before he had chance to take a breath.

...It seems the Church's reliance on using an untested livewire may have been a mistake. A showman with a daytime TV presenter's attitude, Dean 'Archie' Cartwright appears to have little regard for the Church's property. "It's just a head and really, who cares that it was stolen? There are plenty more. We're moving on and the focus is all about getting out there and spreading the word of God

to the people. We're about putting enjoyment back on the menu..."

Nauseous now, Archie pushed the article back across the table. He wanted to say something about it being taken out of context but at that point words failed him. Bishop MacNeath sat opposite, his goggle eyes popping and shining with unrestrained glee. Silently MacNeath collected together the articles as if they were the most precious vellum manuscripts and replaced them in the file. He dropped the file into his bag and leant back in the creaking chair.

Archie took a deep breath in. "It was just an unguarded comment. That's all. I don't mean it, of course I don't. I care about Canute's head. I helped the police. Am still helping the police. And I'm racking my brains to remember more about the thief."

The aged Bishop of Hertfordshire leant forward now and, taking Archie's clammy hands in his own papery cold hands, he looked into his eyes and said in a voice little above a whisper, "We took you on, Dean, because you were supposed to be a breath of fresh air. We were interested to see where you would take us and, from the work you'd done previously, we were led to believe it was all for the good. But this obsession with the media..."

"What? No! I—"

MacNeath chimed in, "Inviting them to sermons, concerts, holding interviews where your professional life and your private life are merged in to one, it's all there, all in the public eye. And the issue we have is that it appears the tide is turning. You can't continue relying on the press to obediently publish your positive images to the public. When it suits them they'll cut you down and, make no mistake about it, they'll bring the Church down with you. And I'm not talking about a contained, local press, I'm talking national press: the *Guardian*, the *Daily Mail*, the *Independent*." He looked to the others. "I can tell you that the Catholic Church is having an absolute field day with all of this."

"But attendance is up! I'm engaging the community and this is how best to do it! I'm using the media to get across to—"

"You cannot *use* the media! That is my very point! The media does not exist to be at your beck and call, Dean! They use you, don't you understand? Let us make ourselves absolutely clear on this; the media will only play along with you up to a point; attend your concerts, list your good works, and so it goes. But rest assured that the more they build you up, the further they'll let you fall and when you go you'll take all of us with you."

MacNeath pulled himself as upright as his globe-like girth would allow. "We suggest you think very carefully about your future *media strategy* Cartwright."

"And we want you to toe the line." The Bishop of Sussex stood up. "You make sure they know you do care about Church property, and that you do care that the head of one of our most famous sovereigns was stolen. How does it look if the Church is seen to be condoning the theft of royal bodies? What then? We'll have Buckingham Palace on the phone, that's what, asking some pretty awkward questions. The Archbishop will be informed of your progress my boy.

We're all taking a very close interest in you."

"Consider this," MacNeath had said, leaning across the table towards the still-seated Archie, "your first formal warning."

Archie swayed to his feet and wobbled towards the pub door, fumbling for the sunglasses that were perched on his head and putting them on. "YouknowSam," he slurred as he clung to the doorframe for support.

"What's that, sir?" The barman came over to hold the door open for him.

"'I...am forced...to restore what I...did not steal.'"

"Pardon, sir?"

"Issa Psalm. Psalm 69. An' it means I'm gonna find that woman who took my king...head of the king thing you know what and I'm going to... Well I'm going to get it back. An' they think the media are...are...no good. But I know. I know...the power of the media... I can harness that *awesome* power. I am, after all, the Mick Jagger...of...the pulpit."

He collapsed onto the carpet in an alcoholic ecclesiastical heap.

Archie tilted his head up.

There was a strong and confident expression on his face. He was a little wary of the nude lipstick but it was always best to trust the experts: the mascara looked good. He carefully lifted the handbrake, checked his mirror, signalled and slowly manoeuvred the Lusso into the Close. Cautiously the car made its way down the road, negotiating the streets at a respectable fifteen miles an hour. Taking its cue from Archie's speed, the open-backed van in front crawled along at fifteen miles an hour, a cameraman perched on the back, filming Archie's sedate progress towards the cathedral, the sound man leaning precariously out of the side of the vehicle, capturing the perfectly tuned engine.

Mirror. Signal. Manoeuvre. Archie pulled in to the Slype, applied the handbrake and checked it was on securely before he got out of the car, flicked his fringe off his face, pouted a little, and headed to the boot. Powerful spotlights illuminated the passageway. Careful to not put his back to the cameras Archie reached into the boot and pulled out his stainless steel meat platter, one of the cleaner's silver candlesticks and another cleaner's old silver-plated tea pot. He conscientiously pushed down the boot lid and locked the car, checked it was securely locked, and then turned, wincing at the painfully white light shining directly in his eyes, and made he made his way to the narrow side door of the Cathedral. He stopped in front of the open door, gasping in horror; his mouth gaping open as wide as it would go as he stared goggle-eyed.

"OK cut; CUT!"

Reaching in to the boot of his car Archie pulled out the stainless steel meat platter, one of the cleaner's silver candlesticks and another cleaner's old silver tea pot. He conscientiously pushed down the boot lid and locked the car, checking it was securely locked, before turning and making his way to the side door. He stopped and, frowning handsomely, he approached the mysteriously open doorway. Loading the Kitchen Items Through the Ages into one arm he tentatively pushed open the door and walked inside.

"Cut! That's great! Much better!"

Inside the darkened cathedral Archie was still frowning heavily and tilting his head to one side. He'd seen enough films to know that this was how to show that you sensed something was up. Looking around suspiciously he slowly placed the KITtA on the flagged floor. "Hello? Is anybody there?"

Seventeen-year-old Alice Pearce, local wannabe actress and A-Level drama student, dashed out from behind the door to the Chapter Room.

"Hold it right there!" Archie made a spirited dash for the bewigged Alice who dodged him and in a kung fu move kicked him in the knee.

"Aaarrrghh!" He fell to the floor in agony, managing to complete one dramatic roll along the flagstones before coming to a halt directly in front of a cameraman, clutching his wounded knee but in a second he was up again, committed to protecting the cathedral regardless of physical pain, running behind the thief, grimacing each time his right foot hit the ground.

"Stop! Stop!" he called, having pulled up in front of another camera positioned at the doorway.

"And...cut! Fantastic, Dean, you're a natural. Hey are you OK?"

"My knee is bloody killing me."

"I'm here with the Dean of Winchester, the Very Reverend Archie Cartwright. Thank you for joining us here on South West Crime Spotters."

"Not at all." Archie shot the presenter his best pulpit grin.

"So, tell us Archie, we've seen the re-enactment you were so good to do for us. Was it at all traumatic to go through what has so recently happened to you and to your cathedral?"

Archie took a moment to consider the question. "You know Alan, I think it was. I can't tell you what it means to me that Canute's skull was taken from my cathedral. I couldn't have been more upset if it was my own skull that had been taken that night."

"Err..."

"CUT! Dean I—"

"Sorry! Sorry! It just came out and the minute I said it I knew it was stupid. Can we cut that bit out?"

"Sure. OK, Alan are you ready? And... Run VT!"

"So, tell us Archie, we've seen the re-enactment you were so good to do for us. Was it at all traumatic to go through what has so recently happened to you?"

Archie took a moment to consider the question. "You know Alan, I think it was. I can't tell you what it means to me that Canute's skull was taken from our cathedral. The theft has gone right to the very core of my being."

"I can understand that, Dean. Now tell me, what state of mind were you in when you encountered this cathedral-thief?"

Archie turned to the camera. "Well what you have to bear in mind was that it was gone midnight and I was returning from a very successful Church conference up in the Midlands. I do a lot of work promoting Winchester

Cathedral and what it has to give, some of which, you may be surprised to learn, is not always appreciated."

"So would you say you were *tired* that evening when you stumbled on the intruder?"

"Yes. I was tired; very tired. I knew that above all else I had to protect the cathedral treasures so when I saw the woman rush out from behind the door..." He shook his head, overcome with emotion.

The presenter looked to camera. "Clearly a difficult moment for the Dean. To take on an intruder after such a punishing schedule." He turned back to Archie. "Tell me, what did you think when you saw that it was a *woman* who had broken in to God's house?"

"Mmmm." Archie nodded, trying to recall what he had planned to answer at this question. Something about equal rights wasn't it? "I don't believe I was any less frightened than I would have been if it was a man, to be honest with you Alan," he said, using his sincere frown for the cameras. "I believe in true equality because I think men and woman *are* equals. And that means the threat of a man or a woman is an equal threat."

The presenter turned to the camera again. "As we saw, Dean Cartwright was badly wounded in the attack and could only hobble after the female intruder. But even so he bravely hobbled for just over two miles, out through the side door and into the streets of Winchester at midnight. We actually have CCTV footage taken from just outside the cathedral that night showing the female intruder as she ran from the building, although unfortunately the cameras failed to capture Dean Cartwright who must have been running out of the view of the camera. This sequence was taken at twelve twenty-two on the night of the attack and the red-headed woman, with a green bag slung over her right shoulder, was running along Colebrook Street and then headed in the direction of Magdalen Hill. The quality of the footage is somewhat poor given it was night-time and raining heavily. Even so we can see she has long red hair, a pale complexion and is around five feet to five feet two inches.

"If you have any information for the police in connection with the Winchester Cathedral robbery then you can give them a call on the number on your screens right now. You can leave a message in complete confidence if you wish, and don't forget there may be a reward if your evidence leads to a prosecution. Remember, it may seem like nothing to you but even the most mundane information can lead to something of very great importance. Did you see someone running through the streets that night? Do you know of anyone who might be interested in taking Canute's head? Do you recognise the photofit the police have issued? Just give us a call." The presenter paused. "Now I'd like to thank Dean Cartwright for getting in touch with us and appearing on the programme today. And we wish you all the best with your search for Canute's head."

"Thank you. Thank you. And *thank you*." Archie looked sincerely into the camera's lens.

"Goodnight, and be safe," the presenter said and, after smiling inanely for five seconds, he then turned to Archie and shook his hand. "Good man. I think we'll cut the piece to camera you just did, and the bit about your skull...but otherwise, it was great. Thanks."

Archie smiled weakly. "Is there a medical person on the crew? I really think my knee may be broken."

Seventeen

"Dean?"

"What is it Margery?" Tapping a Converse-clad foot Archie waited while Margery Down padded towards him. Continental shifts, longshore drift, soil creep; these were all things that moved more quickly than Margery Down appeared to do. Archie chewed his lip while he made the appearance of waiting patiently. He had work to do; his sermon on *The Power of a Faith-filled Life* was not going to write itself. Not only that but once again Canon Littlechild had submitted a vicious and threatening article on *Parking at the Cathedral* for the monthly newsletter, and once again in was up to Archie to turn it into an emotionless and civil document, whilst maintaining good relations with Canon Littlechild. And the Cathedral Marketing Manager had a meeting booked in to discuss the upcoming themed lunches that needed signing off.

But more than any of these things, what he really wanted to do was to hot foot it to his office and try Angela's phone again. He needed to speak to her, even if was to tell her the weekend in Cornwall, planned in haste before he sped off from Lichfield, was now off. He'd promised the bishops that he would make more of an effort to find Canute: swanning down to Cornwall in romantic pursuit of the Dean of Truro would definitely fall outside that particular remit.

And it was useless to think he could try to get away with it: MacNeath had his spies posted everywhere.

As he contemplated Margery's steady progress his mind wandered to thoughts of his impending success at finding Canute. He revelled in the imminent opportunity to demonstrate once and for all to MacNeath and his heavies and in fact to all his detractors just how committed he was to the Church. Because something like this would show them that beyond the tabloid headlines and the flash car there was actually some substance to him. And he was, when it came down to it, a very committed and positive force and they didn't need to be on the offensive with him all the damned time. He would find the stolen head and he would unveil it in a blaze of flashlight-glory to the headlines *God's Sleuth! Dynamic Dean fights back to reclaim Church property!* He would generate sufficient column inches to fill that little brown satchel MacNeath had brought with him. The Bishop would lose the sickly grin and would up the dosage on his blood-pressure tablets and the Archbish would clasp his hands around Archie's own and realise just what a bloody good job he was actually doing down here in Winchester.

And yet...

For all his dreams of glory, rocking up Hamlet-style with the skull in an outstretched arm while beautiful women fainted, the verbal warning he had been dealt had fallen hard.

Everyone had loved him, *everyone*, but now there was his boss and senior members of the Church of England telling him just how disappointed they were with him. And there was the press – the very people who had courted him, publicised and praised him were now turning against him.

He was fallible.

Even the Dean of Winchester Cathedral was fallible.

And that had been the biggest shock.

The impact of his fall from grace had been keenly felt by the Winchester Cleaning Ensemble. They watched helpless as their boy paced the flagstones deep in thought.

But Archie was too caught up in his own melancholy to notice the effect he was having on anyone around him. Increasingly over the past few days, since his tea with the Bishops and the nightmare of the satchel full of press cuttings, he was keeping his own company and when he did emerge from his office it was with his head down, his swagger gone.

What he needed was Angela. He needed the comfort of a woman to help him get through this. Perhaps he could ask Angela to come up to Winchester and help him with the search for Canute? Yes, he might suggest that. He was aching for Angela, he needed her. He needed the feel of her against him, the heat of her skin against his skin and the sensation of her long black hair brushing his face as—

"Dean...what with my bad back would you be so kind as to help me get the box of wind-up-and-glide figurines from the storeroom and take them to the shop? I'm presuming that now the good Bishop and his colleagues have completed their tour of the place we can put them back on sale?"

Margery had finally reached him. Archie took a deep breath. "Of course, of course Margery. And we can get out the holy water pistols that arrived last week too. I'll be with you in a few minutes."

"Oh thank you, Dean."

She paused, and turning back added, "By the way, Dean, the box of Religious Icons Top Trumps cards arrived this morning. Shall we put those out on the shelves too?"

"Yes Margery. Yes. Thank you. I'll come and help you shortly."

He continued pacing, still limping slightly from his run in with the wannabe actress. He was deep in thought, caught up in the kaleidoscope of images that were now overwhelming him; the sensuous warm curve of Angela's neck when he'd brushed aside her long dark hair. The sweep of her shoulder blades, which he'd nuzzled as he worked his way down, down, down the soft smooth arc of her back and untying the ribboned—

"Dean!"

"Yes Mrs Robey! How are you? How's your husband?"

Mrs Robey stared at him, aghast. "He's still dead, Dean."

"Oh. Oh. I am sorry, I forgot. So much on my mind at the moment. You know. Bishops. So sorry. How thoughtless. Forgive me."

Mrs Robey took a moment to gather herself together. "Well. Dean. I just wondered *could* we possibly talk about the flower arranging for this weekend's Services. It's just that Doris says we absolutely cannot get the roses for love nor money and I ought to tell you that if we can't have roses then we're well and truly stumped because the carnations simply won't be enough with—"

Archie put a hand on her shoulder and she stopped twittering and blushed.

"I'm actually on leave from tomorrow Mrs Robey so you'll need to speak to the Archdeacon about these important matters."

"Yes but—"

"I'm very sorry that I can't be of more help." He walked off. Perhaps he and Angela could go away one night? After all, one night away wouldn't make a difference in the hunt for Canute would it? He'd always fancied a stay in one of those mansion house hotels near Bath, acting the country squire. Oversized bathtubs, crisp white sheets on an enormous sleigh bed, a bottle of wine, the lights down low, Angela, warm and firm, yielding when he pressed, gripped, pushed against—

"Dean Cartwright?"

"WHAT? WHAT IS IT? WHAT?!"

"Oh I'm..." Kate stepped back amid the flurry of robes.

"YOU!"

"Yes. Hello. I..."

"What are you doing here again?" Archie glared.

"Well I..."

"Do you know how much trouble that 'Winchester's Saviour' article got me in to?"

"No I..."

"A lot. A lot of trouble. I had the—"

"Hold on a minute—" Kate stepped forward and held up a hand.

"No, let me tell you that when the Bishop—"

"No *you* hold on a minute." Kate jabbed him in the vestments with a newly manicured finger. "There was nothing in that article that wasn't true."

Archie folded his arms and looked at her for a moment. "You didn't have to mention the treasure in the unlocked boot angle. That opened a whole can of worms—"

"Are you trying to tell me how to do my job again?" she cut in.

The cleaning ensemble scuttled into darkened corners.

"Well somebody bloody well ought to!" Archie bit back.

"Fine then! Right! While we're at it shall I tell you how to do *your* job?" snapped Kate. "Why not lock up the cathedral at night because even *after* the break-in it's going unlocked isn't it – is that because you're too preoccupied with your female congregational fanbase to spend time securing the cathedral against more burglars? And while you're at it why don't you deal with the collapsing porch before it kills someone?"

The silence in the cathedral was vast. Somewhere nearby a tourist fled for safety into the Lady Chapel.

Archie shifted uncomfortably. "How do you know about the porch?"

Kate raised a newly-shaped eyebrow. "So, can I have a word with you?" The power had shifted to her and she knew it – it was an incredibly supercharged feeling.

Archie stood helpless, arms by his sides. Where had all this come from? "Urgh. Come on then." Once again he led the way to his office with Kate in tow. She was fishing in an outsized turquoise bag while they walked, eventually pulling out a tiny notepad and pen.

They had reached the office now and he ushered her in, closing the door behind them, but not before he saw two of the cleaners watching from the gloom of a darkened corner, hands on mops.

Archie turned to Kate and was poised to ask if she wanted a drink. But no. Let her thirst. He pointedly walked away from the kettle and over to his chair.

He frowned. Something was different about her since the last time she had been here; there was a change in her.

He sat at his desk and crossed his arms.

It was her clothes, he realised; the shapeless rags had gone and Cinderella was wearing a fitted suit. With a skirt. And she had rather fine legs crossed at the ankle above a pair of new-looking high-heeled patent black shoes. Stilettos.

Kate followed Archie's expression and uncrossed her legs, self consciously tucking them under the seat and out of the way. Nevertheless she was pleased with the attention. She was smart but not primly so. Her figure revealed without being put on display in the manner of Lynn Paget cocktail-dressed tramp. There was another way.

"So..." She flipped open her leather bound notepad and turned to the first page. "I understand that you might be in a bit of trouble with the big boys, is that true?"

She lay her bag on the floor beside her and it sprawled out across the flagstones like a dead turquoise cow. She kicked it under the table and, pencil poised, mustered up her best journalist persona. "I mean, is there going to be some sort of internal inquiry into the head-stealing saga? Does the Church of England have an internal affairs division like the police force?"

"Just hold on a minute—"

"Bishop of Wessex coming on a bit heavy handed is he? They took an awful risk taking you on in the first place and who wants to be associated with the aftermath of all this? And it's not as if you can make a claim against your contents insurance to sort it all out is it? New for old. Who would the insurance people get to replace Canute's head? King Harold's head? Where is Harold anyway? I—"

"Waltham Abbey."

"Oh." Kate was knocked off-course.

Angrily, Archie snatched up a *Christ is Mercy* magnet. "Thought I didn't know did you? Expect me to be some kind of a fraud? A vacuous showman? You wouldn't be the first and you won't be the last." He flicked the magnet between his fingers like a card sharp. "Didn't you used to have brown hair?"

"Yes..." Kate self-consciously put a hand to her newly highlighted bob and smoothed it down. This wasn't supposed to be happening.

"Look, *Kate* is it? You can dispense with the hard-hitting journalist thing because, well, because you're crap at it."

She felt herself turn red.

"Tell me—" Archie leant forward, "—are you going to write an article insinuating just how incompetent I am? Because if you are going to, then I don't really feel very inclined to help you."

Kate tried to regain her composure but felt her newfound broadsheet-image crumbling. "Yes, but if you don't help me then I might get the wrong end of the stick, so to speak. And then I might write a *really damning* article on your position at Winchester."

Archie sighed.

"I just wanted to ask a few more questions about the

woman you saw in the cathedral that night. The one with the head in the bag," she added.

"Yes, thank you. I know which woman you mean."

There was a cautious tapping on the door.

Margery peeped her head round. "So sorry, Dean. Could I have a hand with those figurines and pistols now? Sorry."

Archie stood up. "Of course." He turned to Kate. "If you want to ask me anything you'd better come along. I've got a meeting with the Heritage Trust at half ten and I have to prepare."

"Sure. Fine." Kate gathered her bag and followed him out of the room. This interrogation business was a lot harder than it looked on the television. And far from being the light-hearted, devil-may-care man he'd appeared to be the last time she interviewed him, the Dean was worn-down and brittle now. The visit from the bishops must have hit him hard.

But there had been that flash of the man she had first met as he checked out her legs...

She followed him out of the cathedral, up the steps and into the gift shop, coming to a halt beside the tills where Archie was now employed in hefting boxes from a store cupboard while Margery took out the contents and arranged the figures on the shelves. Kate stood around, not wanting to ask questions in front of Miss Marple – who had every appearance of being absorbed by her task but kept shooting suspicious looks in Kate's direction.

Flicking through the press pack Kate waited for Archie. She reread the first page, scanned the second but it was hard to concentrate, her eyes were drawn to the shop, to what they were putting out on the shelves, and the books, the postcards, the toys. Throwing the police file on the counter she went over to a postcard rack by the door and thumbed through pictures of the cathedral, the grounds, the chancel, and the stained glass windows. Maybe she could send Mike a postcard as a way of letting him know she'd gone when she finally managed to move out? A frosty morning over Winchester. *So long Mike. I've moved on.*

But then he never read his post, so a postcard would sit unnoticed under a heap of oily car junk. Sorting out the mail was another one of her chores, along with nagging him if there was anything he needed to do as a result of the mail. Well, she could always pop back to read out the postcard to him...

Her hand stopped over a postcard of Canute's mortuary chest. She picked it off the rack and studied it. It had been taken close up, the detailed carvings on the side clearly visible, the shield, the untouched lid. She flipped the card over.

THE KING WHO COULD NOT STOP THE SEA BUT STEMMED THE VIKING TIDE ON ENGLAND'S SHORES

That Canute. She had known that there was something familiar about him, apart from being a king of England, and now she realised what it was. He was the one setting his chair on the beach: taking on the idea of divine leadership and getting his feet wet. The Danish leader who spent his leisure time cutting off the noses of people who got on the wrong side of him. Kate's history GCSE was coming back to her and she recalled the image from her text book of the pointy-bearded king sitting on a throne on a beach, crown on his head and arm outstretched bidding the sea to retreat.

Beside the postcard of the tomb was one showing three silver coins. She picked it up and turned it over.

THREE COINS FROM CANUTE'S REIGN 1016-1035.

There were three different depictions of the king on each of the tiny coins. She looked into the face of the man who had so recently had his head stolen. It was an odd feeling because seeing an image of the man made the theft come alive for her. Before that moment the theft had been of some old bones and the focus had been on the thief rather than the head. But these images, literally, humanised him. Frustratingly there was little Kate could glean from the coins as to what the old king had looked like. The faces punched onto the metal were so stylised and roughly stamped that it was all she could do to make out the profile of a face. And he appeared to be wearing a large pointy hat with what looked like buttons running up it. He could have had a moustache on the largest coin, but on the smaller coin he looked clean-shaven.

She ought to buy these postcards, take them back with her to the office and see if they helped inspire her any more. And perhaps the picture desk could locate a suitable quality image for her to publish: if seeing a picture of Canute made the theft of his head more real to her, then it would no doubt have the same effect on the paper's readership. It could help resurrect her story.

She returned to the counter and rummaged around in her bag.

"I'll take these, please."

The Miss Marple shop assistant rang in the sale.

Kate waited for her to tell her how much. But the woman's attention was arrested by the photofit from the press pack that Kate had left on the counter.

"Do you recognise her?" Kate watched the woman's expression and Archie, still holding a Moses wind-up figure, came over to join them.

The old woman didn't take her eyes off the photofit.

"Margery?" Archie prompted.

"Well, it's just, I...well yes I do recognise her as it goes. She's the woman you're looking for isn't she? She's your thief, am I right?".

Kate could feel her pulse racing. "Did the police not question you about her?"

"No. No, why should they? I mean, she was just in the shop. Bought the same postcards that you did as a matter of fact: Canute's mortuary chest and the three coins of him. I remember because she stopped to talk to me about the tomb. Oh my..."

"Is there anything else you remember about her? What else she said. What she looked like?" Kate fished in her bag for her notepad.

"My goodness!" The old lady's hand flew up to her throat. "She seemed so nice, you know, just another pilgrim come to see our house of God. So softly spoken and gentle. Very polite. You know – a real lady. She bought a postcard of Jane Austen too. She was interested in her. Oh my goodness. Well I suppose I should have mentioned it to you, Dean, but you see I only work every other Wednesday so I'm very rarely here, and no-one asked me any questions. Oh…"

"Can you remember what she said? Exactly what she said when you talked to her in the shop?"

But the old lady had gone into a flap, muttering and fumbling with the postcards on the counter. "I really…I… She just talked about Canute. And Jane Austen. I'm sorry."

Archie was frowning, deep in thought.

"It's fine. Fine. Look, here's my card – I'm covering the story for the *Winchester Echo*. If you remember anything more…" Kate said.

"Well thank you Mrs…Miss Grey. But if I think of any more should I not go to the police with it?"

Archie snorted and wound up Moses.

"Of course." Kate smiled, tightly. "But if you would let me know too then we could tell our readers and perhaps it might help the police if more people get involved."

"Oh yes. Of course," Margery bumbled.

"Just one thing. Did she say where she had come from? Was she local? Did she have an accent?" Kate asked.

"Oh I'm sorry. Sorry I don't remember. I can't…"

"It's OK. Don't worry. Thank you anyway." Kate put the change down on the counter and took the unbagged postcards. "Do let me know if you—"

"London! She was from London. I remember now because she visited the cathedral on the day of the big crash on the M3. Because I asked her if she'd enjoyed her visit and she said it had taken her five hours to get *up from London* but even so it had been worth it!" The old lady beamed at having remembered the details.

"The M3 crash was on October the eleventh," Kate said,

more to herself than to Archie or Miss Marple, "so she was here on the eleventh and then again on the night she broke in. Around three weeks later. Tell me…?"

"Margery."

"Margery! Tell me, is the photofit a good likeness?"

"Yes. Sort of. The eyes anyway." She held it in her hands and examined it for a moment. "She was very fine-looking. She was short, mind, perhaps not even as tall as me. Five foot maybe? But she had lovely long red hair in ringlets. And long silver earrings with little green beads in. I remember those. And a bag that she put the postcards in. One of those shoulder bags. Much smaller than your bag Miss. Much smaller. I can't remember much else. She was interested in Canute. And Jane Austen. Oh I'm sorry it must be…"

Kate and Archie exchanged looks and then sprinted out of the shop, down the steps and into the cathedral. Archie parted the waves of dithering tourists, striding purposefully down the nave, Kate struggling to stay in his robe-swishing wake.

He drew to a halt abruptly, eyes fixed to the cathedral floor.

"Jane Austen?" Kate whispered.

He nodded and they looked down at the enormous grave slab embedded into the flag stones. To Kate's untrained eye it looked as though it hadn't been touched. Hadn't the police said as much – nothing else showed signs of having been tampered with. Archie crouched low and ran his hand along the edges of the stone.

Kate crouched beside him. "Has she got to Jane Austen? Has the grave been opened?"

"No. No I don't think so."

Kate didn't know whether to be morally pleased or professionally disappointed.

"Well that's a blessing." Archie stood up and smoothed down the folds of heavy fabric. "Well done for finding out more about our thief," he said. "What are you going to do with the new information?"

The broad smile died on her lips. "I don't know. It's not enough to merit an article. Knowing that she came up from London three weeks before she committed the crime doesn't really give us much more information."

"If it is her," Archie added.

"What do you mean?"

"Well if the photofit is a good likeness. I only caught a glimpse of her. I might have been mistaken."

"But you said the picture was accurate."

"Yes it is. It is." He looked uncertain. "You have to remember that I only saw her in the dark for a couple of seconds."

"I know it's her." Kate had pulled out the photofit and was staring into the beautiful eyes.

"Look—" Archie checked his watch "—I have to get going. Meetings… But I'll let you know if anything comes from my TV appeal. Did you catch it the other night?"

"I did actually. Nice roll. Did that really happen?"

"No," he confessed, "I improvised that bit." He bit his lip. He was doing it again: giving too much away, forgetting that this woman represented the press and in all probability an article entitled *Dean Fakes Action to Boost Cause* would be appearing in tomorrow's local paper.

"I thought you might have done." She was grinning and he knew he could trust her this time.

They stood awkwardly for a moment, watched by politely hovering tourists wanting to see the author's gravestone at their feet. From the short time in which she'd got to know him Kate's opinion of Archie had gone from one of awe at the first moment of meeting him, to contempt for the City boy she took him to be. But now, standing on top of Jane Austen, she saw before her a young man dressed up in robes that weren't truly his yet, in a building that towered above him. For a moment she caught a glimpse of the man struggling to make his place in the world.

"Well then, until the next time you want to come and threaten me." Archie was the first to speak. There was a flash of the man she'd met before. He held out his hand and she shook it. It was warm and firm.

"Tell you what," he added as she started to walk away, "why not come to our interfaith football match on Saturday? See the work I'm doing in bringing communities together. That might be a good article for your newspaper." Archie was never one to miss a media opportunity.

"I might just do that," she lied.

Eighteen

"You look nice." Lynn Paget perched on the edge of Kate's desk, her skin tight dress riding up her thighs. She was eyeing Kate's hair and Kate surreptitiously put a hand to it to smooth it down. It wasn't the usual way of things for Lynn to offer up a compliment so she was wary of exactly how this would go.

"And is there a *reason* for this transformation?" she followed up, a smile on her scarlet lips.

"No. No," Kate said airily.

"So it's not for one *particular* person's benefit then?" Lynn leant closer winked a heavily powdered eyelid. "A *religious* person's benefit?"

"No!"

"That's not what I heard. I heard you can't get enough of the new Dean of Winchester."

"You've got the wrong take on the story Lynn. Again." Inwardly she rejoiced at her *Strong Woman* stance.

"No need to get all brittle about it." Lynn nevertheless looked taken aback at Kate's remark.

"Who's being brittle?" Kate laughed. "I dress for me, not for anyone else. And as for the Dean, I'm up at the cathedral because of the story. I'm uncovering new angles on the skull theft."

"And the fact that the Dean is the hottest thing to hit

Winchester— "

"Is of no consequence," Kate cut in. "Actually I find him quite arrogant."

Lynn laughed. "I'll cover your story. I wouldn't mind the job of interviewing him again."

"It's quite all right thank you Lynn. I'm making good progress." Kate enjoyed seeing the expression on her face.

Lynn quickly recovered herself and stood up, smoothing her skirt down by a centimetre. "Roger told me you'd stalled. Everyone knows you've hit a dead end and you just can't accept it."

The revelation that Dr Evil was bad-mouthing her to her colleagues, particularly Lynn, dealt a blow.

"I've got the front page. Again." Lynn sighed as though it was all too tedious to talk about and Kate shot her a sarcastic smile. "Turns out the farmer and his wife at the Pit Close Farm murders were occultists and the children may have been involved in rituals that went badly wrong. Anyway – I have to serve the whole thing up in the bland, safe *Winchester Echo* style."

"'Hints of macabre activity'?" Kate suggested.

"'A darker angle'?" Lynn offered.

Momentarily the two were united by a common frustration.

"Your hold-up stocking's falling down by the way," Lynn said as she slunk back to her desk.

Nineteen

Kate had been kicking round the house all morning while Mike snored on in his beery-sleep. It was half past ten and she'd already cleaned the bathroom and the kitchen, emptied the bin and ironed the shirts.

Strong Woman, however, remained unplayed in the CD Player: she was trying to go cold turkey.

There was nothing left to do. She sat at the spotless kitchen table with a cup of tea, leafing through a magazine she'd leafed through many times before. Skinny celebrity, fat celebrity, loved-up musicians, warring exes. Why? Why did she buy this meaningless tat? The sophisticated London journalist with her turquoise bag and matching shoes would never buy this rubbish. The London journalist would be perched at her granite breakfast bar leafing through her highbrow Saturday paper, reading the witty articles her friends had written, before lunching with some glamorous male friend in a low key little place just off the Marylebone High Street. So very, very far away.

Kate sighed and placed her coffee mug over Prince William *enjoying a moment of fun with girlfriend Kate Middleton.*

She and Mike were supposed to be going to town this afternoon; she needed more clothes for the office: some smart shoes, a pencil skirt and a belted winter coat. Perhaps a white wool coat like the one she'd seen in the window of Coast? And maybe some earrings. Hold-up stockings; some that held up.

But Mike didn't show any signs of emerging and she knew better than to go in there and wake him up: a day-full of whining was sure to follow.

Her mind returned to the Dean, as it had been doing many times over the last few days. The barbed comment from Lynn stuck in her mind but she knew the woman had got it wrong. There was no way Kate was interested in the Dean of Winchester, other than because of the theft... It was easy for her to believe that her preoccupation with him was solely due to his connection with the story she was pursuing, rather than thinking of him for any other reason. He was on her mind because Canute was on her mind. Nothing more. And, maybe, she was also fascinated by seeing the change in him. Just what had the bishops said that had sobered him up so quickly? And did it mean that Winchester could now expect a Dean that conformed to the traditional model? Could the Lust Red approving, swaggering man she'd first met really change for good, or was it just a reaction to a telling-off and he'd be back to his old self within the month?

Ridding Meadows were to the south of the cathedral and Kate walked towards the pitches to watch the interfaith football match, sipping her take-out Americano and feeling horribly out of place. She had neither young child nor dog with her as an excuse for her presence. And for once her newly tailored look made her feel awkward and out-of-place: she would have felt more at home in the scruffy jeans and jumper of her old self.

Despite this it felt good to be out of doors in the fresh cold air and with the heat-free sunshine of a late autumn morning. Already there were supporters loitering around the pitch waiting for the action to take place, stamping feet and blowing on cold hands. A mixed section of the community was represented here, just as Archie had predicted.

She saw the Dean arrive, jogging along, springing from one foot to the other. He was looking round at the spectators and saw her, waved, and then bounced over to join a group of players who were stretching over by the corner of the field. The Dean was dressed in a red football strip, with loose white shorts to his knees. Kate had never seen a man of the Church in anything but robes before, so to see one dressed as a footballer intrigued her. Somehow it seemed odd that a man of God had hairy legs. Had legs at all. She studied them over the rim of her Americano. They were very shapely and muscular – well, below the knee at least. Not bad at all. She sipped her coffee and contemplated the depths to which she had sunk. Had her growing irritation with Mike – a real man who took cars apart and crushed beer cans in his hands once he'd emptied them – caused a reaction in her so that she was now programmed to find the complete opposite attractive? Had Mike's testosterone-driven slovenliness caused her to swing one hundred and eighty degrees and look with tender eyes at anything in a dog collar? Was she experiencing some deep call of nature – to settle with the safer partner?

No – surely not. Surely this interest, this growing interest, in the Dean of Winchester was because, as Lynn Paget super-tart had pointed out, the man was quite attractive, and would be attractive whether he were an Anglican dean or an average accountant. She surveyed the pitch as the two teams assembled before her. Even in a football strip on a cold bright morning he cut quite a dash. And, after that moment on top of Jane Austen when she had caught a glimpse of what might lie beneath the vestments... something had appealed to her tenderer instincts. A vulnerability within him...

"Come on then you grubby hassocked bastard! Kick it!"

Kate hadn't been to many football matches, and she wasn't absolutely sure what to expect. Nevertheless she had an idea of how football matches *should be*, and this most certainly was not typical of that. The game play was fierce, players skidding and sliding on the ground, pushing, knocking and slamming in to one another, with the referee seeming oblivious to anything but the most excessive, extreme violence. And it was that which was the biggest crowd-pleaser, so he would withhold stopping play at least until the first round of cheering had subsided.

"Come on then Bible Basher!" yelled the Asian captain to Archie. "Let's see what you're made of, you pasty-faced God flogger!"

Kate stared, wide-eyed, but when she looked to her fellow spectators none of them seemed to have even registered the abuse. They were waiting for the next bout of senseless sporting violence.

"Hey, cover the goal you witless Papist! And you, bagel

boy, pin yer bleedin' skull cap down and start playing for a change – I need you in defence."

In between the abuse and violent gameplay there was a lot of backslapping and handshaking amongst all the players – and so it went on: jeering, brutality, camaraderie.

So *this* was what Archie had meant when he said he was bringing communities together in Winchester.

A quarter of an hour on, when the shock of the language had started to fade, Kate, to her surprise, actually began to enjoy herself, glad to be out of the house, glad to be standing in the weak sunshine in the water meadows, entertained by the despicable but imaginative name-calling. There was a particularly tall and serious man who everyone called "Norm the Morm"; he spent the game wandering lankily about the pitch, getting in everyone's way and being shouted at. There were also, Kate deciphered from the creative abuse, Catholics and Methodists and Sikhs. As far as she could make out there didn't seem to be any religious weighting to either of the teams, with members from all denominations on either side. The referee appeared to be an agnostic with members from both teams referring to him as "Faithless Joe".

"Enjoying it?" Archie ran over to her at half-time, catching her unawares as she read a text from Mike: *Where r u? In town? Can u pick up dvd of FleshFiend 3 for me?*

"Oh. Absolutely. Yes." Flustered she pushed the mobile into her pocket and looked up at him, smiling. His face was red with the exertion of shouting obscenities for half an hour. "It's rather more vocal than I thought it would be," she added.

"Vocal?"

"You know – *'Kick it you pagan twat.'*"

"Oh that." He waved it away and bent down to adjust his socks. "Yes, well, I suppose it's got a bit out of hand in the past few months but no-one takes any real offence. We go down to The Swan after the match. Do you fancy joining us?"

She shook her head. "No. I have to get back, thanks." *Get back for what?*

"Well I'm glad you came." He stepped back and made to go and join his team-mates. "Hey, have you had any more thoughts about my head thief?"

"No, nothing. But if I do think of anything you'll be the first to know."

"Likewise." He winked and bounded off.

She watched him disappear into the crowd then picked up her bag and headed off in the direction of home.

He was, she concluded, *recovering*.

Twenty

"But it's too big. It's too big a story just to let go like that." Kate spread her newly-manicured hands out in front of her on Dr Evil's desk. "It's not over yet," she added, more calmly now.

Dr Evil slowly ran a finger along the edge of his desk in one long, irritating stroke. "Kate, I don't see where you can go with this. That's all. We've run your story of the break-in at the cathedral, we've had the missing skull and we've had the photofit of the woman who broke in, but that's it. You want to keep on flogging this thing but there's no story there. People don't want to read a non-story."

"But it's not a non-story! What about the fact that she came from London? And is interested in Jane Austen? What if she comes back for Jane Austen?"

Dr Evil's lazy eye rested on the top of her low-cut blouse. "No-one is going to dig up Jane Austen. And so what if we know she comes from London. Nine million people come from London."

"Well what if we take another angle?"

"What other angle Kate?"

"I don't know…"

"Look…" Dr Evil sat back in his oversized leather chair and placed his hands on his lap. "You keep on to the police and if something new comes up then maybe we'll go with it. I agree with you, it's an intriguing story and yes I think there's more to run on it, but right now they've drawn blanks and blanks don't sell papers. We've done the appeals so now let's just move on. I have this break-in on the Rivers Estate that I need covering. Why don't you head out there now and we can run it tonight. What do you say? It's a good story for my little Jane Austen in the making."

"Sure. Sure." Kate, lips pursed, snatched back the scrap of paper and walked out.

See these shoes
See these heels
'Cause soon baby
They're all you're going to see of me
'Cause I'm a stro-ong woman
And I'm movin' on
I'm walkin' off
Oh yeah
See these heels
See these heels

Twenty-One

The Dean of Winchester lay stretched out along the cold marble steps before the High Altar, his robes falling in thick black folds to the floor. Only the lamps in the choir were left on, leaving the vast interior unlit: the tombs and effigies melting into the black. There was a complete stillness and calm that was never part of the daytime bustle. Now the only movement was the thin coil of smoke winding from his Marlborough Light, up towards the vaulted roof.

It was Friday night. A few streets away the bars along High Street would be filling with the rowdy crowd of sequined girls and cheap-shirted boys. The music would be pumped up, the drinks ordered. But here there was nothing but darkness and silence. All Archie could hear was the faint crackle of the tobacco burning as he drew on his cigarette, and the long breath as he exhaled the smoke up to the roof. The choral evensong was done, the congregation and tourists and members of the cathedral had all left, the building was packed up for the night and he was free to go home. From this point on the Archdeacon was in charge of Winchester Cathedral; a frightening notion. But the man was fully briefed and warned several times over about the perils of leaving the cathedral unlocked. Gabriel, the septuagenarian organist's assistant with the shaky hands, was on full-alert and would secretly be checking that the

Archdeacon had locked all doors every night, so there was really nothing to worry about. Everything would be fine. Heads would be safe.

But everything was not fine. Everything wasn't working out as planned. Not that there was a plan, but if there had been one, this wouldn't have been it. MacNeath had been on the phone earlier that day, wondering what progress he was making with finding Canute. Archie had lied, said he'd visited the Winchester Archaeology Unit when he hadn't, said he'd talked to the police again when he hadn't: he would have said anything to get the big man off his back. He didn't bring up the recent television appeal because he knew the bishop's uncompromising views on the media; let him find out about the programme if it was successful.

But it wasn't just MacNeath plaguing him about the missing head; everyone was at it. The trouble he was in was proving to be crushingly inescapable. After each service half his congregation would mill around, politely asking how he was getting on with locating Canute.

And, just like the Bishop of Wessex, all of them assumed that it was *his* job and his job alone to find the stolen goods and not that of the police who were paid to do that kind of thing. After twenty or thirty suffocatingly polite enquiries – *just wondered how you're getting on finding that head* – Archie wanted to scream from the cathedral tower *it was not my fault the arsing door was unlocked – it was the Archdeacon! Get bloody Cedric to find Canute! It's his fault* and jab an accusing finger at the clueless Archdeacon who would be moonily smiling and chatting and getting away with his crime of omission while he, Archie, had to shoulder the blame.

He blew silent curling smoke rings that vanished into the darkness.

Now more than at any time Archie needed Angela to distract him: taking her to bed would go a very long way to making his life more bearable.

He took another drag of his cigarette.

Angela would not come.

She had called last night after he had left his sixth message on her answer machine (so unlike him to pursue this hard, why was he?) and she had fobbed him off with a feeble excuse about not being able to find adequate cover for the weekend. But he could read between the lines. It was over. He was nothing to her, just a fling at a Church conference, something to relieve the tedium of a few evenings spent in Staffordshire with a group of crotchety old men.

I don't want you to get the wrong idea Archie. Those few days in Lichfield meant the world to me. I mean, I do really like you but...

But what?

It was a difficult time for me right now/ I'm busy/ I'm not looking for anything serious... He knew them all because he'd used them all. But hadn't Angela been different? Hadn't they really had something going on between them? Wasn't there a spark that he hadn't felt before? The revelation of finding a kindred spirit...a Marianne Faithfull of the pulpit to his Mick Jagger of the pulpit, connecting on some deeper, significant plane that transcended anything he had ever felt before? Damn it all weren't those lusty three days in Staffordshire something special?

Clearly not.

No, no, it's not you it's me Archie...

WHY? That's what he wanted to know. Why was it all happening at the same time? Why was MacNeath baying for blood and why were the papers bringing him down and, more than all of this, why was the one woman he thought he might actually have some kind of relationship with giving him the cold shoulder? Why were they all ganging up on him?

At least there was Canute. At least he had a task to be getting on with, something to take his mind off things.

He leant over and stubbed his cigarette out on the step and then, feeing guilty at the image of Margery Down and her mop, picked up the stub and dispersed the ash with his hand.

Where to start on the search for Canute? Where do you go to find a stolen thousand-year-old head? Perhaps he should go to the archaeological chaps like he'd told MacNeath he'd done. That would be a start. And then go to see the police. By doing that at least the lies he'd used to fob off MacNeath wouldn't be lies any more.

He leant back and lit another cigarette, the snap of his lighter echoing off the dark stone pillars caging him in.

Twenty-Two

Edgar cradled the phone between his ear and shoulder.

"There are rumbles my boy."

"Mmm." Edgar was absorbed in drawing brisk, sharp lines across a printed out draft of a press release he'd spent the evening composing. Along the top of the page a stick woman with ragged wild hair flying out behind her rode a sketchy chariot pulled by two giant stick horses.

"Serious rumbles Eddie. From several sources. Trusted sources."

Edgar swapped pens and slashed out sprays of red ink blood behind the chariot; a bleeding Roman squirming under the wheels in stick-man agony.

"Sorry, Dad. What rumbles?"

"They're saying it's not a medieval mass grave at all that the museum's got under the platforms at Kings Cross. They're saying that's just a cover up and they've found nothing less than Boudica's Last Battle Site." The words hung between them. "Eddie?"

"Yes, Dad?"

"Well? Have you heard anything?"

Blood, blood, blood. "No Dad. No-one tells me anything. How's Mum?"

"Goddamn it, don't play with me!" There was a pause as he made to regain his composure, no doubt with his wife giving him *one of her looks*. "So, are you absolutely sure you've not heard anything my boy?" he barked.

Stab. Stab, stab, stab, stab. Armless, legless Romans piled up against the justified righthand border. "Sure. As far as I know it's a medieval mass grave. Where did you hear otherwise?" Edgar asked the question lightly, during which time a blood-mad stick Briton, brandishing a knife, hurtled towards two legionaries hiding for safety behind the bullet-pointed key facts.

"Well, let's just say that Frank from the CLAU mentioned something about Boudica in an email this morning and then, two hours later, Greta Carmichaels from the FMRPCTI called me up to tell me she'd heard there were *Roman weapons* turning up for cleaning and preserving at the finds unit in the University of North East London. Roman weapons Eddie. From a medieval pit."

"Crikey."

He could hear the slapping of a forehead all the way from the South of France. "Eddie..."

"Yes, Dad."

"Tell me! Tell me now!"

"Tell you what, Dad?"

"Don't fuck with me, boy."

"*Graham!*" the shocked voice of his mother could be heard in the background.

Edgar paused mid-Roman, his pen hovering over the smashed shield. His father never *ever* swore.

"Dad, I..."

"Where are you?"

"At work."

Oops... The words were out before he had time to think.

"And why are you still at work at nine on a Wednesday evening?"

He stared at the postcard of Edward Thornycroft's statue of Boudica he'd discreetly pinned to his noticeboard, horses straining, chariot thundering and Boudica, triumphant, arm outstretched, careering in to battle. "Filing, Dad?"

"Edgar!"

"Filing. I told you! Filing"

"Look Eddie I..."

"Dad, stop bullying me for Christ's sake! I don't want to be here at work so late, so just let me get on with what I'm doing so I can go home." He paused, heart racing, astonished at himself. "I told you Dad – I don't know anything about anything. What am I except the tea-boy? You said yourself I'm starting at the bottom and working my way up, so who am I to know if there's any secret squirrel stuff going on? They're hardly going to tell the tea boy are they? I'm sure you know loads more than I do – you always have done. If I know anything I'll tell you. Goodbye, Dad." He hung up.

Returning to his press release he sighed.

His carefully drafted words were heavily scrawled over with stick-man carnage. Boudica was determinedly driving straight over his opening paragraph with blood obliterating his first sentence and a pile of Romans butchered over a quote from Professor De Lacey.

Resignedly Edgar printed out a new copy and began another read-through.

Twenty-Three

"Hi, I'm here to see Sergeant Swain." Kate ran a hand through her bouncy bobbed hair. "I have an appointment." She smiled: her hair felt cool and soft and springy to the touch. Dressed in a pale blue jumper and long swooshy skirt she felt impressively confident with herself.

The dour-faced policewoman on the front desk was not as enthusiastic about Kate's appearance. She watched her with narrowed-eyes, her lips pursed tight together, as Kate continued to preen herself and admire her reflection in the bullet-proof glass between them.

The policewoman picked up the phone and dialled.

"He's busy," she said after a moment, dropping the receiver down sharply.

"Pardon?" Kate's hand stopped mid-smooth.

"Sergeant Swain sends his apologies but he's now busy and he can't make your appointment."

"But..."

"Something has *come up*." She saw the look on Kate's face and couldn't resist adding, "Things like that happen in the police force: we aren't able to schedule criminal activity as yet."

Kate smiled through gritted teeth and decided to make the best of it; maybe this new thing that had come up was a lead to another story after all — she should get in there before Lynn got it.

"So what's come up?"

"He didn't say." The policewoman returned to her paperwork and Kate stood drumming her manicured nails on the desk.

"Fine. Fine. Well can I speak to another officer working on the cathedral theft then, *please*?"

Without looking up the policewoman snatched up the receiver again.

"Hello there!" a familiar voice rang out behind Kate and she spun round on her heels.

"Dean Cartwright!"

"Archie, please!" He caught a look of genuine pleasure on her face at the sight of him, which was quickly replaced by something far more detached. "What are you up to here Kate? Hunting out new stories for your paper?"

"Mmm, sort of." She twisted her hair between her fingers, measuring up the man before her with his shabby greatcoat and long green wool scarf that reached to his knees. Part London rock-thing and part old-school churchman. "What about you?"

"I'm here to do a bit of my own Sherlock Holmesing, see if I can't find out whodunit on my head theft."

"Really?" Kate perked up. "Are you here to see Sergeant Swain?"

"Who? I don't know."

"You don't have an appointment?"

"Heck no. Do you need one of those? I thought this was the police station not a deli counter. Do we have to take a numbered ticket?" He shot the policewoman on the desk a grin and when Kate turned she just caught the woman's blushing smile before it was quickly wiped from her countenance and she went back to being sour-faced.

"Anyway…" Kate felt like a disapproving mother talking to her son and resented him for making her feel that way. "When you've quite finished, I was going to say – I'm here for the Canute theft too."

"Maybe we could pool resources and crack this thing together?"

"Maybe…" However much Archie was involved in the story, *was* the story, she wasn't sure how closely she wanted to work alongside him. A man so hungry for media attention was bound to bring his own particular problems along and she didn't want them getting in the way. However much she was enjoying seeing him…

Kate found herself surprised at her own strength of feeling; but four years of having to work against Lynn Paget had sharpened the competitive instinct in her, a desire to work alone and prove herself to the world.

But perhaps in this instance working with someone would be no bad thing, even if it was Archie Cartwright. He appeared to have his uses: within five minutes he had got them the use of a room and the promise of a policeman to take them through the cathedral theft files and answer any questions.

The policewoman paused on her way out of the door.

I don't believe this Kate glowered *she's actually going to ask him if he wants a coffee.*

But the policewoman caught Kate's expression and, leaving the door open, she left them caffeine-free.

Kate sat her bag on the table and pulled out her new Blackberry, a leather-bound notepad, a silver fountain pen, a pencil, the police briefing documents and her own file on the head theft.

Archie smiled as she fished out the items, one after another after another.

"What?" Kate caught him watching her.

"Oh nothing. Nothing. I was just wondering when you were going to pull out a personal assistant from that enormous sack."

"She stays in there – doing the filing."

Kate carefully set about arranging the items in front of her on the desk in order of size. "Have you done any more investigating on the case, other than turn up at the police station this morning?"

"Some. Sort of." He shrugged and leant back in his chair, "I went round to the Winchester Archaeological Unit yesterday but they were less than useless; quite rude and patronising as it happened," he added, "probably because they think I'm responsible for losing the head."

"Well you are." Kate arranged the pens in line.

Archie balled his hands up under the desk. It was no use arguing with the woman. "I also went down to the City Museum but there was nothing there either. They hate me too."

"You're feeling very sorry for yourself aren't you?" Kate said, "I'm sure they don't really hate you."

Archie gave a short bitter laugh. "They do hate me. They all hate me because they all blame me." He was well aware that he sounded like a brat, but that just made him even

160

more aggravated by his situation.

"Oh well, pull yourself together." Kate shrugged. "You either let yourself be brought down by it or you rise above it. It's your choice."

Archie looked at her, wide-eyed. Had his inner resource of strength got so low he was now taking advice from an upstart female journalist?

"Do you have any theories?" Kate asked, amused at the expression on his face following her admonishment.

He pulled himself together. "No. None. The whole thing is totally beyond comprehension." He leaned forward and picked up her pen, turning it round in his hands. "How could someone get away with stealing the head of an important person? That's what I want to know. There must be some DNA, or whatever it is, lying around to give a clue as to whom the thief was. Someone must recognise the photofit you published in your paper."

"Not if she's not local," Kate said. "None of the national papers published the photofit so no-one outside Winchester would have seen the pictures. Anyway, you said yourself that the photofit wasn't excellent."

"Yes but it wasn't that bad. It definitely captured something about her."

"I think it captured something of your fantasies more than anything else." Kate raised her eyebrows. "Long red hair, full lips, big doe eyes. Wasn't it your trousers thinking?"

Archie snorted. "My *trousers* thinking?"

"How would you have put it then?" Kate asked defensively.

"Well, there's a whole array of expressions which

could—"

"Hello there!" A shiny-faced young policeman bounded into the room and shook their hands. "Cathedral theft is it?" He placed a large box-file on the desk before him and began rifling through it. Kate opened her notepad to her preset ordered list of questions.

Half an hour later and it was obvious to Kate and Archie that their visit to the police station had been a complete waste of time. They had been taken through exactly the same material they had seen before with no new snatches of information to take them any further forward. The police file lay between them on the table and Kate strained to read what was written in it: there must be something the police knew that they weren't passing on to the media. Surely.

"What we need—" Archie was slumped in his chair and looking dejected "—is something like that." He pointed to the shelving unit beside them. Up on the top shelf beside box files and stacks of papers sat a clay bust of a woman watching them with cold glass eyes.

Kate shivered. "Who is that?"

"It's a Jane Doe." The policeman began to place his papers back in the box file. "An unidentified person – you know, John Doe, Jane Doe. That particular woman was in a very bad state beside the river just outside Winchester. No-one could identify her as she was, so we had her face reconstructed from the skull. It brings the victim to life, as it were. Another way to prompt a response from the public."

"I remember!" Kate exclaimed. "Didn't they call her the Hampshire Ophelia?"

"That's right."

"And someone called in didn't they? Someone recognised her."

The policeman nodded. "When we have these made up they have about a 75 per cent success rate."

"So..." Kate stared up at the haunting face above them, an idea forming. "It was done by someone here at Winchester?"

"No. We used a freelancer to do it."

Ten minutes later Archie and Kate left the police station with a spring in their step, clutching a slip of paper with the phone number and address for Bob Gilroy, Medical Artist, on it.

Twenty-Four

"Hello Edgar? Eddie? It's your father here. Pick up if you're there. Eddie! *Honestly dear he can't hear you it's a mobile phone not a landline; you don't hear it when people leave messages on mobile phones.* Yes, thank you Brenda. EDGAR! I think you know what I'm talking about with this dig, so give me a call back on my mobile. Your mother and I are flying in to Gatwick – *Heathrow dear* – Heathrow early tomorrow morning and we'll be staying at the Belvedere – *No we couldn't get in there remember Graham? Edgar darling we're at the Roehampton instead. They have nicer rooms anyway* – Yes, yes. OK, now listen Edgar, we're coming back to England to see this dig for ourselves. Medieval plague pit be damned – there's something big going on there. Can you get in touch with my old colleague Hilary De Lacey at the Museum and mention my name, get me on the pass-list at the dig. Call me back my boy – *Love you honey. We've bought some real olive oil for you, sweetie.* – for God's sake Brenda..."

Twenty-Five

Holding an enormous bag of white seedless grapes like an entry-ticket, Edgar navigated the strip-lit hospital corridors in search of his boss. Hospitals held a particular horror for Edgar. At the impressionable age of seven he had been left in a room alone with his insensible great-grandmother while his parents went out to get a cup of tea. During that time the death-white old woman had come round, had one of her *funny turns* and had leapt off the bed, hobbled over to him half-naked screaming *the bin men are coming, the bin men are coming.* Even now as he passed frail elderly women wheeling their drips he shrank away, terrified there would be another inappropriate assault.

It was early evening with barely an hour left of visiting time and he felt the frustration mount as he tried to navigate the endless corridors to obscure places with names that meant nothing to him: *cardio-neurosis renal care, auxiliary ambulatory paediatrics.* Edgar had studied James Joyce during his A-levels and, wandering the linguistically obscure corridors, he wondered whether the sign-writer had taken his inspiration from the man.

At last he found Ward 38. He peered inside. His boss, instantly recognisable by the swoosh of black quaffed hair like a World War II RAF pilot, was over by the window, propped up and reading *Hello* magazine.

"Eddie!"

"Hi Uncle Richard."

"*Pardon*?"

Edgar put his finger to his lips and, leaning in, whispered, "Remember when the Sister took the phone off you last week?"

"The first time?"

"No. The second time."

"I think so…"

"Well before she hung up she made it very clear to me as the caller that you were to have no stress and absolutely no contact with work for the next fortnight."

"Ah ha! So you must be my newfound nephew!"

"And so I am! How are you Uncle?"

"Oh, you know. Middling. They say my old boy will be fully operational in six to nine months, which is great, but the skin grafts are – oh I'm sorry Ed you didn't want that much information did you? Well, let's just say I'm fine. Great. Can't piss in a straight line, but hey ho… Better than the other two who I hear are going to be off work for some time eh? Ha! Serves them right for shooting me in the bollocks doesn't it? So, what's new with you, how are things back at HQ. Sorry I haven't been there to break you in gently."

"Well I sort of need your help." Edgar settled himself down in the visitor's chair beside the bed putting the grapes on the side table, which was tragically devoid of cards and flowers.

"Kings Cross causing you trouble is it?"

"Mmm."

"Been reading about it in the papers this morning. Can't tell you how much I wish I was there in the thick of it. But hey ho. Fire away then. What's on your mind Ed?"

"It's… well…the dig…it's not what it's made out to be," Edgar whispered and, getting up, pulled the curtains around the bed.

"Hey, you know those things don't actually block out sound don't you? It's just normal material."

"I know that."

"Fine. Right. Well, they've found a plague pit haven't they? That's what it's all about, reading between the lines. Isn't that right? They're saying it's plague free but really they've gone and found the Black Death? The eejits. I knew it. I see what you mean – this is one hell of a public relations disaster what with—"

He stopped, seeing Edgar shaking his head.

Richard frowned and leant forward, grimacing slightly as the pain kicked in. "Go on then, nephew – fill me in."

Ten minutes later when Sister yanked back the floral curtains she saw the patient and his nephew sitting in silence, both eating grapes, both frowning.

"You know the patient's not supposed to be stressed in any way," she muttered, picking up the notes from the bottom of the bed.

"Of course." Richard grabbed another grape.

She walked off, looking back at them suspiciously.

Richard leant towards Edgar. "Well the truth is bound to get out. The Museum's as leaky as…well as my cock to be frank with you."

Edgar winced. "But what do you think I should do?"

"I think you should have a little more confidence in yourself, that's what I think you should do." Richard took another grape. "You're doing just fine. You've gone out and seen for yourself what's happening. Those goons at the Museum are playing hush-hush with it all but you needed to know the truth and now you do. They've always been bastards about not telling the press office anything and then expecting us to cope when all hell breaks loose. So well done you for actually having the balls to go and find out for yourself. I admire you for it. And now you know that in a week or so you'll be able to break the story, or it will be broken and you'll know what you're fielding, so if I were you I'd start preparing some press releases. But keep them confidential. Make sure everything is password protected, not on the shared drive and on no account print anything off and leave it lying about."

In hushed tones the boss imparted his knowledge to the office junior and the office junior scribbled notes furiously in his pad.

Twenty-Six

"It's the funniest thing," Archie said.

"What is?" Kate kept her eyes glued to the motorway.

"Fifth gear."

"I'm in fifth gear!"

Archie did a mock double-take, looking down at the gear stick. "I didn't know you could go so slowly in top gear."

Kate, lips pursed, shot him a disapproving look. "The car gets the shakes if it goes above sixty-five."

"We should have gone in mine." Archie, resignedly, sat back and watched the grass verges of the M4 glide past very sedately.

The journey from Winchester to Bristol was dragging on. He had nothing better to do with his time off, so there was no pressure to be elsewhere, but the snail's pace she was travelling was driving him to distraction. Not even the opportunity to admire her legs was sufficient in staving off boredom.

He gave a long drawn-out sigh.

"Look," Kate snapped, "I am *sick* of your self-righteousness and your sarcastic little comments. If you haven't got anything worthwhile to say then just keep quiet."

Archie stared at her, agog. She might look appetising enough, be all smiles and friendly chat but she was developing this habit of snapping at him at the least provocation.

"I am perfectly happy to pursue this story on my own," she was continuing, "as I was doing, in fact. So, if you want to tag along then fine, but don't start whining at me. This is *my* car and I'm going at *my* speed."

Archie hung his head.

They trundled on, past the exit for Chippenham: past Leigh Delamere Services.

"Sorry," he muttered.

"No, no, no!" Bob Gilroy was shaking his head. "You've got it entirely wrong, I'm sorry but there you have it." The old man gave a chuckle and lit another cigarette; his third since they had arrived at his Georgian townhouse twenty minutes before.

"Urgh!" Archie sighed. "We're not getting anywhere with this; it's impossible!"

"I'm sorry," Kate apologised for Archie, "it's just we've come rather a long way. And…well we were so sure this would give us a new angle on the story."

Inwardly Kate was kicking herself. She should have checked things out on the phone before they'd trekked all the way over to Bristol. Any good journalist would have done their research before committing to such an expedition. If she'd obeyed that simple rule then they wouldn't be sitting here now at a dead end, wasting everyone's time.

Dr Evil had been less than thrilled when she had proposed the trip to Bristol in the first place, even though she'd promised him a new and exciting angle on the head theft story. And now she would be returning to Winchester without any new lead and that would not go down well. She had been convinced that she could have arranged for a bust of the head thief to be made up, and, as in the case of the unidentified John Does and Jane Does, the article with the picture would prompt a response from the public. If the poor quality photofit had got a result from the woman in the cathedral shop then surely a 3D model would have the potential to generate something greater.

But now they were told that it was impossible. And the depth of her disappointment was tangible.

And no doubt Dr Evil would keep her on an even tighter leash, entrusting to her only the most mundane of local stories, with heavy supervision. And that flirty, pouty Lynn Paget would have even greater free rein, picking up the stories that would have gone to Kate.

"I'm sorry, young lady," Bob Gilroy flicked the ash from his cigarette on to the filthy quarry-tiled floor of his studio, "but I don't work like that. You can't give me a description and I make a facial reconstruction of her up for you. You'd want some sort of modeller for that I imagine: an artist in the more traditional sense. But even then you wouldn't get anything of any value as a tool for identification: you'd be left with an artist's impression of another person's impression, which I imagine, and I may be wrong, would be too far removed from the actual reality to be of any real use to anyone."

"I 'spose so." Archie swung his legs on the bar stool.

"It's a terribly interesting exercise though, from a purely hypothetical point of view you understand. I'm afraid you've had rather a wasted journey today."

Kate turned to Archie for direction but he was captivated by a horrific half-skeleton half-human face on the dresser nearby. Perched on a high table atop a pole was a plaster skull with pegs pressed into it and glass eyes stuck in its skeletal sockets. With bands of wax muscle and semi-fleshed nose it was infinitely more dreadful than the haunting face from Winchester Police Station that had started them on this wasted journey.

"What *is* this?" Archie got up to take a closer look. "Is this for some kind of horror show?"

Bob Gilroy chuckled before descending into a fit of phlegmy coughing. Archie, who had been dying for a cigarette, felt the urge leave him. Kate tried to blank out the disgusting noise as well continuing to blank out the gruesome model, the other skulls arranged on shelves, the terrifying array of instruments, the hammers and saws and bowl full of glass eyes. She did this by staring at the floor and examining the exquisite detailing on her new turquoise suede shoes that rested above accumulated strata of filth. She *really* wanted to go home now.

"That—" Bob Gilroy finally recovered from his coughing fit "—is an unclaimed person found in woods just outside Newport in Wales two weeks ago. I've been commissioned to build the face from what was left of the man's remains."

"Eww, Kate, this is a really gruesome isn't it?" Archie leant over to her to get her attention.

"Mmm." Kate squinted at the head from the corner of her eyes.

"What is it exactly that you do then, if you don't mind me asking, how does this become a proper head?" Archie leant in to examine the model closer.

Bob stubbed out his cigarette and reaching into a box beside Kate's elbow he pulled out a blackened skull. "I don't mind you asking. Well, first things first, I started with this chap here."

"OH MY GOD!" Kate shot up from her chair and backed away. "Oh that is *so* disgusting."

Bob turned the toothless skull to face him, looking at it critically. "No he's not disgusting – poor old chap don't you listen to her. He's just rather tragic that's all. And besides, the skull isn't a disgusting thing: you and I have one; in fact we'd be buggered without one I can tell you. No, these things are fascinating."

"Can I?" Archie reached out to take the skull from the medical artist, cradling it in his hands, running a finger over the fissures on its smooth surface, and around the rougher edges of its sockets. "Look – he's grinning at you Kate. I think he likes you."

"Shut up Archie!" *Beautiful, beautiful, turquoise suede shoes...*

Bob Gilroy winked at Archie and held out his hands to take back the skull. "Well, there was nothing found with the body that could be used to identify him, so they called me in to do a reconstruction."

"How do you know he's a chap?"

"From examining the pelvis and also from a look at the skull itself. This one is broader across the brow than a woman's would be. What you see here on the table is my work midway through the reconstruction process, using a cast of the original skull." Kate inched closer, still disgusted but her journalistic curiosity piqued.

"First of all—" Bob gently pushed the model towards them "—I make a cast of the skull and I work on the plaster cast from that point on. Some artists use the skull itself to build on but I think that's a little distasteful and a cast is just as effective. And of course it means I can return the skull to the police or whoever employs me, rather than return the made-up model with the skull still buried underneath."

"Amazing. Can I?" Bob nodded and Archie ran his finger gently over the ribs of wax muscle.

"These little pegs you can see all over the skull," Bob continued, "well they mark out the average tissue depths at each location so that I can build up the muscle and fatty tissue and finally the skin in the right proportions."

"Wow that's incredible!" Archie gingerly reached out and touched the nearest peg on the cheek of the skull. "So do we all have the same tissue depths then?"

"Not at all. It depends on your age, whether you are male or female and also on ethnic origin. I'm looking at a Caucasian male, I would say, twenties to thirties, so I use the calculations for average tissue depths of that type of person."

"Wow!" Archie looked back to Kate. "Kate that's amazing isn't it?"

"Mmm." She squinted at the skull again.

"So what other tricks do you have then?" Archie asked.

"Well young man—" he bent to light another cigarette from the stub of his last "—the shape of the eye socket can determine whether eyes were level or turned up or down. And the shape of the lower jaw can indicate a cleft chin, which this chap doesn't have as you see."

"So you really can get a good picture of what someone looked like, then."

"Well, yes, it's an impression. It's still an art form you must remember, though, not a true science. But there is a scientific approach to it that forms the basis of the craft. See here – the nasal bone gives me a clue as to the angle and the shape of the nose. The mastoid process, just behind the ears here, is a good indicator as to the shape of the lower ear – a straight one means the subject has dangling ear lobes just like you have, one that bends forward is a sign that the ears blend smoothly in to the side of the face. Just like your friend." He looked at Kate.

"I think *my friend* is in denial that she even has a mastoid process." Archie grinned at Kate.

Kate shot Archie a sarcastic smile. "The Jane Doe you did at Winchester was a success pretty much as soon as you did it wasn't it? Is that usual?"

"Winchester, Winchester..." Bob Gilroy searched his memory. "Do you know I don't recall working on a Jane Doe in Winchester. At least, not recently. Maybe a couple of years back..."

"But you did a Jane Doe this summer."

"Did I? Did I? Ah I know!" His brow unfurled, "I *didn't* do Winchester as it happens. I was in Canada at the time with an old college friend, so another freelancer was given the work in my place. You're right, I do tend to work the West Country and Wales, being based here in Bristol, but in that instance it went to a medical artist based in London. Cora Montgomery. We're a small fellowship us freelance medical artists – we know each other fairly well, and I recall she did a very good job didn't she? But then Cora *is* very good and her reconstructions are rated for their authenticity." He stood up and went over to a sideboard. Leaning over to a shelf he took down a framed photograph.

While his back was turned Kate mouthed *I want to go now* to Archie who gave a 'five more minutes' sign. He was captivated by this other world that they'd stumbled in to.

"Well thank you very much…" Kate took charge, not wanting to be surrounded by it all any more. She stood up, coat in hand. "It's very interesting—"

But Bob Gilroy continued regardless of her tone. "In this picture are almost all of us gathered together – a rare occasion." He passed the photograph to Archie who took it politely and went through the motions of studying it. "We're at the 2007 Ethics and Reconstruction conference. You see how few of us there actually are in the UK. There's me in the front row, and further along are Bill Worthing, Pat Murphy, Cora Montgomery – she's the one who did the Winchester job you were taking about just now – and at the end there is Roger Whitley-Jones. Interesting conference as it happened. Certainly gave me some food for thought. And then on the back row there is Dick Paltrow…"

Kate and Archie had both tuned out of what Bob was saying, mesmerised by the woman in the photograph, seated on the front row. Cora Montgomery: the woman who had done the reconstruction at Winchester. Cora Montgomery who was looking straight at the camera, straight up at them, half-smiling with her unmistakable cupid's bow mouth.

"…and then Pat Murphy was bold enough to question

whether we should—"

"Excuse me," Archie interrupted. "Cora Montgomery..."

"Cora? Do you know her?"

"Possibly," Kate said, her voice trembling. Looking to Archie she could see that he too was affected by the woman in the photograph.

"Lovely lady is Cora, always so smart and well presented," Bob Gilroy was saying, "as you can see on that photograph you're holding. She's there wearing a suit and the rest of us are just in our jeans and t-shirts – she puts us all to shame. We had a good laugh at that conference and even Cora joined in with us, which wasn't very like her, she's one of those quiet types, you know, that keep to themselves. I've always said she would do well to have a husband she would, get her out a bit more, get her involved in things, you know? She just seems to bury herself away in her work and in our line of business... Well, you can be shut off from the world for days if you're not careful. Lovely woman though. Very skilled, as I said. In fact she has different opinions on the average tissue depth measurements that I was talking to you about, only slightly different opinions but I think I'm more and more coming round to her way of thinking. Why do you ask?"

"Oh. Nothing. I just thought I recognised her. Maybe not though," Kate said, feeling herself turn red.

"Well here's an interesting thing about Cora, she crosses over into the world of archaeological reconstruction. Now where was it? Oh, I know, the University of North East London – one of those hyped-up colleges from the eighties – anyway, they get involved with a lot of digs around London and the South East and I think she does some work with them on recreating the faces of some of the people they dig up. Frightfully interesting I should think. As it happens I've been wondering for some time now whether I should get in touch with my local archaeological offices in Bristol and see if there were similar opportunities here. I imagine there are never any grants available though. These archaeology chaps work on a pittance..."

As he rattled on, Archie lit a cigarette with trembling hands and took a long, hard drag. And then he leant over and lit the cigarette Kate had taken for herself.

Twenty-Seven

It was dark. Very dark. An inky, pitch-like black.

Groping along the wall Archie reached the light switch. So bright! Pain! He whacked the switch off. Stumbling blinded in to his living room he walked into something squishy, and then collapsed onto it. It was the sofa.

What a great night. But it did feel odd to have spent the entire time with a girl and to be going home alone: it wasn't the usual way of things. Still, he was in no state to bring a woman back; in fact he was aware that he was in no fit state to bring himself back and he tried to recall how he'd made it from the King's Head to his house.

No. It was gone.

Kate.

Kate Kate Kate Kate Kate Kate Kate.

There was something about her. But what? He closed his eyes. The room was spinning.

It was odd because she was quite good looking, really. Very good looking after she'd done her hair and had got rid of the housewife get-up he'd first seen her in. Quite a rapid transformation from frump to...what was she? Non-frump. He couldn't think.

He dozed blearily. But there was something wrong. Something was beeping.

He propped himself up on his elbows, collapsed, and

tried again.

It was the answer machine.

From his position on the sofa he could just about curve his arm around the table and hit 'play' before sinking back into its welcome feather-filled depths.

"Hi, Archie, it's Angela here. Look I'm really sorry about the phone call the other day. I do want to see you again darling, it's just that well I'm sort of with someone at the moment and...well...we're breaking up. But I wasn't sure but now I am and oh what am I trying to say? I'm trying to say yes! I'll come over to Winchester and I—"

Without a second thought Archie whacked the delete button.

"Me again! I just remembered what else I had to tell you! Remember when you drove off from Lichfield the other day? Well you sprayed gravel over the place and you hit Smithson from Rochester Cathedral in the face. Cut his cheek actually. He's fine about it though. Just thought you ought to know. Only two stitches apparently. Byeee. See you soon! Call me! Mwah!"

Archie flailed around before managing to hit the delete button a second time.

And passed out on the sofa.

It was 9am and Kate, seated at her desk, massaged her temples, wondering whether one of her colleagues had a paracetamol.

Or a hammer.

She had the urge to crawl into a dark place and sleep, but she had work to do, and what she really wanted to do was spend this time enjoying her success in finding the thief that stole Canute's head.

Their success.

Gingerly she took a sip of coffee.

Yesterday had been a triumph beyond anything she could have ever imagined. To have found the woman who had stolen Canute's head when everyone else had failed! Even an entire police team had failed to find the thief – a thief who they had worked with just months before on an unidentified person case. OK so the highly fantasised photofit had not been the best means of identifying the thief, but surely someone at the police station could have made the connection...

Kate put her head in her hands and took a few deep breaths. Why had she drunk so much yesterday? How much *had* she drunk yesterday? She tried to recall the events of the previous twenty-four hours.

She and Archie had left Bob Gilroy's house quietly and politely shortly after seeing the photograph of Cora Montgomery: the woman who had broken in to the cathedral. Bob had been all too eager to share his world with them, and before they knew it there were albums, letters, newspaper cuttings produced about his work. In the end, when he was absorbed in finding a folder in his filing cabinet, Kate had dialled Archie's mobile and he faked a call, the outcome of which was, *So sorry, but we have to go right this minute. Something's come up. So sorry...*

Together the two had walked sedately down the front path. They mechanically got into her car. Backed up. Waved goodbye to Bob Gilroy. Pulled away, drove down the road, pulled in, stopped, looked at each other and then whooped like American teenagers.

"Oh my God!"

"It was her!"

"Cora Montgomery!"

"She's a medical artist!"

"Who does archaeology work!"

Archie stared at Kate for a moment. "And she's going to recreate Canute!"

"I know!"

"She's actually going to peg out Canute's skull and remake his face!"

"*If she hasn't already!*"

"The sick woman!"

"We've done it!"

"We're going to find Canute!"

"We're geniuses!"

"Let's celebrate!"

"But I have to drive."

"OK. Let's get back to Winchester and then celebrate there!"

"Good idea!"

"And Kate…"

"Yes Archie."

"Can we *please* go fast enough to make the car shake?"

Sighing Kate booted up her PC: now she had the task of learning more about Cora Montgomery. She rubbed her temples once more, trying to knead away her headache. Goddamn Archie. All she wanted to do was sleep. She checked her watch. It was half nine.

There was a commotion behind her and she turned. A gaggle of women from the office had descended on one desk nearby where Lynn Paget, keen to demonstrate she wasn't solely a shameless career-whore and was, in fact, a sensitive mother type, was awkwardly clutching a tiny red-faced newborn baby in her scarlet-nailed hands and grinning like a lunatic to show how comfortable she was with a floppy-headed baby.

"Omigod, he's just so cute!" Laura from accounts cooed and Lynn looked up, shooting Kate a smile that belied the terror which was writ large across her face.

"Hey! Come over here Kate! Meet Janet's son Toby. Isn't he…adorable!" Toby started to wail.

"Mmm – yes he is. I just have to check some things." Kate turned back to her PC and surreptitiously angling it to avoid being overseen she began her search.

She opened up the internet, took a deep breath, and typed in CORA MONTGOMERY.

She hit *enter*.

The results page flashed up.

Checking behind her one more time, Kate scanned the page:

BBC News/ UK/ Murderer caught by artist's skill
Cora Montgomery has worked on anatomical reconstruction for over ten years…if it were not for the skill of artist **Cora Montgomery** a killer might have escaped…
News.bbc.co.uk/3ah/343ahdh.stm – 25k Cached - Similar pages - Note this

Amazon.com: **Cora Montgomery** & Terence Peters: Books (Oxford Medical Journals Paperback March 2002)…artist **Cora Montgomery** and Professor of Forensic Science Terence Peters discuss facial reconstruction as a means to…

www.amazon.com/s?=464/ search & type = cora&Montgomery – 145k Cached - Similar pages - Note this

Ms **Cora Montgomery**

Ms **Cora Montgomery** Department of Biological Sciences, North East London University, redefined the nature of forensic reconstruction with her paper on the assessment of tissue depths and …

www.nelondonuni.ac.uk/biosciences/forensics/55?=23–2k Cached - Similar pages - Note this

[PDF] T34346 RepAccs A3 CP *View as HTML*

Head reconstruction produced by **Cora Montgomery** of North East London University, School of Biological … Police Station on 4 June 2006. The Then Transport Minister John…

www.btp.police.uk/documents/ annualreport/ btpannualreport23.pdf – 88k Cached - Similar pages - Note this

The expensive coffee beside her keyboard went from scalding hot to warm to cool to cold. Caught up in her frenzied search across the net Kate clicked from page to page. She scanned papers in medical journals that Cora had submitted, read about a recent conference in Dublin Cora had attended, visited the School of Biological Science pages on the website for North East London University where Cora was a lecturer, and then, finally, went on to a map page.

She had to see Archie, right now. It was ten – surely he would be up by now. A memory of last night flooded back. Slumped with Archie in a booth at the back of a grubby backstreet winebar, drawing cartoons of a headless Canute, giggling like children. Pressed shoulder to shoulder, hip to hip, drowning in a sea of gin and tonic. Perhaps, she considered, Archie would not be up by now...

"You're not leaving without coming to see the little man are you?" Lynn called over to her, frowning. She was still clutching the infant, as though her attempts to demonstrate what an earth-mother she was were some kind of endurance test. Kate admired her persistence.

"Actually Lynn I have to go follow a lead right now. Big story I'm trying to crack."

Lynn looked at her with a sharp, hunted expression. Cracking stories was not something one did at the *Winchester Echo*. The facts were presented and you wrote them up.

"What lead? Where?"

"Oh you know..." Kate began, vaguely, grabbing her white wool coat and turning to shut down her PC. She was so caught up in her own thoughts that she didn't hear the screams until she had switched off the screen and was picking up her bag. The office was pandemonium. Little Toby had thrown up what looked like several pints of semi-digested milk all over the slinky dress Lynne was wearing to the office that day. Three women were running to get tissues, while others were trying to distract Toby who was bawling at the top of his voice, his tiny purple face screwed up in the effort. Kate stopped in front of Lynn and peered down at the screaming infant, writhing in his own vomit. "So cute!" she cooed and stalked out of the office before she got anything on her scarlet shoes.

Twenty-Eight

"Right then." Edgar sat at his desk and spun round in the chair. He pulled to a halt in front of the phone and hit '1'.

"Erika, can you come in here for a minute."

Scanning through the files on the system he found a template and opened it up. Time to write up the Mayor's report.

"Hi Ed-gar. How was Richard? Is he still in hospital?" Erika wandered into the office and perched on the edge of his desk. Edgar was looking unusually smart and *collected* this morning, she noticed, and there was a confident expression in his eyes. And since he had lost the puppy fat a new, sleeker, more determined man was emerging.

"Richard's fine. Just about. Well, you know, as good as can be expected. That sort of thing. Anyway, I have a plan of action."

"A plan that Richard suggested?"

"No, actually," he bristled, "it's mine. As it happens Richard agreed with what I was proposing."

"So what is it?"

"Well, the plan requires you to field all phone calls from the reporters."

"Oh Ed-gar! They are so rude to me!"

"I know. I'm sorry. If it makes you feel better I think they're rude to everyone. I need to write up this report so you must make a note of who wants what and tell them a new press release will be emailed to them by the end of the day. Five o'clock. Oh, and make sure you get their email addresses. And double-check the spelling. If anyone else calls that isn't a journalist or reporter of any sort, tell them I'm out of the office, unless it's the Head of Marketing and Communications and in that case put him through to my mobile."

"So what is this report for?"

"The Mayor's Office. One of his evil henchmen threatened me into writing it."

"What *is* it with people? I think London is a very rude city you know?"

"I know." Edgar thought for a moment. "Actually, can you contact the secretary of the Head of Marcoms and get her to book ten minutes with him for me at lunchtime today. I need to go through the report with him before I send it off."

"What if he's booked up?"

"Oh he will be. Tell his secretary I want to see him about Project Rebel and we'll stick to ten minutes max. He'll make time for me."

"Fine." She scribbled it all down. "Anything else?" She let the words hang in the air and inched nearer to him along the table.

"Could I have a cup of coffee please?"

Edgar sat opposite the Head of Marcoms in his office, waiting while the big man read the Mayor's report he had spent the last two hours drafting. Rigid with nerves, Edgar perched on the chair and spent the time looking at the framed photographs on the office wall. There were several of a large yacht, one of which showed the Head of Marcoms at the helm looking theatrically nautical in a stripy jumper and sailor's hat. Another photograph captured a group of children outside a large villa somewhere hot, a short cross woman lurking in the background and scowling at the camera. And then another photograph of the short cross woman again but this time behind a fuzzy filter, with garish make-up and wearing a vodka and orange smile. Treasured things to the Head of Marcoms: the yacht, the villa, the children, the wife.

Edgar scanned the back wall, looking for pictures of Henri the swarthy male receptionist. There were none.

"This is very good, Edgar. Very good indeed." The Head of Marcoms put down the Mayor's report and looked at the young PR man, impressed. "You've gone as far as we've advised you go and explained yourself very well. And I like the reference to the cost per day that they keep bandying about to the newspapers. Very clever, turning it back on them. But what I want to know is, as the leader of Project Rebel, who put *you* in the loop?"

Edgar bit his lip.

"Was it James Anderson?"

"Not as such."

"Peter Ryknield?"

Edgar shook his head. "Actually sir…I put myself in the loop." And, in a voice shaking with nerves, he confessed to snooping on the secretary's desk and having blagged his way through security at the dig site.

The Head of Marcoms listened, wide-eyed.

"Well!" he said when Edgar had finished. "I must say I'm rather shocked. But well done you – I think that your actions demonstrate remarkable strength of character. And I think, weighing it up, well, it's the right thing given the circumstances. Good man." He slapped Edgar on the back. "But I must warn you that you keep this *absolutely* to yourself, do you understand. We're not ready to share the true nature of Project Rebel with anyone other than those in the loop and I need to be able to trust you completely on this matter. Can I trust you completely?"

"Absolutely sir."

"Good man! Well, now that you're in the know you ought to be aware that we've got a briefing tonight at eight at the Royal Gardens Hotel in Covent Garden and I think you would do well to attend. Totally hush-hush, of course... A few of us at the Museum of London, the Archaeology team, Frankie from English Heritage and a small contingent from the Government."

"Tonight, sir?"

"It's the only time when all the key people are free. It's round-the-clock working for us on Project Rebel, Edgar, and we need to make ourselves available when the opportunity arises. Not a problem for you, is it, working on a Friday night? You don't have any plans to go out sniffing drugs and cavorting around on sweaty dance floors until the early hours do you?"

"Absolutely not, sir." But there had been a plan. There was a screening of *Orlando* at the Prince Charles: he was planning on asking Erika if she was interested.

But, he knew, he would never pluck up the courage to ask Erika out. And besides, she probably had plans of her own for Friday night. It was all a dream; a hope. What *might be* if he did have the courage to ask her out. And was devastatingly handsome enough to attract someone as beautiful as Erika. She probably had some hunk of a Scandinavian lumberjack or tennis ace tucked away at her flat – girls like her were never single. She wouldn't look twice at an English would-be textile designer.

"Good stuff!" The Head of Marcoms went on, "Carry on fielding calls and hopefully we'll all have some more direction after tomorrow evening. And well done on this report for the Mayor's Office!"

Edgar stood up and began to walk out.

"Oh Edgar..."

"Sir?"

"One more thing."

Edgar turned and walked back to the desk.

The Head of Marcoms paused and clasped his hands in front of him. "Your father..."

"Ah, yes sir." Edgar sat back down. "He's called me actually."

"Yes, I thought he might. So what does he know about the *battle* elements to our 'medieval' dig at Kings Cross?"

"Nothing from me. But...well you know, sir, he's still well connected with people at the Museum of London."

"Yes." He nodded. "You see Edgar, your father, well, he was a very important man here. Still is a very important man of course," he added quickly, "and he had his fingers in...well, in a lot of pies, as it were."

Edgar nodded, not quite sure where this was going. He thought he had it up until the bit about fingers in pies.

"Well," the Head of Marcoms searched for the right words, "your father, Edgar, was *one of them.*"

"One of them?"

"He was an archaeologist Edgar. And you must know what those archys are like. They keep themselves to themselves. Very cliquey you know; comes from being on the receiving end of trouble when project timings slip or when funding goes tits up. And it also comes from standing knee-deep in crap most of the time."

"I understand, sir."

"Well of course you do. But what I'm trying to get at, and what you have to understand, is that those bloody archys are a very close community, and they don't always see eye to eye with us desk-bound stooges. Think we have an overly cushy time of it, which of course we do. And we're enormously grateful to them for being outside in the elements doing our dirty work while we sit in plush offices and bark at them down the phone. So you see there is this *divide* young Edgar; them and us, and, well, what I'm trying to get at is that your father, if he knew about this dig, would have no qualms about ignoring our wishes here in the office to keep a tight lid on it. He would feel no compunction to follow our instructions. He would be, and from what you've told me he probably *has* been, on the phone to scores of his contacts, and they would be on the phone to their contacts and the secret would be out in the open in the blink of an eye. And we don't want that. We haven't properly recorded and secured the site yet and it would be disastrous if the pubic knew what we have without being able to put it all together."

"I understand," Edgar said.

"So, what does your father know?"

Edgar took a deep breath. "He called me last night. Asked why I was working late."

"And you were…"

"Filing, sir."

"Good man."

"And he said that someone connected with the North East London University finds unit had mentioned to him that there were Roman artefacts turning up in the medieval mass grave and he wanted to know more about it."

"Ahh. And did he name his source up at North East London?"

"No sir. And I'm sorry but I didn't think to ask him."

"Not to worry. Best not to draw attention to it. I take it you denied everything."

"Yes, sir, I told him I didn't know anything. I am after all the office junior."

"Well, I haven't seen much evidence of that my boy." He leant over and patted Edgar hard on the shoulder. Edgar tried not to beam with pleasure.

"Would it be too much to ask if you continue to keep what you do know about the dig from your father for the next couple of weeks until we break the story? I know it's a lot to ask of you but I don't want uncontrolled leaks on this."

Edgar thought briefly of his boss Richard lying in hospital with his own uncontrolled leaks. He bit his lip.

"Sir..."

"Yes, Edgar.

"I did tell my boss. Richard. I went into the hospital and told him about the dig and asked for his advice. I needed to. I'm sorry. But I really believe he won't tell anyone," he added.

"No problem. Richard's a good man. Fifteen years at the Museum of London and I trust him completely. If he was here, and not in hospital with his balls broken, then he'd be on Project Rebel without a second thought. But as it is, you are."

Edgar breathed a sigh of relief. "There's no-one else."

"Good. Good. So just keep your father out of it as much as you can. And let me know if he starts asking more knowledgeable questions."

"Well, sir, he's actually coming to London."

"When?"

"Tomorrow I think."

"Can you avoid him?"

"I think so. For a little while."

"Well I leave it up to you to deal with. Can't give you any father-son advice but you know where we stand."

"Yes, sir."

"Good man then. As you were."

Edgar nodded and walked out, pleased with the back patting (so long as that's where it stopped), delighted with the praise, and petrified by the impending arrival of his father.

Twenty-Nine

Outside the old warped glass windows the dazzling sunlight bathed autumnal Winchester in a golden glow. Around the corner on College Street the poet Keats had composed *Ode to Autumn* in celebration of just such a magnificent, life-affirming morning.

Archie leant over to the window and yanked the curtain closed.

His head was *banging*.

He had two hours to decide on the cathedral's new mission statement before emailing it to marketing so they could sign-off the print run of brochures.

Two hours.

He was getting too old for this drinking into the early hours nonsense. He wondered how Kate was faring that morning, having matched him gin for gin she must, surely, be suffering. He had been impressed: most girls he knew wimped out after the tenth drink.

Sitting himself heavily at his desk Archie picked up the brief he'd given to marketing with regard to proposed mission statements for the cathdral. "Something dynamic," he'd told them, "to the point, gripping, but more than just a sound bite. I want it to be meaningful. I want it to strike to the very core of our purpose here at Winchester. Key themes are Godly, Jesus, love – yes I know but try – history, entertainment."

And now, also on his desk, in the dimly lit room, lay the fruits of their labours.

York Minster – the cathedral that was such an anathema to him – had an impressively lengthy nine point mission statement but no gripping strap line. He paced the room, reading York's individual bullet points and 'pah'-ing at each in turn. He flung it down on the floor and picked up Lichfield's.

Lichfield Cathedral walked all over York Minster with its bumper sixteen point mission statement. He liked the idea of the sheer volume of missions. But he wanted something snappier.

Canterbury was fair: *To show people Jesus*. And Exeter: *To love God and to love all people*. It was more inclusive. Less Jesus-centric. Durham wasn't even trying: *The shrine of St Cuthbert*. That was just for the tourists.

Archie flung them down and picked up more.

Fantastical family fun!

Alton Towers seemed to have the measure of it.

What he wanted was Alton Towers, but also Canterbury. And Durham. And he wanted something better than York Minster. It *had* to be better than York Minster.

He looked over the outputs from the Marketing Department, listed in the memo.

Winchester 4 me! Winchester 4 everyone!

No.

Winchester: it's a God thing

No.

A thousand years of Glory to God

Better, but no.

He threw them down and looked at the last offering and its associated notes.

See it for yourself. Save it for the future.

Good.

But, he scanned the notes and re-read the strap line, pacing the room as he did: where was God in *See it for yourself Save it for the future*? Was God lurking in the eternalness of time, in the saving for the future? Or was that line simply relating to the fabric of the cathedral and nothing more. In which case it was going for the tourists again, just like Durham. Archie couldn't decide.

He contemplated it for a few minutes.

It would be fine.

He took out a pen and signed the strap line off. He'd drop it in to the office after he'd had a shower. There was no way he could be seen, or smelled, in public in the state he was in. It had been a very good night though...

There was violent thumping at the front door. Archie leapt.

Half expecting MacNeath he opened it slowly, but there stood Kate Grey with a broad smile on her face.

"Oh for goodness sake!" He held open the door and Kate bounded in looking annoyingly groomed and bright. "I thought it was something serious. Why didn't you just knock like a normal person?"

"Urgh, you smell vile!" She skipped past him, taking in the dishevelled state of him. "*And* you're still wearing last night's clothes!"

"Thank you." Archie bowed low. "You look haggard like a

she-tramp. Now we've exchanged pleasantries do you want to go home?" He lit a cigarette and hunted for an ashtray under a pile of Winchester Cathedral newsletters.

"Sorry. But, listen to this, I found out lots about Cora Montgomery. Lots and lots. I printed it out to show you but do you have internet access? I could show you now. This hasn't printed very well."

Archie groaned. "As much as I really want to find Canute's head and keep my job, couldn't you show me in a couple of hours' time? Or tomorrow maybe. I have to go and see my duvet."

Kate clapped her hands together making Archie leap. "Oh come on, wake up! Listen to this – Cora Montgomery lives in London, has a studio in Kings Cross, and I found her home address!"

"You're kidding?" Archie stopped hunting for the ashtray and looked up.

"Nope! Now get your laptop out because I need to show you this."

"Fine, fine," he muttered, "seeing as I'm not allowed to go to bed." He walked over to the bookcase and yanked a laptop down from the very top. The bookcase wobbled ominously, threatening to fall and scatter shelves of cloth-bound books on religion and trashy paperback thrillers.

"Are you supposed to read things like that as a man of the Church?"

"Like what?" Archie was engrossed with the laptop, inserting cables.

"*Red Hot Babes* magazine?"

Like a shot he was over the other side of the room and

tore the magazine from her grasp. "That's none of your business."

She laughed. "Beats those waffling newsletters you put out though, doesn't it?"

"Shut up, Kate."

"You should put her on the front of the cathedral newsletter. That would increase the circulation. Or maybe you could have a 'Readers Wives' section!" she snorted.

"Yeah that's funny. Just show me that website."

"Sure." Kate came over, still grinning. She clicked through web pages so rapidly that Archie had to look away, the blur of images was making him nauseous. "Here," she said finally, "Cora Montgomery, 32 Battlebridge Crescent, Kings Cross N1, and her phone number is here and – *get this.*" She clicked on an icon and a map popped up. "Ta da! Directions to our head thief!"

They sat back on the sofa and looked at each other. "You've found her."

Kate nodded, full to the brim with pride. "See? I am a good journalist!"

"So what should we do now? Go to the police?"

Kate considered it for a moment, "I think we should... *not* tell the police."

Archie gave her a doubtful look.

"Really," she emphasised. "I think we should do a bit of investigation ourselves. I mean, if the police become involved then they'll just take over—"

"As they legally should do."

"Yes, I know, but don't you want to do a bit of delving yourself? Find out who got you into all this trouble with the

Bishop of Wessex?"

Archie looked at her, exasperated. "Will you *please* tell me how you know about the Bishop getting involved in all this? Or is it just an educated guess?"

"I'm omnipresent," she quipped. "Like God. Only younger and not three people. And female of—"

"Seriously Kate. How do you know about the Bishop of Wessex?"

"One of your cleaners is my aunt."

"Fine. So long as you're not lurking round the cathedral and spying on me."

"As if..." Kate affected a haughty expression. "Anyway, going back to our head thief, in my opinion, there would be nothing to gain by going to the police at this point."

"How do you work that one out?" Archie said.

"Well you wouldn't get the credit for actually, physically finding Canute would you? They would. And I wouldn't be able to ensure exclusivity on the story. I'd only be briefed alongside all the other journos. Where's my exclusivity? Where's my selling point?"

"I'm still not convinced," Archie said. The prospect of doing the wrong thing, yet again, loomed large. There would be another afternoon spent with MacNeath and his fellow angry bishops in the kitchen, going through the newspaper cuttings about Archie withholding evidence from the police.

"Hmm." Kate considered her proposal. "We could always plead ignorance. If the police started to ask questions about why we didn't involve them earlier, we could say we weren't sure and were just following hunches and only realised right at the last minute that we were on the right track."

"Yeah. Maybe." Archie was coming round. "And me being a man of the cloth they're more likely to believe me."

"Of course. Your dog collar is our get-out-of-jail-free card. I'll just pootle in the background at that point. Nobody trusts a journalist."

"Can I meet you later today?" Archie said. "As much as I want to crack on with this, I really do need to go to bed. And then have a shower."

"Fine." She stood up. "This evening then?" Mike would be out and she hated being in the house on her own.

"But no alcohol," Archie said.

"None?"

"None."

"A small *some*?" She headed towards the door, opening the latch. "*Hair of the dog* and all that?"

"A very small *some* maybe." He was smiling.

He was still smiling when he'd closed the door and headed to the shower. It was her energy and drive that he noticed most, he reflected. And her fine figure, of course, particularly when it was pressed up against him in the back of a dark-lit winebar.

Thirty

"You can talk now you know. No, I'm waiting for the beeps Brenda. *The beeps were ages ago. Graham you really ought to get your ears checked out again.* Goddamn it, I hate these phones Edgar! Eddie it's your father here. Your mother and I are at the hotel and we're heading in to Central London in about half an hour to see you. We'll be at the Museum at around three. Meet us in reception will you? Call me back on this number. *So excited darling! Can't wait to—"*

Thirty-One

"Rickshaw?"

"No thanks," Edgar pushed through the masses outside Covent Garden tube station. Already there were groups of tourists congregating; shiny excited young Europeans out for a night in the capital. A bar further down James Street had customers spilling out onto the cobbled pavements, and the performance artists were calling and whooping to the crowds. Men juggled fire, escape artists broke out of chains and statues came to life petrifying toddlers and making their parents laugh.

"You want a rickshaw?"

"No. Thanks."

Edgar yawned: he was past tired. Tiredness was something he had flirted with earlier that week. Now he was entertaining full-on exhaustion. This feeling of exhaustion was, he considered as he crossed the cobblestones, rather like being drunk: you're aware you're upright and walking, but you can't quite feel your legs. Unlike being drunk though, it wasn't something he could simply sleep off. Since visiting the dig site his nights had been filled with the nightmares of trenches teeming with corpses; eye sockets with soil crumbling out of them and bony fingers scratching at him. The enormity of his job was weighing heavy, more so after he'd spent the last hour in Waterstones flicking through books on Boudica. Boudica and the Romans, Boudica and the Iceni tribe, Boudica's world, Boudica's culture, Boudica's Britain...everyone wanted a piece of Boudica. Each new article on the warrior queen brought home the fact that the Museum had uncovered *the* British warrior of all time. That his problem was a very big one. Lying just a couple of miles north west of him was the woman who *burned Roman London to the ground*. Not a few streets, not an area, not a district. The whole of London. All of it.

Edgar recalled a memory from his distant childhood; his father looming darkly on the edge of his bed, holding the empty glass from which he'd drunk the last sleepy mouthfuls of milk. Half-lit by the landing light his father was talking softly, spinning him fabulous stories, which featured archaeology in a starring role, and would often break off from marvellous tales and plunge into mind-boggling fact and statistic. But they had been wonderful tales; tales of ancient ships buried with their treasure under windswept grassy hills, coin hoards from the warrior Vikings, magnificent temples that still lay hidden under London pavements and, of course, the story of Boudica. That whenever anyone dug deep down into the soil in London, really deep down, where the original Roman London had been, there you would see a layer of blackened soil. And that layer of blackened soil was all that remained of the devastation Boudica had wreaked on the Roman people *two thousand* years ago; that black layer under your feet was all the burnt Roman buildings and all the burnt Roman belongings and all the burnt Roman people...

And at that point Edgar's mother had to come in to calm

him down while his father was bundled out of the room muttering *well the boy can't be shielded from it all his life.*

And now there she was, exposed, bang up against the ticket machines at Kings Cross Station with her war horses beside her and thousands of her people thrown into pits nearby. And he, Edgar, was going to play a role in breaking the story of her discovery to the world.

"Rickshaw?"

"No! Just stop it with the Goddamn rickshaws!"

His heart was pounding now. It was such an enormous responsibility for him; so much rested on his inexperienced shoulders and was he really up to it? OK, so he'd used a bit of cunning and good fortune to get in to see the dig and find out what was happening but so what? Blagging only went so far. And now he had to actually do a good job and take responsibility and all these important people from the government and the museum would be expecting the earth.

And then there was the threat of his father, an unseen and menacing shadowy figure pursuing him, taunting him with his incompetent phone messages. He was now in London, hunting him down and wanting to know the truth. Because his father was not stupid. His channels were open and receiving signals from all directions that something was definitely 'up' with the Kings Cross Dig, and Edgar knew it would be impossible to lie to his father once he started asking questions.

Would his father check out the Bloomsbury flat? He would do if he had brought the spare set of keys with him. If that was the case then Edgar would most definitely not be safe. At least his mother was coming too – hopefully to provide some tempering influence to counteract his father's predictable anger.

Edgar drew to a halt.

Without knowing how he'd done it, he had arrived.

The Royal Gardens Hotel was before him; polished brass and potted geraniums, a stripy awning hung with strings of tiny white lights. A doorman appeared and opened the door.

"Good evening sir and welcome to the Royal Gardens Hotel."

Edgar entered, trembling.

Thirty-Two

"Evening…sir." Sam eyed Archie suspiciously as he walked up to the bar. The last time Archie had visited the King's Head he'd downed seven double G&Ts and needed to be carried back to the Deanery. Sam had then got one of the local boys to fetch the Archdeacon to let him in. *How was tonight going to shape up* he wondered.

Archie perched on a bar stool and unwrapped the long scarf from around his neck. "Cold out, isn't it Sam? Two G&Ts if you please. Doubles."

That was how his evening was going to shape up. Reluctantly the barman reached for the glasses. "Bishop been round again has he, sir?" The prospect of having to cart the Dean home at closing time weighed heavy but he didn't want to say anything to a man of Archie's standing.

Archie frowned at Sam and was about to say something when Kate walked in, perching on the bar stool beside him, distracting in skinny jeans and funky boots. Archie gave her a very visible once-over and grinned. She was *glowing*.

"I got you a G&T hope that's OK." Archie pushed the drink to her. "You look nice. I like your hair."

"Oh." Kate patted her bobbed hair. "Thanks. So do you." He had *vastly* improved since that morning: clean shaven, bright-eyed and smartly turned out in a grey wool jumper and the right sort of jeans. "Let's take that table in the corner. We don't want to be overheard."

"So…" Archie rallied after a swig of his drink and settled in snugly next to Kate. "We should discuss what we're going to do about *you know who*. I think we should call this Cora Montgomery."

Kate looked up from her arranging of pens and notepad on the table. "I *don't* think we should call her."

"Why not?"

"Because you're not one hundred per cent sure it's her are you?" she said slowly.

Archie contemplated her for a moment. Was he really so readable? It had only been a small niggling doubt in the back of his mind that, perhaps, Cora Montgomery was not the person who had thrown him down in the cathedral that night. Had it been so obvious to Kate that he was having second thoughts on the head thief?

"No," he sighed. "No I'm not."

"But you were so sure when we left Bob Gilroy's house…" Kate said. "What's changed your mind?"

"I don't know." He prodded the lime in his drink. "I was carried away with the idea that it *was* her. And it probably is…she's petite, and she has those big eyes and a cute little mouth. And she's got a professional interest in the heads of dead people…"

"So now you're talking yourself into being one hundred per cent sure?"

"No I am not one hundred per cent sure. But if you can put aside being a statistician for a second then I can say that deep down I *do* think that she's our woman. Deep down."

"I still don't think we should call her, Archie."

"Why?"

"Well firstly," Kate began, "what would we say? *Hello is that Cora Montgomery and did you steal Canute's head from Winchester Cathedral?*"

"Yes...you might have a point."

"And secondly, if we called her we might scare her into doing something with Canute's skull that might be...well... detrimental."

"OK then. So what do you propose?"

Kate shrugged. "I think we should go to London and see if we can catch her in action. Peek inside her house; see if there's any evidence of her having stolen skulls. We could even trail her. Personally, the more of the situation I can uncover for myself before we involve the police, the better my scoop will be. And you want maximum glory for recovering the skull, so this way we could achieve both aims."

"And you think we're more likely to get Canute's head back if we go down there and snoop around first?"

"Lordy, Archie, I don't have all the answers. I'm just giving you my best guess. I think phoning her would be difficult and could put us at a disadvantage. We should go up to London to get a better idea of what she does. And take it from there."

"OK then." He put down his drink and contemplated her soberly. "On one condition."

"That you drive?"

"That's remarkable Kate, how did you guess?"

"A woman's intuition. Now buy me another drink."

For a man so obsessed with image and style it amused

Kate to see there was a very charming bounce in his step as he headed back to the bar to buy her a drink.

Thirty-Three

Edgar wasn't quite sure how he'd ended up in Bar Italia in Wardour Street.

The place was a bright-lit Formica-countered island filled with the layers of many Italian conversations and the chink of espresso cups. It was an island of safety in the nefarious seas of Soho. Never mind that he'd upset the owner by trying to order a grande skinny caramel macchiato; he'd barely registered the look of horror on the old man's face and had not even batted an eyelid when the thickset son had needed to come and take over the transaction, dealing with him in a far from civil manner and eventually presenting him with a black coffee.

For now Edgar was content to be sitting on a bar stool staring out of the window ostensibly watching the strange and wonderful late night Soho, but actually not seeing any of it. The pack of shiny-shirted lads stumbling towards Tottenham Court Road and the man with the red roller boots in a purple lycra one-piece bopping and weaving his way down the street were invisible to him, as were the hen weekenders dressed in bikinis tottering by unnoticed.

He did a double take.

They really *were* only wearing bikinis.

My God they looked good.

Edgar forgot his heavy thoughts for a moment and

focused on watching the six girls as they tottered past the window, each one a vision of loveliness, albeit tinged with a November frost.

"Ed-gar!"

"Erika!" He stood up and nearly toppled over the barstool. Erika, dressed in a green bikini and silver high heels teetered in to Bar Italia. Even the espresso machine fell silent.

"Ed-gar but what are you doing here? On your own on a Friday night? Are you meeting someone? A girl I know it!" She clapped her hands and her breasts wobbled.

He blushed and tried very hard to keep looking at her face. Recovering the power of speech he said, "No. I... there was a meeting. With work."

"Oh this Project Rebel..." Erika laid a hand on his shoulder.

"*Shhh!*" Before he could think Edgar put a finger to her lips. "People aren't supposed to know!"

Erika was taken aback for a moment. "But you told me about a Project Rebel this week. And told me to tell the Head of Marcoms you wanted a meeting with him to discuss it. And Henri from reception knows all about it. He told me they've found a very important person under the station and Project Rebel is all about keeping it secret. Is that so?"

Edgar looked round at all the customers staring in their direction and winced.

"Erika." A white-blonde bikini girl walked in. "Skynda på! Det är kallt!"

"Vänta!" she shouted, and turning to Edgar said, "So, should Henri really not be telling people any of these things?"

Edgar gaped, horrified. "No! Not at all!"

She leant in towards him. All of the male customers in Bar Italia wished they were in Edgar's shoes at that moment.

"So this Project Rebel down at Kings Cross," she whispered, her face next to his, "would it be serious if a lot of people knew?"

"Erika!"

"No, no," she whispered, "not me! I just heard from Henri what I just told you; but you know what he is like. No, I just wondered because he has a housemate who I met at a party once. Well, I dated him, he was a pig but there you go. Anyway, he works for a big newspaper, I think it is the *Daily Mail* and I bet Henri would tell him somethings. You know?"

Edgar bit his lip. Caught in a no man's land between the dread of potentially calling the Head of Marketing and Communications to discuss the possibility of his gay lover's indiscretions, and the sheer joy of being so close to the soft plump curves of Erika's body, he didn't quite know what to feel.

With an eye to her freezing friends at the window she said, "I must go now Ed-gar." She stood back but not before she had planted a lip-gloss kiss on his forehead. "So! We will be at Bar Salsa if you feel like joining us. It is just round the corner there. Here, let me give you my mobile number." She jotted it down on a corner of the receipt for his coffee and passed it to him. "Not that I will hear it! But I can check if you leave me a message you know…"

Edgar hastily shrugged off his jacket. "Take this, you

must be freezing."

Erika laughed at his worried expression and held it out for him to put on again. "No, I will be fine Ed-gar. But thank you. I come from Sandviken; it gets pretty cold up there." And she tripped out of the café in her glittery heels.

Edgar watched her go in a haze, mechanically folding up the receipt with her mobile number on and putting it in his wallet. Well, at least he could rest at ease knowing that she would not have gone out with him to the cinema this evening. She definitely had other plans. He was an idiot to think she would have preferred sitting with him in a shabby old cinema rather than be out on the town with her friends.

He sighed and stirred his coffee with the tiny silver spoon. He'd been invited to go to Bar Salsa, but he knew that he wouldn't go. Why wasn't he the type of man who would go out and pursue that beautiful, sociable woman? Why, he wondered, why wasn't he confident enough to think that he might be in with a chance with her, to know the moves if he was in with a chance with her. What kind of a man would he be then?

He would be the kind of man, Edgar realised, like the men who were leaving the café, walking en masse in the direction of Bar Salsa in search of bikinis and glittery high heels.

The owner of Bar Italia stood in the centre of his now-empty cafe with his head in his hands. Through the gaps between his fingers he stared over at Edgar with a look of a man who had just been shot.

Edgar watched the last of them file out of the door,

smoothing down their hair: preening.

No.

He stood up and grabbed his copy of the Site Report. Erika had kissed him, the smear of her lip balm was on his skin still. Surely that meant something. Surely, having invited him to the club, having given him her phone number, then she wanted him to be there.

Still standing on the threshold, the last man left in Bar Italia, he looked down at the report in his hands. And he knew he would not go. If Henri was about to – or *had* – spilt the beans, then something ought to be done. And the responsibility lay with him.

He sat back down and put the pack on the table.

Of course, he realised, Henri would know all about Project Rebel. During the illicit meetings between Henri and the Head of Marcoms there must have been a pause for breath, surely, during which time the Head of Marcoms would have had the opportunity to boast that he was responsible for the most exciting event the museum had encountered over the past decade. Henri must know *everything* there was to know about the project. And now Henri was telling Erika all about it, and, quite possibly, his journalist housemate.

So Edgar knew he had a choice to make: either he could keep quiet and assume that Henri, who had already blabbed to Erika, would for some reason hold back relating this monumental piece of information to his housemate, or else he had to tell the Head of Marcoms that his boyfriend was blabbing, in which case the museum would have to put in hand the emergency procedures to cope with an early break in the story before the official launch.

Crap.

Deep in thought he stirred his coffee, tinkling the spoon in the cup round and round and round.

He needed some proper help now. What would Richard do? Should he go to the hospital again and do the uncle/nephew thing once more? Could he buy grapes in time? What time was it? He checked his watch. Quarter past midnight. So that was out. Hospital security was super-tight at the moment after the fake clown/assassin debacle that had been in the news, so he would never get away with sneaking in and waking his boss.

There was the possibility of another solution. He stirred slowly. Could he tackle Henri? Could he, in fact, have a word with Henri to tell him to keep a lid on it?

No.

It wasn't his place to be doing that, and besides the Head of Marcoms would no doubt have pressed upon Henri, amongst other things, the need to be discreet about the Project Rebel dig. And if Henri hadn't paid attention to his senior management lover then he probably wouldn't pay attention to a jumped-up press officer who'd only been in the job a fortnight.

He stirred quicker.

The Project Rebel meeting earlier that evening had been fascinating, exciting, terrifying. At first he'd walked in to the plush ballroom and all those important looking men and women had turned to him with expressions that clearly said *Is he here to take my food order*? But the Head of Marcoms had put an arm round him and had propelled him around the room, introducing him to everyone. *Here is our new hotshot from the Press Office, very resourceful is Edgar, thinks on his feet* [nudge, nudge] *eh?*

Edgar paused in the so-far ceaseless stirring. The café was plunged into silence.

"Mia Dio!" came a strained voice from behind the bar.

Edgar turned to look at the barman holding his head in his hands at the counter. He must have worked a long day – he looked tired and wild-eyed. Edgar smiled but the barman narrowed his eyes and muttered something else in Italian and stamped away towards the back of the empty café.

Edgar turned back to the window and continued to absent-mindedly stir his coffee again.

At the meeting earlier that evening the Head of Marcoms had distributed updated copies of the Project Rebel Site Report for which they'd had to sign. His copy was the last one, number twenty-four. The document started with a page dedicated to threatening the recipient of the report against disclosure. Edgar scanned it: written in the sternest and obscurest legal jargon it promised everything bar a plague of locusts would befall the person who leaked any details of Project Rebel *or, in full knowledge, allowed details to be leaked.* Edgar understood quite clearly what that meant. He quickly skimmed through the rest of the report. There followed a summary of progress up to Friday night, a timetable of activity, disaster-recovery plan and a page of contacts including, he was rather pleased to see, his own name: Edgar Thompson, Senior Press Officer. *Wouldn't do to have your actual job title in there,* the Head of Marcoms had whispered as he was handing out the reports, *but play your cards right on Project Rebel...*

Putting the spoon down Edgar drank the cold remains of his thoroughly stirred coffee and flicked through the report. Emergency Procedure stated that in the event of early disclosure to the media *or threat of early disclosure to the media* immediate action must be taken, starting with notifying the Project Manager – i.e. the Head of Marketing and Communications. A press conference must be convened, the site secured, viewing facilities set up and a media event managed within twenty-four hours of the actual or suspected leak, to ensure the preferred and contained story made it into the papers, and not an unofficial uncontrolled story: thus enabling maximum control of the message, accuracy of information and also maintaining valuable media relationships.

He checked his watch again.

He looked back down at the Emergency Procedure page of his report and then flicked through the pages to the very back page, drawing out his mobile and running a finger down the list of contacts until he reached the Head of Marketing and Communications.

He really did not want to be making this call. One street away Erika was dancing in a bikini with a café full of young Italian men keeping her company.

Life was so unfair.

"Come in, come in, dear boy." The Head of Marketing and Communications, dressed in a plush velvet dressing gown, which could have been a smoking jacket, stood aside and Edgar walked in.

The house was a magnificent Victorian villa in St John's Wood, all stained glass windows, mosaic-tiled floors and large brass lantern lights.

"Like I said, I'm sorry sir to have—"

"Aubrey, please. No standing on ceremony at..." He peered at the grandfather clock in the corner of the hallway "...five to one in the morning! Now, come on through to the kitchen and I'll endeavour to make us a pot of tea." He closed the front door and ushered Edgar down the long wide hallway and on into an enormous chandelier-lit kitchen. Edgar felt like he'd walked onto a film set for a Victorian period drama. "Now then, Darjeeling, Earl Grey, *Lady* Grey, Green Tea, Lapsang Souchong, we've got it all. Organic, Fair Trade, caffeine-free my Lord we've probably even got tea-free... My wife Constance is a bit of a tea buff so we have just about every tea stocked by Waitrose on the Finchley Road. Now let me see." He looked Edgar up and down and Edgar smiled nervously. "You look like a Lady Grey sort of a chap. Am I right or am I right?"

Edgar laughed nervously. "Er...just anything really. Just tea like builders drink. Nothing fancy."

"Nothing fancy eh? A sort of proletariat tea-drinker are you? Builder's tea – I like it!" He winked and closed the cupboard, crossing the enormous kitchen and heading to a pantry, emerging a minute later with a box of Tetley Tea. "It's her guilty pleasure," he said, fishing a couple of bags out. "Not one she serves up for the fair ladies of St John's Wood I can assure you. So, Edgar, what's on your mind? You sounded pretty fretful on the phone."

He gestured for Edgar to take a seat at the breakfast bar.

The chairs were high and wobbly, seemingly made from a single piece of silver metal scooped and curved with a tiny red leather seat at the top. Edgar clambered up and held on to the seat with both hands.

"Well, sir...Aubrey...ahh...it's about Project Rebel."

"As you mentioned." Aubrey put the oversized cup of tea before him and pulled up another stool, expertly manoeuvring his bulky body onto the seat without wobbling or looking uncomfortable in any way. "So what about Project Rebel then, Edgar? Out with it."

"Well...I think there may be a *leak*."

Aubrey sipped his tea and raised his eyes to Edgar.

"I was with a friend this evening who knows about Project Rebel." Edgar fiddled with the handle of his mug. "And she shouldn't know."

Aubrey put his mug down and looked straight at Edgar. "Who is the person, may I ask, who threatens my well-planned project?" There was anger behind the softly spoken words.

The clock in the hallway chimed. Edgar took a deep breath.

"Erika Jonsson, she's a PA in the press office with me."

"And she found out from..."

The Head of Marcoms was leaning forward on the counter now, looking Edgar straight in the eye, waiting to hear the name.

Edgar stared at the counter. "She said that she found out from the receptionist..."

"From Henri?"

Edgar nodded.

The two men looked at each other across the breakfast bar.

"I see." Aubrey was now the one to look uncomfortable. "Thank you for your discretion, my boy. I can see we understand each other perfectly on the situation. Now... Well... We need to take action... I see you still have your copy of the Project Rebel documents with you."

"Yes, here." Edgar, relieved at having now got through the worst, pushed his copy between them on the counter. Aubrey flicked through it and, tearing out a sheet from a nearby shopping pad, he began to write.

"OK, so I'll speak to Henri immediately – no need for you to follow up anything there. And—" he looked up at Edgar while he spoke "—I'd appreciate it if this delicate state of affairs was kept between ourselves, and that you didn't speak to Henri on the matter."

"Of course." Edgar looked away and focused on the silver bin in the corner of the kitchen.

"Good. This project is my baby and I will be the one to resolve this problem with it; the blame lies at my door. But we must follow procedure and bring the press event day forward now. It's no good waiting to see if Henri has spilt the beans or not – we need to ensure we're in control of every aspect of the project and the media need to be fully managed. I want them eating out of my hands, I want them listening to me and my team for information and not relying on leaks from ill-informed gossipers to tell half-stories and not promote the sheer brilliance of our work at the Museum."

Edgar was nodding, still biting his lip.

"I retire in eighteen months, young Edgar," he was saying, "and I'll do it on a high note. We bring the launch forward and we keep control."

In the vast kitchen in the early hours of the morning the two men bent over the report and re-read the emergency plan, making notes and discussing it in hushed voices. From down the hallway Edgar could hear the deep *tock tock* of the grandfather clock which, during the course of their planning, had struck half past one, quarter to two and two o'clock. He yawned.

"Well then, Edgar. I think we've just about cracked it." Aubrey rubbed his eyes and closed the report, pushing it back to its owner.

Edgar took the copy and put it in his satchel. "I'll go into work first thing tomorrow morning – later this morning – and type this up. Shall I email a copy to you so we're both clear what the next steps will be?"

"Absolutely. But password protect it please: 'Project Rebel'. I'll be in the office around seven all being well. And we'll take it from there. I'll call Larry in the next ten minutes or so and set the ball rolling on the ring-around. In two hours I should think everyone involved in Project Rebel will have been made aware of the need for the emergency timetable. So you won't need to call anyone and tell them. I'll try to organise it so that we're all about for a meeting at half eight in the Museum boardroom. Sound good?"

Edgar nodded and stood up shakily, frightened of sending what must have been almost a thousand pounds' worth of bar stool crashing onto the slate floor.

"Taxi!"

The black cab shot past.

Damn. Edgar stepped back onto the pavement and trudged onwards towards the Marylebone Road. It was eerily silent so close to the centre of town: there wasn't much traffic along the seemingly endless tree-lined streets of St John's Wood at three in the morning. He wondered what Erika was up to now. Still at Bar Salsa in her bikini? Chatting to someone, laughing, putting a soft hand on *their* shoulder, a lip gloss kiss on *their* cheek? He tried to blank it from his mind and to focus on the pressing need to be getting back to his flat.

There was another taxi, hurtling down towards him, light on.

"Taxi!"

It sped by.

Why? Why would an on-hire taxi go past without picking him up? His familiar self-doubt loomed large. Was it *him*? Were the taxi drivers avoiding him personally? Did they sense his spinelessness and ignore him? Would they have stopped for a man like his father?

He turned. There was the sound of another car coming down the road. A taxi! It's yellow light a beacon of hope speeding right towards him.

"TAXI!"

It hurtled past.

"YOU FUCKING BASTARD!"

He stood in the gutter, furious, shaking his fist at the disappearing taxi. He climbed back onto the pavement and looked around, feeling ashamed at bringing down the tone of NW2. No-one shouted *you fucking bastard* on roads as nice as this.

He should, he knew, have ordered a private taxi when he was at the Head of Marcoms' house. But that 'Would you like a sherry before you leave, my boy?' comment at the end of the night had really thrown him. The closeness of the Head of Marcoms to him in the hallway. The gradual loosening of the velvet smoking jacket. *What was underneath? And, more alarmingly, why was he even thinking about what was underneath?*

No, as sensible as it would have been, ordering a taxi at that point would have meant waiting. And waiting would have meant sherry. And sherry would have meant...

Well, probably nothing. In all likelihood the Head of Marcoms was simply being friendly and it was just that familiar paranoia creeping up on him again. Smothered as a child, indulged as a young adult and now so recently abandoned for the plains of Italy, Edgar was still reeling from the fact that he had to find his own way in the world. Suddenly there were no parents to slip him a couple of hundred quid, loan him a car, host him for a weekend and send him back with a week's worth of prepared meals, washed clothes and money.

He was frightened by it: terrified.

But now, oddly enough, at half past three on a Sunday morning, walking through deserted St John's Wood, he wondered if his current predicament wasn't *so* bad after all? Because when he was with his parents he was a son, a boy, a person who was told what to do and how to do it. But now he was making his own decisions; good (no sherry) and bad (no Bar Salsa). But at least they had been his decisions, and it was all working out.

So far.

The prospect of being responsible for the press packs for the Boudica dig terrified him so much he felt sick to the bottom of his stomach. But, he knew, it would pass. All he could do was his best, and that was exactly what he *was* doing. And, with a bit of luck, it would all come together in the end.

He was at the Marylebone Road. The roads here were busier, even so early on a Sunday morning, and he could see at least two taxis with their lights on. But it was too late for that. For now he was content to walk, with a bounce in his step. At this rate he'd be at his flat in Bloomsbury in twenty minutes. He could have a shower, grab some toast and head in to work a new man.

Squinting in the gloom of the early morning Edgar jammed his key into the lock of 15 Kedleston Square and, grasping the old brass door knob, pulled and pushed the heavy green front door, willing it to open.

15 Kedleston Square really let the side down. A tall brownstone Georgian house in a plot of tall brownstone Georgian houses: it wasn't architecturally deficient, it was its state of repair and general *wantonness* that made it stand out from its superior, polished neighbours. The front door was shabby. The windows were Victorian, mostly painted shut, the panes of glass wobbly and distorted and not the sympathetically-styled, double-glazed, self-cleaning, solar

reflecting windows sported by the other properties on the square. And there was no high-tech security entrance system to 15 Kedleston Square, just a series of bells attached near the front door, some of which worked and some of which didn't. Edgar's, currently, didn't.

15 Kedleston Square was Bloomsbury thirty years ago. A lone survivor among the million-pound executive-rented apartment neighbours that faced onto the shared communal gardens. It was the penniless scholarship kid in the exclusive public school.

Edgar's father had bought the flat in 1960s. Back then Bloomsbury had not been fashionable and the top floor studio flat had been unremarkable and cheap. He'd lived in it for five years and then rented it out to a series of tenants that had escalated from students, progressing to post graduates, then academics, high-paying professionals and finally to a businessman from Paris who stayed for six years until he was jailed for fraud and sent back to France leaving most of his antique furniture behind.

There was a click and the front door finally opened. Edgar pushed open the door and punched the timer switch, dashing up the stairs before the light went out and plunged him into total staircase-tumbling darkness.

The flat itself was tiny, perched right at the very top of the house and converted from what had once been the servants' quarters. It consisted of a single-bed-shaped partition off a tiny living room, a small shower room, and galley kitchen. But Edgar had come to love it. And he loved it because it had one secret feature that would never make it on to any estate agent particulars as it was highly dangerous and against every health and safety ruling known to man. If he hoisted himself up onto the worktop in the kitchen, shuffled across the kitchen drainer (supporting his weight on the edges of the worktop) and opened the stiff old sash window, he could clamber out onto the roof of the five storey building where a wide strip of boarding was nailed in place. And there he would be in a bricks and mortar tree-house: his *Mary Poppins*-style bolt-hole. From there he could see the rooftops of the whole of London; or so it seemed. He could see the Barbican and Swiss Re towers of the City, the London Eye and even the very tips of Tower Bridge down near the river. It was to the makeshift roof terrace that he planned to retreat now, to huddle up against the tall chimney with a cup of tea and a stack of toast; to watch over his city in the peace of a cold, clear dawn.

Edgar reached the front door of his flat and inserted the key, hitting a second timer switch in the shared hallway again to buy himself more time to get into his flat.

He opened the door and stepped into the sitting room, putting a hand out to the light switch. But stopped. Something was wrong.

In the dim light from the hallway he could make out a large travel bag by his feet. And another leaning against the wall in front of him.

And his father was sprawled across the sofa.

With a click the hall light turned off. Edgar was left in the dark, hardly able to breathe. His father was fast asleep and presumably his mother was on the single bed behind the partition wall. Or was she still in the hotel? Step by small step he backed out of the flat, letting the door close behind him with a terrible, resonating click. He stood for a moment in the black hallway, both hands resting against his apartment door, listening for sounds from the other side that would indicate his father had woken up. Nothing. Groping around, he found the timer switch and pressed it on, the lights flickering into action. He turned and fled down the stairs, holding on to the shaky metal banister and throwing himself down two, three, four stairs at a time. Outside on the street he raced in the direction of Tottenham Court Road, his mobile in his hands. He turned it on and sure enough there were three missed calls and one text message waiting for him.

Hotel a disgrace. Will camp down at yours for night if OK. See you 9ish.

He flew through the darkened streets and emerged, panting, on to the strip lit Tottenham Court Road with its stream of night buses and reeling party goers.

"TAXI!"

Within two minutes he was on his way in a cab to the City.

Thirty-Four

It was half past ten in the morning and Archie was enjoying his third breakfast.

The first breakfast of the day – cereal – had been at home while he leafed through a copy of *York Minster News* and made facetious notes in the margins.

<u>What a carillon! The addition of 24 new bells to the Nelson Chime – York Minster has become the first cathedral in England to possess a full carillon of bells.</u>

Ding
Fucking
Dong

The second breakfast – toast – was taken at Kate's house as he waited for her to get ready for their trip to London. He stood in the kitchen with Mike, who seemed surprisingly uninterested in just where Archie was taking his girlfriend for the day. *I used to go to church* was his only concession to conversation, *bloody hated it.*

Speeding along the M3 Archie was tucking in to a bacon and egg baguette as Kate sat silent beside him, absorbed in paperwork.

"What are you doing?" he asked with a mouthful of service-station breakfast.

"Checking our itinerary."

"Very sensible. So what are we doing now? Are we on time?"

Kate ignored the sarcasm. "I have *depart Winchester ten a.m.* so we're on time."

"And once we get to her house what do you have timetabled in for us then?"

"Well," Kate sighed, "I did have trouble there. I don't know what's going to happen so I've just got alternative things for us to do. Maps and directions to North East London University where she works, and to Madame Tussauds, which might be useful for background research? Also the nearest police station if we need it. Phone number, address, map…"

"Impressive."

"You really can stop with the sarcasm." Kate had hoped he would have been impressed at her methodical approach, and his attitude upset her.

"No. I'm impressed." Archie caught her expression. "Honestly. I wish I could have some of your attention to detail and the like. I'd get a lot more done. Deans should be good at planning."

Kate stared ahead at the ribbon of everlasting motorway. For a while they were silent.

"Can I ask," she said eventually, "what prompted you to become a Dean?"

Archie briefly looked at her. "You have no idea how many times journalists have asked me that question."

"Well I'm sorry to play the unimaginative hack," Kate said, "but I want to know."

"I tell the *hacks* that I had a calling. That usually worries them enough to move on to another subject – they're not comfortable with vague things like divine callings: it's not their world."

"And did you have a divine calling?"

Archie laughed. "No. If you must know I started out on this path because as a young boy I was very, very bored."

She waited for him to elaborate but he was caught up in negotiating the traffic at high speed. "Do your superiors know that little nugget of information?" she prompted, not wanting to let it go.

"Surprisingly not." He quickly glanced in her direction, suddenly frowning. "Kate I hope you're not on duty. Am I having this conversation with Kate Grey the journalist, or am I having it with Kate Grey fellow head-hunter?"

She held her hands up. "Absolutely not on duty. Anyway you're yesterday's news now that Cora Montgomery has turned up."

"Fair enough." He settled back in his seat.

"Go on then...you were saying that you were very, very bored," she prompted.

"You really aren't going to let this go are you? Well, I was left to my own devices a lot as a child, and one day I picked up an enormous copy of the Bible. It was one of those family heirloom ones, you know the sort? Well it was so different from anything else in the house – I can still remember the dark embossed binding, and the feel of the stiff metal clasps. And I remember thinking *this is cool* and looking through it."

"For the rude bits?"

"You seem to have the measure of me."

"And you found them?"

"A-plenty."

"Go on then." She sat back and folded her arms. "What rude bits did you find between the brass clasps?"

Archie thought for a moment. "Leviticus was a good one. 15:18: 'When a man has an emission of semen he must bathe his whole body with water, and he will be unclean till evening.'"

"That's really in the Bible?" Kate was incredulous.

He nodded, engrossed in the business of cutting up a BMW.

"I don't remember them teaching *that* at school. Mrs James never read out anything about semen in assembly. And we only ever did collages of Jesus on the cross or walking on water."

"Well there you go. You didn't get the full glory of the Bible did you? But then," he considered, "it would be very difficult to do a paper collage of a man ejaculating wouldn't it? You'd need to get the expression just right and how do you do that with bits of scrumpled-up coloured tissue paper and flour and water glue?"

Kate snorted. "I would so have loved to see my mother's face if I'd brought home a collage of a man having an emission of semen. It would have been priceless!"

"Well maybe one day schools will build in the Old Testament stuff. What about this then, from Song of Songs: If only you were to me like a brother, who was nursed at my mother's breasts! Then, if I found you outside, I would kiss you, and no-one would despise me."

"Yes, but that's just taken out of context. He doesn't mean *kissing* as a sexual thing, surely. Just like as a friend. A peck on the cheek. A manly peck on the cheek."

"But it goes on to say, 'I would give you spiced wine to drink, the nectar of my pomegranates—'"

"*The nectar of my pomegranates!*" Kate snorted, and then immediately tried to compose herself again. Snorting was not something sophisticated journalists did.

"'...his left arm is under my head and his right arm embraces me...do not arouse or awaken love until it so desires.' Heady stuff for a nine year old."

"Well it's no *Hot Babes*, but it is racy. So you really were on a mission looking for smut?"

"Yes, Kate, I really was that shallow a nine year old. But somewhere along the line I got to reading the stories, the instructions, the bits in between the smut, and then one day it all came together. You could say I got into it by accident. It helped that at the time the national news was obsessed with the finding of the Dead Sea Scrolls, so it seemed like a very exciting subject to a young boy. I never had a passion to be an astronaut or a fireman, so this was the only true calling I ever had. Dad was happy that I wasn't going into welding like him, and Mum was just grateful I wasn't buying drugs or getting women pregnant."

"At *nine*?"

"No – I think she had in mind when I was older."

"So you were a very good little boy?" Kate smiled.

"Very."

"Quiet?"

"And reserved."

"So what happened?"

Archie laughed. "Five years in a squat in South London with a woman called Tallulah."

"Oh." Kate looked out of the window, feeling very Middle England.

"It wasn't all her doing." Archie interrupted her thoughts. "It was getting to the capital and realising the enormous potential of it all. The limitless horizons to be found in grubby streets. Bars. Gigs. All of it. It's like I sort of woke up. But I still wanted to be involved in the Church: the capital didn't turn me into a Sloane Square advertising executive or a Finsbury Circus bank boy."

"Hmmm." Kate stared out of the window. "Do you think many men in the Church today received their calling through reading the rude bits in the Bible?"

"I would have to say probably not." Archie swerved to overtake a Mazda, itself doing ninety.

"But don't you think—" Kate paused, trying to relax despite the extreme driving. "Don't you think you're just a little bit of a fraud?" She had started as a journalist but couldn't stop her own values from surfacing. Archie was such an enigma to her and she wanted to understand him. To put him in a clearly labelled box and know where she stood with him. But he absolutely refused to be categorised.

"No." Archie's answer, when it came, was measured.

"But you're not involved in the Church because of a great love of God are you? You just got into the Bible and took it from there."

"I'm sure there are lots of men of the cloth who, like me, are fascinated by the textual side to it and wanted to spend their lives absorbed by it."

"But it's not *academia* is it? You're out in the field so to speak aren't you? Shouldn't you care?"

"I *do* care!" He had conversations along these lines with tedious regularity.

"But shouldn't you be a Dean because you care what's actually in the Bible, rather than solely being fascinated about the Bible itself? Aren't you supposed to exude love and compassion, not go through the motions because you have to do it all? What about all the people who look to you for guidance? What do you give them? A glossy brochure with your mission statement printed up and a voucher for the cathedral restaurant?"

"Of course I care! Of course I listen and help," Archie snapped, "but that never makes it into the papers – you don't hear about that side of my role do you? What you hear about is just a snapshot of my working life. How could you know all of it? How dare you presume to know all of it?"

"It's just that you come across—"

"I know how I come across! But so what? See beyond it! Be the first! You know I am actually doing a half-decent job at Winchester."

"But treating the Church so obviously as a business..." Kate persevered regardless; although he was upset she could sense she was getting somewhere.

"Why not treat the Church as a business?" he retorted. "Think of the Cistercian monks."

"Never heard of them."

"Fountains Abbey...Rievaulx...Tintern..."

"Nope." Kate affected a blasé attitude but felt the full force of her own religious ignorance. It was the private club all over again.

"The Cistercians were 12th Century monks and they mined and farmed and managed estates and bingo, they were millionaires by today's standards. They were holy and Godly and, crucially, they were *businessmen*."

"Yes but didn't Henry VIIIth dissolve them?"

Archie laughed. "He did. But you can't imagine that these days; Mrs Windsor isn't going to come along and shut us down for being too successful."

"Ahh, yes, but if you take the business analogy too far—" Kate was on firmer territory here "—then you could be seen as a good investment, an asset. The Church of England could be involved in a hostile takeover."

"Are you insinuating that our friends from the Catholic Church might want to merge the two faiths for cost saving purposes?"

"You're laughing, but why not? If you want to businessify the Church then how far do you go? Where do you draw the line?"

"'Businessify' isn't even a word."

"You get my meaning."

Archie shrugged. "All I'm saying is that applying some sort of modern business management to the Church wouldn't be wrong in today's society. You want facts?"

"I want facts. I like facts."

"OK then, attendance is dropping year on year. It's down five per cent over the last four years and we're expecting this year's figures to show an even more marked trend. We're appealing to fewer and fewer people in the community, relevant only to a dwindling minority and how can we just sit back and let that happen? We need to give people what they need – a focus, a sense of community. Yes there's all that love and hand holding and bless-you-my-child stuff that you think constitutes the Church. But ultimately it's my opinion that we need to be a commercial success as well. We need to widen our appeal."

Kate looked out of the window again. "I can see why you have so much trouble with the Church establishment."

"The Bishop of Wessex thinks I should be one of those sing-the-hymn-and-hide-in-the-vestry type chaps. What good is that to people? Anyway, let's move on shall we? What about you?"

"Oh…"

"Come on, you know all about me and my life, what about you? What made you stoop to become a journalist?"

"Ha! Stooping! You're really very funny."

"Well…go on."

"It was because I like writing, that's it. Very dull. Nothing as exciting as your story, I'm sure," Kate said, uncomfortable now that the focus had turned to her. She was on unfirm ground with her transformation into a sophisticated journalist still little more than clothing-deep. "I like hunting down stories," she added, seeing that Archie wanted more, "when I get the chance – which is why I'm in your car heading in to London. And I was lucky and got a junior position at the local newspaper when I left university. So that's why. You know, if you're so interested in taking a business and turning it round you should have become a management consultant. Did you ever consider that?"

"No. But don't divert the attention back to me again. We had about fifteen miles of talking about me and we have a good twelve or thirteen left to talk about you. Are you happy being a hack?"

She smiled ironically. "Yes. What's not to love? Crap pay, back-stabbing colleagues and a boss who calls me *my little Jane Austen in the making,* patting me on the arm and telling me to go write a story about kittens that dance."

"Really?"

"Well, not the dancing kitten bit. But my boss is one of those men who thinks women should really stay at home and keep the pantry stocked, and the only reason young women should be allowed in the workplace is to have an opportunity to meet a man and once that's accomplished then it's off to the maternity ward and don't-you-keep-your-man-out-of-the-office-too-long."

"That's a crying shame," Archie reached over and laid a hand on hers, affecting a look of gravity whilst keeping an eye on the road. "My poor child. How you've suffered. Let me pray for you."

"Oh sod off." She shook her hands free. "Hey, where are we?"

"Clapham? I'm not sure. Maybe you ought to direct me. The map's in there."

Kate scrabbled in the glove box for the road atlas.

"We don't want to upset the timetable do we?" she conceded with a smile.

Thirty-Five

From the other room Edgar could hear the thud-thud-thud of the photocopier flinging out copies of his press release. He leant back in his chair and rested his feet up on the table.

The first draft, written when he'd got into the office at four in the morning, went to Aubrey at seven. Aubrey had read it and the two of them had discussed it, rewritten several sections and then circulated it to the remaining Project Rebel members at the hastily convened emergency eight o'clock breakfast meeting.

Edgar had been entirely unprepared for the dissection by committee that his work had undergone. He should have known, of course, he should have expected that something so vital to Project Rebel would be examined minutely. But it had still come as a shock. Sitting at the foot of the boardroom table, like a shoeshine boy seated before his customers, Edgar was instructed to cross out, amend, re-amend and then reinstate every other word in his three page press release turning it from a meaningful coherent whole to a catalogue of linguistically tortuous but technically accurate statements that followed no pattern or progression, rather they assaulted the reader like a bad poem.

The Project Rebel team seemed to have been sourced

from a pool of the most pedantic and obstinate people in the industry.

Shouldn't you use "likely" rather than "probably"?

Well I prefer "likely".

So do I. "Likely" is preferable in this context.

But "probably" is a stronger word and correct me if I'm wrong but what we're talking about here is "probably" the remains of a horse's harness?

Well can't we say "very likely" then if you want to be more definite? It is "very likely" the remains of a horse's harness. Edwin – write that down.

No don't write it down Edwin.

Actually isn't it Edgar? And Edgar – don't write it down.

Well, whatever, I prefer "probably".

If I may interrupt you gentlemen, when we talked about the finds associated with the platform eight bodies we talked about the two objects being daggers "in all likelihood". Don't you think that for the sake of consistency we should apply the phrase "in all likelihood a horse's harness" here?

Oh no. I don't like that. Very tabloid. Can we go back and change "in all likelihood" to probably.

I prefer likely.

Finally, at nine o'clock in the morning, the uncompromising suits from the legal department were happy, the pedantic archaeological unit were happy, and the meticulous English Heritage staff and the Government were satisfied with what was produced. While they had moved on to discuss the site emergency launch procedure Edgar had sat at a side table with his laptop and typed up the changes, struggling to make sense of his notes: *while most now ~~believe have~~ ~~concluded come to believe believe have come to conclude~~ think …*

Printed copies of his revised press release were signed off in the boardroom while a break was convened. It was during this time that everyone breakfasted on a platter of fresh croissants and pastries the secretary had brought in. Edgar looked on, famished but too busy and too polite to help himself, gathering up the signed copies: *Thank you, that's great, thanks, thank you.*

And now, heavily modified though the press release was, it was still his baby and he patted the multi-signatured copy that lay in front of him as he leant back again in his chair and listened to the satisfying thud-thud-thud from the other room.

"Here." The sour-faced secretary emerged from the print room. "I made this for you." She plonked a mug of black coffee on his desk and then thrust the half-emptied platter of pastries from the board room before him.

"Oh!" Edgar gazed at the wondrous selection of food. "Oh, Barbara." He could feel tears prickling behind his eyes. "Thank you!"

The secretary's face cracked with the strain of a smile, which she concealed by marching back into the print room to supervise the photocopier and savagely staple the copies for the press packs.

Edgar gorged on Danish pastries, launching himself first on the crisp pain-au-chocolate and then moving on to a soft, moist almond croissant, pausing midway through for a doughy bite of a sticky cinnamon swirl. He stopped short of holding the giant platter up to his mouth and tilting it, but only just. It was such an age since he'd eaten anything and he'd been up for so very long. Twenty-eight hours. Without a break.

For the past two hours, while Barbara had copied and bound the documents for the press packs, Edgar had been working his way through the Press Office Emergency Guidelines. Since half past nine he had been calling up the contacts on the media database, putting calls to office phones. But, as it was the weekend he was constantly being redirected to home phones, mobile phones, emergency contact numbers, out of hours numbers before getting through to the right people.

And when he did get through to the contact he launched into the same pre-approved script time after time.

There's been a new development at the Kings Cross archaeological dig. No – it's important – nationally important. Globally important. No it can't wait until Monday morning. No, I can't tell you any more at this stage – well I'm sorry to hear that, but the Prime Minister himself will be on site at one o'clock this afternoon to make a speech. You are *able to attend, well that's great. Bring your press identification with you. Yes, you get there by going round the back of the mainline station; do you know it at all...*

Again and again and again.

With each new call Edgar felt a little more in control, a little more confident in himself. It was liberating calling up all the people who had, over the past fortnight, been barking unanswerable questions at him down the phone. Now the power lay with him. Unguarded, taking an unexpected phone call in their home at the weekend, the journalists were suddenly a lot more friendly and amenable – with their *how are you*s and *good to hear from you again*.

"Enjoy the buns then did you?" The ex-military man who headed up security for the Museum of London popped his head round the door.

"Er…" Edgar glanced guiltily at the empty platter.

"Oh don't you worry about that. I was going to take one after the meeting finished but Barbara slapped my hand from the plate. Someone's looking out for you aren't they? I didn't think anyone got in her good books, you'll have to tell me your secret some time. So how's it going with the press and the TV?"

"Oh fine. Fine. Everyone I've spoken to so far is coming or a representative is coming on their behalf. We've got the papers, the main TV channels and radio as well. They all suspected that there was something up with the dig site so now it's being confirmed they're hungry for the story. I told them midday but some are going to be there within the hour. Sorry, I just couldn't stop them."

"Well, that's not a problem. As a matter of fact I came up here to tell you that the site is now secure so it's no problem if your media people start arriving. The extra cameras are online, additional security is all in place, the police presence has been confirmed, although we don't have exact numbers yet, and the barriers have all been reinforced to withstand crowd pressure and covered with additional razor wire. The security around the site is as tight as a gnat's chuff. There isn't anything that could get in there."

Except a male gnat thought Edgar.

"Edgar!"

"Professor De Lacey!" Edgar stood up and shook the professor's outstretched hand. He was pleased to see her.

"Well done young Edgar, well done." She beamed at him. "You've managed to put together a top class press release."

Edgar smiled and sat back down. "Well, it was thanks mainly to you and the time you took to go through everything with me. Really I'm so grateful!"

Hilary pulled up a chair and sat opposite him. "Pish! Now, young Edgar, there's something I ought to tell you." She leant forward and Edgar looked at her, quizzically. "It's about your father. He's in town."

"I know," Edgar said, "he's staying in my flat."

"You've seen him?"

"Well not to speak to. He was there last night. This morning. But he was asleep and I sneaked out before he woke up. I came straight here. How do you know he's in England?"

"He called me. Wanted to know about the dig of course; wanted access to the dig, no less. He's well connected here and from the very brief conversation I had with him he seems to be very well informed about what's going on, although I suspect he doesn't know the full story."

Edgar was shaking his head. "I haven't said a word to him. In fact I've been avoiding his calls."

"Hmm. Well. I don't think Aubrey would have wanted this to come between father and son. But if that's the course of action you felt was most appropriate to take, then that's your choice. But despite your efforts your father has friends all over the country and I should think one or two up at the finds unit in North East London University have tipped him off. Anyway, he was asking after you."

"Oh?" Edgar bit his lip.

"And I said that apart from a few words in the office I hadn't spoken to you much since you'd arrived at the Museum. And I know Aubrey won't mention your involvement with the project if your father gets in touch with him."

"And has he?"

"I should think so." Hilary laughed. "Your father likes to be in the know about things like this doesn't he? And he's more than good friends with Aubrey. Now, if you'll excuse me, I want to do a last site check before we parade our finds to the world. Apparently they're installing stadium lights all over the place and I want to make sure the roadies leave my excavations well alone."

Alone in the office Edgar checked his phone. There were no messages. He checked again.

"Champers?"

"No." Edgar waved it away. "Actually, yes. Thanks." He reached towards the silver tray that Erika was holding out to him and, gingerly took a glass. He was on the brink of saying something, something about Saturday night and how he'd really really wanted to go to Bar Salsa when the Head of Marcoms waddled up.

"Good man!" The Head of Marcoms slapped him on the back sending him head first into his Krug. "You'll be needing a couple of glasses of the good stuff to get you through the day, believe you me."

Edgar wiped the champagne off his face. "So I imagine, sir."

"Down the hatch!" The Head of Marcoms tipped his head back and drained his glass.

Edgar sipped his champagne, watching Erika work her way around the Finds Room, a venue that had been hastily put together in the old station waiting room. She had reached the English Heritage group. They were dressed in casual suits and lounging in the chairs in a corner. They took the drinks and toasted one another self-assuredly. Across from them were the men and women from the Government, in their tailored black and charcoal suits, standing rigid by the drinks table and looking serious with their vodka and tonics. And then there were the worker ant archaeologists, identified by the pint glasses gripped firmly in each hand, wearing jeans and t-shirts stating *Dig Andalucia 1985* and *I was there at Sutton Hoo '92. Where were you?* They had a grateful, awkward look about them, glancing around and waiting for someone to tell them to *get outside and dig Goddamn it*. Alone in her mingling was Professor Hilary De Lacey, archaeologist primarily but with a foot in the opposing camps, moving between the Government types, English Heritage and the archaeologists, resplendent in a plum-coloured wool suit and matching high-heeled shoes. She was putting everyone at their ease and enjoying the moment. She looked over at Edgar and raised her glass to him.

Edgar raised his glass back.

"Fine woman, De Lacey." The Head of Marcoms had noted the exchange. "Anyway, you must excuse me I just want to speak to security and go over the Prime Minister's arrival. Can you make sure the press packs are out and that someone's on hand to distribute them. Did you have enough printed?"

"Five hundred, sir," Edgar said smartly.

"Is that enough?" The Head of Marcoms looked concerned.

Edgar's confidence faltered. "I believe so."

"Fine. Fine. You're the expert. Right, well, good luck Edgar. And don't forget to enjoy the moment – bask in the glory of it all. You've done a good job my boy so bask away!"

"Thank you sir." Edgar was clutching his champagne glass stem in a vice-like grip and staring at the volume of press packs that now looked hopelessly deficient.

"Oh yes and one other thing. Don't forget that we're to have the press in the dig site first. We allow twenty minutes for photographs and broadcasting in there or whatever they want to do, and then straight away we're bringing them into the media briefing room over there to explain what we've done. Can you round up the troops if they look like they're not playing ball? I want everyone properly briefed by the panel of experts on the dig site; I'm not allowing the press to go making up what they think the story is. I want them in there, getting the full story from the right people. Control Edgar, I want total control."

"Of course, sir."

"Good man!" He whacked him on the shoulder. "You've done well today."

"Thank you, sir."

The Head of Marcoms waddled off and left Edgar alone

and fretting about the number of press packs.

It was eerily quiet in the main dig site – the calm before the storm. Edgar could hear the threatening clamour of the press outside, and the menacing rumble of the invisible trains pulling into the still functioning platforms beside the dig site. It felt as though a storm were coming.

A lone archaeologist in one of the ubiquitous white boiler suits was climbing up from the trenches after what must be some last-minute site preparation. She scurried off through the double doors leaving Edgar alone in the vast site. He wandered to the wooden railing and took a deep breath in, the champagne having taken the edge off his anxiety. He surveyed the scene before him, smiling now. He could do this. Now that the site was stadium lit, the scene before him looked more like a film set, which was what it was at this moment in time. The cameras were coming and the scene before him would be filling television screens imminently. The bright white lights picked up the gleam of human bone against brown-black soil and the glinting of a thousand tiny marker-pins pressed into the earth, each marking the site of a find, twinkling like stars against the night sky.

Boudica's grave was picked out by powerful spotlights suspended on scaffolding from the corners of the old station roof; it appeared to glow in the intense brightness, the luminous white horse skeletons arched over the bright white bones of the headless body between them.

Edgar's fingers stiffened, gripping the wooden railing hard, the whites of his knuckles showing through his skin.

His stomach in knots he leant forward, surely...*surely* he was mistaken.

He wasn't.

He stared open-mouthed at the flood-lit grave.

Boudica's head was gone.

Boudica's head was *gone*.

She had no head.

The briefest, incredulous pause and Edgar was tearing back to the Finds Room, stopping just before the double doors, taking a deep breath in – calm, calm – and in he walked, in to the dim champagne-filled space that resonated with the rumble of light conversation and laughter.

Edgar scanned the room. He spotted Hilary instantly, beside the bar, chatting to Erika with a glass of champagne in each hand. He made his way to them as quickly as he could. Calm, calm.

"Hi Erika. Er...Professor De Lacey...could I have a word?"

"Of course, young Edgar. Excuse me." Edgar led Hilary back to the double doors and out into the site.

Coming to a halt Edgar turned to face her and taking a long shaky breath said, "Professor De Lacey – has Boudica's head been taken away from the dig site for some reason?"

She paused, meeting Edgar's eyes. "No."

Edgar stood unmoving, debating what his next line would be.

"Edgar," Hilary cut in to the silence, "you're not trying to tell me Boudica's head is missing are you?"

Edgar looked into her eyes. He nodded.

In a split second the two ran to the viewing platform.

"Oh holy mother of God!" Hilary slapped a hand over her mouth and steadied herself against the railing.

"I couldn't believe it when I saw it!" Edgar wailed. "Or rather when I didn't see it!"

De Lacey had turned a blue-white; lit by the stadium lights she looked ethereal.

"OK there people? Basking in the spectacle of it all eh?" Edgar and Hilary leapt as the Head of Marcoms materialised behind them and gave them both hearty slaps on the back. "I can tell you that I have just seen the Prime Minister and he is a man who is raring to go and announce our sensational news to the world! We've got a hungry pack of media wolves scratching at our door so why don't we head back in and get this show on the road eh? Come on now you two – no need for nerves. We've pulled together like…" He petered out of clichés. "What? What is it? Why are you both looking like that?"

Hilary and Edgar looked back down into the grave. The Head of Marcoms, searching their faces for some clue as to their expressions, looked into the grave with them.

There was a long and painful silence.

"Where is it?" he rasped.

Hilary bit her lip. "That's the thing Aubrey. We don't know."

The Head of Marcoms gave a high-pitched manic laugh. "Your boys haven't taken it somewhere for testing have they Hilary? Cleaned it up? Given it a good buffing? With a duster eh? Photographs? Eh? Eh? Bit of a jape. Bit of a laugh? Hmm?" The mania sparked in his eyes, small circles of red appeared on each cheek. "Archaeologist playing a prank? What? Eh? Wouldn't put it past the *bastards*…the bitter grudge-bearing *bastards* with their—"

"Aubrey!" the calm of Hilary's voice, a good octave below that of the Head of Marcoms, cut into his stream of nonsense. "Someone must have taken Boudica's head and it's got nothing to do with me or my team. It's not been moved in any official capacity. We must be absolutely clear on that point – Boudica has not been disturbed in any authorised way."

"So you're saying," the Head of Marcoms stuttered, falsetto, "you're saying her head has been stolen?"

Hilary nodded. Edgar looked on wide-eyed. "It would appear so, sir," he managed to muster.

The three looked down at the headless warrior.

Edgar let out a long, shaky breath. "We're going to have to call off the press announcement aren't we?" he said into the silence.

"LIKE FUCK WE WILL, BOY!" The Head of Marcoms suddenly rallied. "There is no DAMNED WAY on God's green earth that I'm going to let some PETTY little bone thief piss away my project on some last minute JAPE by GOD!" He spun round and looked wild-eyed at Edgar. "Edgar my boy I want you to get someone from security, PRETTY DAMNED QUICK. Bring them here because I want to know what the HELL they were doing when—" He held his hand up. "No! Wait. I have another plan."

He manoeuvred his bulk past Edgar and Hilary and over towards the ladder leading down to the ground level of the dig site. "Yes...yes, this could work. Hilary, Edgar I want you two to swear to absolute secrecy on this – are you with me?"

"Yes, but—"

The Head of Marcoms held his hand up to stop Edgar in his tracks. "I have," he began, descending the ladder and panting for breath with the exertion, "a loan on a yacht...worth half a million pounds...a holiday home in Cyprus requiring complete renovation...and a wife who shops...in Harvey Nichols...I am damned if I'm leaving the organisation...in disgrace...without a penny. I am leaving with my head held high...with a golden handshake with a Goddamn bonus...I am leaving with the possibility of future board duties...at magnificent remuneration... when I retire...in eighteen months...then all hell can break loose...and you can bloody well...lose the lot as far as I'm concerned...but right now...right now this is my project... and I am not going to have...the world's media...capturing the most monumental COCK-UP...known to man."

By the time he had finished ranting he was down at soil level, walking heavily over to the grave, kicking bones out of the way, wiping his forehead with the exertion. Stooping down to grab a skull and jaw bone on the way he jumped into Boudica's grave and placed the new skull at the top of the body. "Hilary, your help please. Was this the correct angle?"

Hilary, who was gaping in horror, turned to Edgar, unable to speak.

"Hilary. Pull yourself together woman!" came the voice from below their feet. "This is just a temporary fix until we find the right head. Come on now, how important is the damned skull itself anyway eh? Eh? Eh? What's key here is the context. Big picture. You archaeologists are so *bloody* preoccupied with the little stuff. We've got the bloody Iceni army down here so who gives a toss if Boudica's head isn't the right one. So – was she looking more to the left? Like this? Hilary! Hilary for God's sake close your mouth."

Hilary took a deep, shaky breath in. "The head was angled more to the left." She managed to croak, "But you've got a male skull there Aubrey."

"Oh for FUCK'S SAKE! You come down here! NOW, WOMAN! You come down here and pick out a woman's skull..."

"No I—"

"DE LACEY!" Specks of foam had appeared around the corners of his mouth.

Shooting Edgar a terrified expression Hilary climbed down the ladder, her heeled shoes making the descent difficult, eventually lowering herself onto the soil and, picking her way steadily to a mass grave, spent a moment examining the skulls. After another coarse expletive from the Head of Marcoms, she gingerly removed a skull. Walking slowly over to Boudica's grave she knelt down and almost lovingly placed it above the shoulders of the body.

"Good woman!" The Head of Marcoms threw his own selected male skull and jawbone over his shoulder where it clattered into a mass grave and, stepping on the horse skull he jumped up and headed for the ladder. "Now you two – not one word. Do you understand? After the media frenzy we'll catch up and work out just what we're going to do here but until then, not one word..." He mounted the ladder, panting as he climbed back up, and stalked out of the room. "I'm going to get the PM."

Hilary was visibly shaking, climbing up the ladder as best

she could with trembling hands and stumbling feet. Edgar reached out to help her.

"He's gone mad," she muttered. "Aubrey's gone bloody mad."

"The man has a lot to lose." Edgar paused. "You don't think we'll be caught up in any trouble if this thing goes public do you?"

"I can't see how it can fail to go public. Any minute now and there are going to be thousands of images of Boudica with this head on her neck and only a fool wouldn't notice that it's not the right one. The size of the skull is utterly disproportionate to the—"

There was a sharp bang.

Pandemonium broke out.

With a violent roar the journalists flung themselves through the double doors and hurtled towards where Hilary and Edgar were standing. The two watched in horror at the army of bodies advancing, arms outstretched wielding Dictaphones, note pads, microphones, the scene made all the more surreal by being strobe-lit by flashlights.

Just in time they fled for safety through a side door.

Hilary and Edgar were in the corridor, backs to the double doors. The raucous din from behind them was formidable. On the other side of the doors there were cameras capturing images of the body with the wrong head. Media correspondents were talking through the scenes for their audiences at home, the camera crews recording in high definition the substitution that had just taken place: *we can actually look into the eyes of the famous warrior queen for the first time in two thousand years...*

"Edgar I—"

"Professor De Lacey!" The still-purple Head of Marcoms burst through a door and waddled briskly over to them. To his left walked a man Edgar recognised as Sir Marcus Pethwick, the Head of the Heritage Trust.

"Well then!" The Head of Marcoms winked at Edgar and Hilary. "Fancy finding you two here. Shall we go to the media briefing room, *the old station café to you and me,*" he added mock sotto voce, "and launch this to the world, eh? What do you say?"

Edgar stared at the purple face pressed in to his. The glint in his eye was that of a man not entirely at home to sanity.

"Come, come." He slapped a hand behind Edgar's and Hilary's back and propelled them towards the media briefing room. "I don't know Marcus – biggest find we have in a century, give or take Sutton Hoo, and these two get all nervous about a little press conference. Now you two – *in, in, in.*" And with a firm hand still behind their backs he thrust them in to the room.

Once inside, Edgar was abandoned and could only watch, helpless, as the professor was manhandled past the rows of seating, up to the front of the briefing room, up the stairs and on to the podium. Journalists hungry for the full story, were pressing into the room. TV crews were hastily setting up around the edges and a soundman was checking the cluster of microphones at the front table at which sat the three men and two women who were there to present Project Rebel. In the centre was the expansive Head of Marcoms, beaming and winking and appearing to enjoy every moment. To his left was a grey-faced Professor

De Lacey who was now occupying herself by attempting to pour water into her glass, her hands shaking to such an extent that the water was splashing on the museum-red tablecloth. To the left of her was the mean-looking representative from the Government who had been the most pedantic over the wording of Edgar's press release. On the opposite side sat the Head of the Heritage Trust and beside him a woman Edgar recognised as being from English Heritage.

Within minutes the room was full and the doors flung open to allow more journalists to listen in from the corridors. Edgar was squeezed into a hot airless corner at the very back.

Looking to his colleagues on the top table the Head of Marcoms checked they were ready and then held up a plump hand. The excited hum of voices died down.

The media briefing was about to begin.

Slowly and with a tone of enormous pride, the Head of Marcoms welcomed everyone to *what must surely be one of the most significant archaeological discoveries of all time*.

The cheers and applause seem to be never-ending.

Edgar stood, rigid with nervous tension, watching as the event played out. After the initial introduction each representative at the table spoke on their involvement in the project codenamed Rebel, exactly as had been planned at the emergency meeting. Hilary came across better than Edgar had expected. Her indistinct voice wobbled and faltered to start with but as she immersed herself in her subject she rallied. And with the growing confidence in the Professor's ability Edgar felt himself relax too, his shoulders dropped and he took deep lungfuls of the hot, fetid air. The questions were going to be tough but for the moment the professor was managing. She wasn't going to crack.

Edgar had been nervously watching her, but now he shifted his focus and looked over to the Head of Marcoms. He was startled to see the man looking straight at him. From up on the podium the Head of Marcoms winked imperceptibly at Edgar and, raising his eyebrows, gestured in a barely negligible nod over to the other side of the room. Edgar looked over to where he was indicating.

And there, against the opposite wall of the media briefing room, behind the press of journalists, stood Edgar's father. And he was staring right at him.

Thirty-Six

"And how are you Edgar? TAXI!"

"I'm very well thanks, Dad. How are you?"

"I'm fine. TAXI!"

"And how is Mum?"

"She's very well. TAXI! What is it with the damned cabs in this city?"

"Taxi! Where is Mum?"

"That was quick!" Edgar's father looked at him incredulously as a black cab pulled up. "You get in first. Your mother's waiting back at the flat."

And that was the extent of the conversation between father and son from the time they stood waiting for the taxi on the crowded, press-filled Euston Road to the point where they entered the flat in Bloomsbury.

Until recently Edgar, would have felt the need to fill the silence with nervous babble, talking and chattering and saying anything in the hope of dissipating his father's obvious anger towards him. He would be caught up in explaining himself, reasoning with his father and apologising for not having told him about his involvement in Rebel, pleading with him to understand the situation. All in the hope that by firing indiscriminate rounds of justifications, one would hit home and pacify him.

But Edgar, to his surprise, was not troubled by the strained atmosphere. Instead, numbed by a shortage of sleep and an excess of stress, he slumped in silence in the taxi, staring out of the window and watching drab North London slide by. He was physically and emotionally exhausted. Even the theft of Boudica's head and the panic-substitution had lost its significance in his numbed-out mind.

Edgar sensed his lack of concern was not purely down to mental fatigue. It also came from newfound confidence: a new and welcome feeling of job satisfaction. Of pride, even. And it was that, as much as exhaustion, that was ridding him of his anxiety over what his father might think of him and his actions over the past few weeks. He knew what he had done, regardless of what his father might think, had been the *right thing*. And more than that, he had proved his worth to the Museum by taking part in Project Rebel: nepotism may have landed him the job of press officer, but the work done on the Boudica dig was all down to him. So whatever his father thought, Edgar, in his befuddled and fuzzy state, was more than happy with the way things had turned out. Give or take the odd missing head.

"Edgar...we've missed you!" His mother pounced on him in the doorway to the flat, clutching him to her like a magnet to a fridge and planting a wet kiss on his cheek. "But you're so thin love!" She pulled back and examined his face. "Oh my darling, *look at you!*"

Edgar was surprised by how happy he was to see his mother. The warmth of her hug and the familiar scent of Lily of the Valley mixed with the smell of her hairspray. All this in stark contrast to his father, who hadn't so much as smiled at him.

"Hi Mum." He gave her a kiss on the cheek and then, walking into the flat, he took off his jacket. "I'm thin because I haven't eaten properly for a while."

"And you look so tired!" She flapped around him, taking his jacket and hanging it on the coat stand.

"Yeah, I haven't slept for a while." He flopped down on the two-seater sofa and his mother perched opposite on the arm of the easy chair.

Edgar looked around. Even in his daze he could sense there was something different about the place. A stack of books had returned to the shelves, the carpet had lost its crunch and there was an overpowering smell of pine forests wafting from the direction of the kitchen.

His mother looked at him, unsure of herself.

Edgar relented. "I'm sorry Mum...Dad. I'm just. I'm so tired right now. I haven't slept for ages..."

"Brenda." His father was still standing in the doorway to the shared hall. "Our son...was part of the team...that managed Project Rebel!"

Was it Edgar's imagination or was his father *emotional*?

"Graham, no!" His mother looked from her husband to Edgar. "You weren't were you Eddie? Were you?"

Edgar smiled sheepishly. He was watching his father who was advancing into the room and now came over to where he was sitting, laying a hand on his shoulder. It felt odd. And good.

"My son!" his father repeated, his voice wobbly and his eyes looking alarmingly wet. "I'm so very proud of you!"

Edgar gawped.

"You are talking about the Kings Cross Dig?" his mother

asked. "The one on the telly just now. With Boudica! You were right Graham, it *was* Boudica wasn't it! Were you part of all that Eddie?"

Edgar, still clutched in the grip of an emotional father, relayed what he'd done. The media pressure. The Project Rebel reports beside the egg sandwiches. Visiting the site and then earning his place on the team. He chose to omit the part about the missing head. They listened in silence, agog.

"Well," his father said when Edgar had finished, "I think this calls for a celebration. Brenda – the whisky, if you please!"

Edgar watched while his mother scuttled in to the kitchen area and pulled out a bottle of whisky from the cupboard. "Gatwick's finest!" she quipped, searching for glasses. "I bought it for you, but I'm sure you won't mind if we all have a toast will you?"

"Not at all…"

"Come on, my boy." Edgar was being pulled up by his shoulders. He allowed himself to be led towards the sink and watched dumbfounded as his father unscrewed the window catch, clambered on to the kitchen work surface, and winched himself out onto the narrow roof space.

Edgar shot his mother a quizzical look but she just shrugged and went about pouring measures of duty-free whisky into mugs.

Nonplussed, Edgar hoisted himself through the window and joined his father on the roof. It was late afternoon and the light was fading. Below them the city looked dreary and overcast, from the slick hard towers of the City to the barren winter squares of Bloomsbury.

"Here!" His father thrust a cigar at him and put another in his own mouth. He cupped his hands around it as he lit it, passing the matches to Edgar. They puffed away in mutual silence, looking out over the chimney pots of North London.

"Whisky's up!" his mother chirped through the window, holding out two mugs for them.

"Thanks Brenda. You coming out?"

"Oh no. I'll call Auntie Sarah I think, she'll want to hear all about this. Mind if I use your phone love?"

"Not at all!" Edgar took the whisky from his mother and she blew him a kiss.

"Cheers." His father clinked his mug against Edgar's. "It's nice to see these boards are still shipshape." He stamped his feet on the wooden planks. "My God…it's a long time since I was up here. I used to love it out here."

His father used to come out here? It was hard to imagine his father as anything other than the serious-minded sergeant major of a son-manager he had become, certainly not as the sort of young man who shimmied over the kitchen drainer and perched on the rooftops drinking whisky.

The pair smoked in an amiable silence.

"I'm very proud of you, son. I really am."

"Thanks, Dad." Edgar took a gulp of his drink and felt it burn its way down his throat. He wished he wasn't as tired as he was and could appreciate fully that first moment, up there among the chimney pots, when his father was truly proud of him and all he had achieved. As it was he was now almost wholly overwhelmed by exhaustion and Gatwick whisky. He clung to the lead guttering to stop himself from falling off the narrow walkway and onto the pavement three storeys below.

"Well, I bet you're glad that you took that job at the museum that I set up for you eh? Not poncing around with fabrics eh?" His father laughed.

"Mmm," Edgar said into his mug, draining the last of the whisky.

There was a faint wisp of smoke rising from a chimney over towards Russell Square. He watched it for a moment as it curled and snaked upwards and then vanished to nothing.

Thirty-Seven

There was an ellipse of dense vegetation in the centre of Battlebridge Crescent, fenced in by high Victorian railings. The gates were open and so it was there, in amongst the bare London planes and the waxy rhododendron bushes, that Archie and Kate sat, their eyes focused on number 32, waiting for Cora Montgomery, Medical Artist, to emerge. Partially screened off they sat in silence, Kate wiggling her feet as they threatened to go numb with the inactivity of sitting unmoving on the hard wooden bench on a cold November morning.

Time passed achingly slowly and the two silently sank from their high expectations to doubt and then to plain boredom at the lack of any action. Kate had been convinced that, once they had arrived, they would see Cora leave her house and they would then be able to go in for a snoop. As it was they had no idea if this was her house, if she was even the right person. For Kate, boredom was stretching in to despair.

"Have you ever been to York Minster?" Archie broke the silence, not taking his eyes off the glossy front-door.

Kate looked at him, irritated that his thoughts could be elsewhere. "A while ago."

"And?" He turned to her. "What did you think?"

She shrugged. "I don't know. It was good. What has it got

to do with us being here?"

"How good? Was it very good? Fairly good? Do you think it was better than Winchester? Did you eat in the café?"

"Archie!"

"What?"

"I was about eight. I can't remember. I probably wandered around and then bought a pencil."

"I think they're too elitist." He turned back to stare at the front door. "Their donation charges are higher than ours: we made an effort to keep them as low as possible. And the goods in the shop up in York Minster are too upmarket in my opinion. It's not what the Church is about. We're about the common man."

Kate shrugged and attempted to return to her thoughts.

"What do you think about 'See it for yourself, save if for the future'? Do you think that's a good strap line for the cathedral? I didn't come up with it, the marketing team did. I'm warming to it. It's quite clever really, with the—"

"Archie shut up!" She saw his expression and quickly added, "I'm sorry. But too many questions! I don't know the answer to any of them. It's useless asking me, I don't understand your world."

"Ahh you see..." Archie raised a finger. "That's the whole problem – *your world*. It should be your world too."

Kate took her eyes off the front door and turned to her companion. "Look, Archie... It's not my world. It's never *been* my world. It will never *be* my world. I am a journalist." She said the words but they sounded false to her. She'd never truly considered herself to be a journalist. She considered herself to be employed by the *Winchester Echo*. It didn't follow that she was employed journalistically.

Archie sighed and went back to staring at the front door, lighting up a cigarette.

"There was an alleyway. Did you see it?" Kate asked, trying to bring Archie into the world that she was inhabiting. She didn't take her eyes off the front door, its shape and colour now burned on to her retinas so that even if it did open and Prince William and Kate Middleton emerged, having shared a moment of fun together, she was sure she would only ever see that single image of a closed front door, a letterbox, a doorknocker in the shape of a fox.

"Do you mean the alley with the archway entrance?" Archie said

"That's it. It must run behind the houses. Maybe there are outbuildings or something. Would these houses have had stabling? How old are they?"

Archie shrugged. "Georgian? I don't know. I can't date things if they haven't got transepts."

"Well we could be waiting here for hours. She might not even be here today. Or even this week."

The pair looked at one another.

"I hadn't thought of that," Archie said eventually, not wanting to admit he hadn't thought about any of it. He knew he should, he realised that, but he was more enjoying the company and trying to work out how he would be able to convince Kate to stay overnight in the capital with him.

"It only occurred to me just now." Kate's heart sank. "I should have called her number before we left Winchester."

"Hold on a minute." Archie sat up. "Wasn't that the very course of action that I suggested last night in the pub? I distinctly remember saying we should call her and you said—"

"I'd just put the phone down. That way we could be sure there was someone *in* rather than make all this effort to come to the capital and wait outside an empty house."

"Oh who cares… It's all a good jape anyway," Archie said.

Kate stared at him. "Aren't you bothered that there's no real plan or thought gone into this? Don't you agree we'd get somewhere more quickly if we spent time thinking things through before we raced off?"

"Well you did. What about your super timetable? You obviously spent time planning."

"Yes but big picture!" Kate wailed, "I was so caught up in the detail that I didn't think big picture."

"Well, if we had always thought things through at every level," Archie attempted to placate her, seeing she was turning hysterical in the manner of a dumped girlfriend, "we wouldn't have made it this far would we? If we'd have researched what that Bob Gilroy bloke actually did, then we would never have gone to see him. And if we hadn't seen him we would never have seen that photograph of Cora Montgomery. And then we would never had the pleasure of sitting in a dodgy Kings Cross garden square in November.

"Well it bothers me," Kate huffed. "I used to be so careful, you know," she continued, more to herself than to her companion. "That was one thing I was known for, my meticulous attention to detail. Dr Evil was—"

"Dr Evil was promoting you?" Archie cut in.

Kate paused. "No."

"Was giving you the big breaks?"

"No," she added, sullenly.

"Well then." Archie crossed his arms. "Sounds like your boring attention to detail plan, or whatever it was, wasn't actually getting you anywhere."

Kate stood up and grabbed her bag.

"Kate!"

"No. I've had enough!"

"I'm sorry Kate – I didn't mean to be so rude. Please... we're here now..." He chased her out of the park and into Battlebridge Crescent.

She turned to him and there were tears in her eyes. "You're right. It's lame isn't it? I get lumbered with the shittiest jobs and not even—" she gestured wildly at her new appearance "—this new...whatever...I still get passed over and treated like the office junior! I've tried to change. But all that's happened is that I don't even recognise myself any more," she wailed, trotting down the road in the direction of Kings Cross Station. "I'm just...I'm completely the opposite of what I used to be. And even now I'm not good enough."

"Hey." He grabbed her arm and slowed her down. "Calm down. Kate?"

"I wasn't that bad was I?" She burst into fresh tears and stopped. "Was I? Do you think so? Did I need to change every single thing about myself?" She wiped the tears away with her sleeve. "Why do I have to try and be everything I'm not?"

She looked to Archie, who felt the full weight of her breakdown upon him, and dared not speak for fear of saying the wrong thing. He simply held her fast and let her rant.

"I don't recognise myself any more," she cried and allowed herself to be pulled into his arms. She sobbed while he held her.

"This way," he said gently and moved her nearer the kerb as a pedestrian sidestepped them to get past.

Kate briefly looked up as a woman thanked Archie and walked on. Ashamed, Kate dried her eyes with her sleeve.

"Come on." Archie held her hand and led her along the street.

They walked a few steps in silence.

Petite. Long red hair. Old fashioned beauty. Click-clacking her way down Battlebridge Crescent. "That was her wasn't it?" Kate whispered.

Archie winked and squeezing her arm he propelled her into the alleyway entrance, a mere five doors down from the house Cora Montgomery had just entered.

Thirty-Eight

Archie still had his arm around Kate. She was glad of it. Her hysteria of self-doubt had quickly given way to the shock of coming within centimetres of Cora Montgomery: the very object of their attentions had just walked right past them and in to the house they had been watching.

If Archie had taken his arm away now Kate knew she would have collapsed in a heap on the cobbles. She breathed deeply and concentrated on keeping upright as they made their way down the alley.

After the gentrified exterior of Battlebridge Crescent, and the imposing stone archway entrance leading to the alley, the alley itself was a sharp contrast. They picked their way slowly over a filthy cobbled path, skirting rotting rubbish and clumps of ragged weeds. On either side dark brick walls loomed upwards, topped with razor wire and smashed bottles pressed into cement; this was the true face of Kings Cross lurking behind the elegant facades of the houses.

"That was definitely her wasn't it?" Kate broke free at last and skirted a mound of old carpet.

"Definitely. Without a doubt," Archie said.

"Did she recognise you from the break-in?"

Archie thought about it for a moment. "I don't think so. When she saw me in the cathedral I had the cathedral's little black dress on. I look completely different out of uniform."

"I don't know..." Kate began, eyeing him up. Yes the long coat and jeans were worlds apart from his robes. But he did have the same tousle-haired, part angelic part cad-about-town look about him, regardless of the clothes he wore.

"She might have recognised me, if she'd seen me in Winchester," Archie continued, "but not here in Kings Cross. I'm out of context aren't I? Stop a second."

They looked at the back of the houses on Battlebridge Crescent and Archie counted down. "Here. This must be the back of number thirty-two." Unlike most of the others they had passed the wall still had its back entrance, a thick door with peeling black paint secured with a padlock and two other locks. Above the door was a small dirty window shielded behind a rusted metal grill.

"These two houses still have brick sheds in their back gardens butting onto the wall," Archie was mumbling as he searched for something to stand on.

"I don't know." Kate looked sceptical. "The doors look derelict to me. They're probably bricked up behind."

"It's still worth a look." Archie tested a partially rotted wooden crate. It held his weight and, moving it to a position in front of the padlocked door he climbed on to it. "Can you keep a look-out?" he said.

Within a minute he was level with the window, wobbling on the old crate, which creaked ominously. He steadied himself by holding on to the metal grille.

The glass was smeared with decades worth of smoke and dirt. Archie peered inside. Using his sleeve he wiped a circle of filth off the pane.

"Oh..."

"What?" Kate called out below.

"One minute." Archie widened the circle of cleaned glass he had made and looked in again. The outbuilding leaning up against the back wall was a studio. In sharp contrast to the derelict appearance from the alley the inside was clean and orderly with white painted walls and a bright concrete floor reflecting the natural light from huge windows in a lean-to roof that sloped into the garden and towards the house. A large table stood blocking the doorway to the alley, on top of which sat a bust, pegged out but not completed, just like at Bob Gilroy's house. The sight of it sent a shiver down his spine. No doubt Canute was just inches away from where he was standing. He turned and gave Kate the thumbs up before turning back to clean more glass so that he could see more of the studio.

He looked into the newly cleared area. There were shelves of heads.

He leant back in fright and the crate threatened to collapse.

Kate rushed to steady it. "Are you OK?"

"I'm fine." He shot her a nervous smile. "It's just like Bob Gilroy's studio. Heads on shelves, bags of clay. Books..."

"Can I look?"

Archie took a last glance through the window and slowly got down. "Be careful. It's very unsteady." He helped her up and held her by the hips as she stood on tiptoe and looked through the window for herself. She gasped and held tight to the metal grille.

"Thirteen heads!" she said as she took in the site. "Which

272

one is Canute do you think?"

"Who knows? I want to get in there for myself."

"We can't. No way. There's a heavy table against this door and besides, Cora Montgomery might come in at any moment."

"We could wait until tonight."

"And get knifed down an alley in Kings Cross? No way." Kate climbed down from the crate, taking Archie's hand, and then dusted herself off. "Thank you," she added.

"Pleasure." Archie grinned and Kate chose to ignore him. She hated the way he made her feel so prudish. If only she felt able to respond in kind.

Archie moved the crate back to its original position. "Don't want anyone breaking in."

"So..." She waited until he returned and they started back down the alleyway. "The police?"

He shrugged. "Have you got everything you want for your big story?"

"I guess so. If we tip the police off then we can watch them go in and arrest her."

"And what about Canute?"

"You'll still get the credit for finding Canute," Kate reassured him as they emerged with some relief into the elegant street once more. "But what else can we do? We can hardly go in there, accuse her and then ask for Canute's head back."

"Why not?"

"She'd just deny it. And we can't enter her property without permission. She might not let us in."

"Well perhaps she'll be glad to show us. Or feel a sense of

shame at what she's done and confess."

"Mmm, very likely." Kate shot him a withering look. "I say we call the police, wait to see what happens and maybe, since we're in the capital, I saunter down to the *Guardian* and see if they're interested in my scoop..."

Kate had imagined the moment soon to come a thousand times over the past few months – how she would walk in to a newspaper's head office, ask to speak to a member of the newsdesk about *a very important story*, take a seat on a luxury sofa in the foyer, check her lipstick in her compact mirror. A man would approach her, intrigued by the beautiful woman with the big story, shake her hand.

I hear you have something on the 'insert important story'...

Yes, yes I have.

Well come up then, Miss...

Grey – Kate Grey.

Hey, man on reception, get Miss Grey a pass...

Thirty-Nine

At nine o'clock on Monday morning, at Edgar's request, Erika had gone to the nearest newsagents on Moorgate and bought every edition of the morning papers. Together in the press office the pair now pored over the front pages spread out on the tables like a giant tabloid tablecloth.

"Look! Here is one of Aubrey! Doesn't he look like Santa, don't you think Ed-gar? I think so. And look, Professor De Lacey is behind him. She looks very ill I think. So pale. Hmmm...let me see, are there any photographs of you Edgar? Surely, there must be." She rifled through the pages. "Skull, skull, body, horses and body, statue, skull..." She reeled off the images from the front pages as she cast them aside. Edgar looked on, silently.

He'd barely done any work for the last three hours except answer the very few calls that had come in, mostly about the public opening of the site, which had taken place that morning amid yet another frenzy of media attention. Oddly detached from it, he'd watched the news as he got ready for work: excited members of the public who had been queuing throughout the night, huddled in sleeping bags just to be among the first in to the dig site, *Oh my God we're just like sooo excited about seeing Boudica you know? It's like sooo amazing that they found her...*

"Here you are!" Erika thrust a copy of *The Times* at him.

"This is you Ed-gar, behind Professor De Lacey, entering the media briefing room, I think. You look very handsome in your suit. But you are not smiling I see. You look very worried in the photograph don't you think?" She looked at him across the table and seeing his distant expression she slowly lowered the paper. "What is it Ed-gar? What's up?"

"Nothing." He attempted a smile. "I'm just tired, that's all."

"Of course you are! Do you want a coffee? Will that perk you up?" She lay a hand on his shoulder and Edgar had the overwhelming urge to rest his head on it and maybe feel the trailing of her long fingers through his hair.

"I will get you a coffee. Stay right there!" She tripped out to the kitchen and Edgar, head in his hands, stared at the jumble of articles before him. The enormity of the skull-swapping had hit him as he stared at the high resolution colour images before him, deep into the hollow eye sockets of the unknown woman that was most definitely not Boudica. What was going to happen when someone from the dig realised that Boudica's actual skull, which had been uncovered and recorded, photographed, measured, and examined minutely, was a different one from the skull that was on the front pages of most of the day's papers? What was going to happen then?

For the second time that morning his mobile rang. (The first call had been from his mother *Congratulations, darling, we're so proud. Your father and I are so immensely proud of you...* to tell him that she'd booked a table at Rocket off South Molton Street, in Mayfair, at seven. Could he meet them for drinks at the Bunch of Grapes? Yes, he'd said, he could.)

"Edgar? It's Hilary De Lacey!"

"Professor!"

"Look, I'm sorry to call you but, well, I'm up at the dig site at the public opening and…well…" Her voice dropped to a barely perceptible whisper. "I need to talk to you."

"I'm just looking at the papers now," Edgar said, "the photographs are so clear…"

"I haven't slept a wink," Hilary said. "Look, when can you get here? There's no chance of me making it to the office today because they want me to stay on hand here. But I can meet up for a coffee with you somewhere near the dig?"

"I can come now." Edgar was already standing up. "Do you have anywhere in mind?"

"What about the Costa on Brill Place?"

"Fine. I'll see you there in twenty minutes?"

"Great."

Erika had come in with the coffee and a plate of Jammy Dodgers. Her face fell when she saw Edgar putting on his jacket and overcoat.

"You're going…"

"Erika, I'm sorry." He walked over to her and, without thinking, he placed his hands lightly on her shoulders. Leaning over he planted a light kiss on her cheek. "I'll be back."

She watched him walk out of the office and down the corridor, her hand glued to the place where he'd kissed her.

Forty

"Put your phone away! We have to be smart about this," Kate said as they walked briskly down the road away from Battlebridge Crescent.

"What do you mean by smart? We tip off the police, they raid Cora's studio, and then we write up the story and collect the heads when the police have finished with them. Isn't that plan smart enough?"

"We can't tip off the police from a mobile phone. That's as good as giving our names and addresses. They can trace the numbers back to us."

"Is that such a bad thing? I thought we wanted to be involved in finding Canute." Archie was getting increasingly exasperated, more at himself for being upstaged by Kate constantly than with his inability to understand the subtleties of her plan.

"Supposing – just supposing – it's not her. Suppose Cora Montgomery isn't the one."

"But it is her!"

"Thinking this through...perhaps it would be the best idea to not reveal to the police who tipped them off. Just in case things don't go according to plan. If all this goes horribly wrong do you want all the press that would come with it? What would the Bishop of Wessex have to say?"

"So you do have a plan," Archie said. "The woman who said

she'd given up attention to detail and planning has come up with a plan." He mock-punched her on the shoulder. "See – there was no need for all that fretting earlier on."

Kate found herself smiling. "It's true: I do have a plan. Of sorts. We ought to go to Kings Cross Station and use a public payphone. But we'll have to keep our heads down. Literally. We mustn't be caught on CCTV."

Within minutes of their return to the park in Battlebridge Crescent, two police cars careered down the road and pulled to a halt in front of number 32.

The doors to the first police car had now opened and two officers were emerging, placing their caps on and talking into radios pinned to their uniforms. With agonising slowness they walked to the familiar red front door and knocked.

"I hope she's not gone out," Kate whispered, her voice trembling with the force of her heart hammering in her chest.

The second policeman looked around as they waited at the door, looked up and down the street, across into the park. Archie and Kate quickly looked down at a newspaper Kate had suggested they buy, hardly daring to breathe.

Cora was at the door. She was wearing an apron, and looking the very picture of domesticity, red hair scooped back and glasses on. The policeman nearest to her was talking, his colleague added something and they all laughed. She stood back and let them in.

The door closed behind them.

The policemen in the second car remained in the vehicle.

There were two officers in the front.

"Do you think they'll bring her out handcuffed?" Kate said.

"I shouldn't think so."

"Look!" Kate pushed a rhododendron out of Archie's sightline. "Policeman at the window! Top left."

Archie looked over at the house and saw the policeman, he was saying something to either Cora or to his colleague. The man looked out of the window briefly and then moved away.

"So they're looking in the house? I thought you told them the heads were in the studio outside."

"I did. They'll look there too. I guess they're doing a thorough job."

Time passed and the pair continued to wait. The second police car backed up slightly to occupy a position directly blocking the alleyway. One of the policemen got out, and walked down the alley.

"Do you think she's trying to do a runner?" Kate whispered.

Archie just snorted and continued to watch the front. Kate's experience of stakeouts was obviously drawn from bad seventies TV series.

A few minutes later and the front door opened again. Out in the bushes Archie and Kate watched.

The two policemen from the first car walked out of the front door and behind them Cora emerged on to the doorstep.

She was saying something and one of the policemen laughed. He was now shaking her hand. The other shook her hand. They walked away, the first touching his radio and speaking in to it. Gesturing to the other police car they got back into their vehicle and within a minute had pulled away. The policeman who had investigated the alley had now returned and, stepping back into the second police car, the police quit Battlebridge Crescent.

Cora watched them go, then stepped back in to her house and shut the front door behind her.

Archie stared at the taillights of the retreating cars. "Shit."

Forty-One

"It's impossible," Hilary De Lacey said, running a hand through her grey hair and leaning in towards Edgar. They were seated in a corner of Costa Coffee, two untouched cappuccinos on the table before them, Edgar folding, twisting and plucking at sachets of sugar with nervous hands.

"But what can we do?" Edgar put down a torn sugar packet and pushed it across the table.

"Everyone knows that there's been a switch," she said flatly.

"Has anyone said anything to you?" Edgar asked.

"Not to me. But I know they suspect my hand in it. I can tell from the way people are acting that it's common knowledge among the archaeologists. Aubrey was an idiot to think he could deceive so many professionals by substituting a different skull."

"Perhaps he really thought it was only going to be an hour or so before the real head was found?"

Hilary scoffed and stirred her cold coffee.

"The head you found wasn't that close a match, then?" Edgar asked after a moment.

"Nowhere near. Edgar I had to think quickly and I did what I could but... Well, for a start I had no way of being sure I was positioning the skull correctly. And the lefthand horse suffered damage to the lower mandible when Aubrey stepped on it, so I'm afraid there are clear signs of the grave being tampered with."

"Yes but—"

Hilary shook her head. "Beside the question of tampering, the skull I chose – within the time limit – was utterly different from the original. The supraorbital ridge was more pronounced in the original skull, any fool could see that. *Here.*" She pointed to her brow after seeing Edgar's expression. "And the eye sockets had more of a squareness to them in Boudica's skull: she had quite masculine markers."

"Any other differences?" Edgar asked, after all maybe the lack of squareness to the eye sockets wouldn't be spotted by the world's media…

"Plenty!" She sank back in her seat. "The arrangement and condition of the teeth would almost certainly be different between the two skulls – although both skulls had few teeth and all those remaining in a poor condition it would be nothing short of a miracle to expect the same teeth in the same state of decay to be present in both."

Edgar ripped open a packet of Demerara. "So what can we do?"

"Go to the police?" Hilary looked up. "I don't know Edgar. I just don't know. I was going to retire in five years. And now – well when all this starts up then maybe I'll be forced out right away. Without a proper pension. And I'll be a criminal in the eyes of my colleagues, when they find out I was an accomplice. Edgar?" She stopped abruptly.

Edgar had stood up. Sugar scattered in all directions. His chair clattered backwards onto the floor tiles as he turned and walked away.

Hilary rose to her feet. "What is it? Edgar? Edgar!"

She called in vain.

Edgar had gone.

Forty-Two

"Aren't you going to eat your panini?" Archie pushed the squashed beige sandwich towards Kate. She couldn't have been any less tempted had it been a tramp's sock. She pushed it back.

"I'm not hungry."

She sipped her cappuccino and stared listlessly at the oversize picture of coffee beans on the wall opposite.

"It was a good plan, Kate."

"No it wasn't," she moped into her cocoa-sprinkled foam.

"Of course it was." Archie laid a hand on hers and she looked up, close to tears again but desperate not to cry. "It just didn't work for some reason," he added.

"Why not? Why didn't it work?" she nearly shouted, making him jump. "It was her! It was definitely the right woman! You know it! I know it! She has a shed full of skulls out the back and she matches the photofit and she was in Winchester before the theft. Of course it's bloody her!"

"Well, it must just mean she hides the skulls away." Archie bit into Kate's sandwich. "You must try this. It's lovely."

Kate looked at him in despair. "How can you be so…" She searched for the right words. "So damned *hungry?*"

"'To those who by persistence in doing good seek glory, honour and immortality,'" he said mid-bite, "'he will give eternal life.'"

"Pardon?"

"*Romans* 2:7."

"OK great. I feel so much better now."

"Kate, just because that plan didn't work—"

"I'll get eternal life? Great. Whose were all those skulls then if they weren't Canute's and others' like him?" She returned to her argument.

"Scene of crime skulls? Victims? Mr and Mrs Does?" Archie offered. "You know she works for the police. They were probably there from her day job. Come on – if she works for the police she's going to have a get-out-of-jail card isn't she? Waft some paperwork in front of them, account for all those skulls and it's going to look like some busybody was spying on her and her weird career and got the wrong impression."

Kate eyed Archie up from across the table. "You knew it was going to play out like this didn't you?"

"Not as such." He wiped his mouth with a napkin, having finished her panini.

Kate stared at him, agog. "Can you just wipe that Cheshire grin from your Goddamn face too?"

There was a sharp bang at a table nearby and Kate and Archie turned to see a man striding towards them. In a moment he was at their table, his hands resting on the Formica table top.

There was a moment when all three stared at each other.

"Can we help you?" Archie's voice had a threatened middle-class ring to it.

"I'm sorry." Seeing their expressions the man stepped back and crouched down to their level. "I didn't mean to surprise you. My name's Edgar Thompson, I work for the Museum of London."

Kate and Archie looked blankly at him, nonplussed.

"The dig?" Edgar waved his hand in a general motion behind him. "Boudica?"

"Oh I know! Wow – so you're involved in it? That must be amazing." Kate put aside her melancholy and perked up.

"It is…" Edgar began.

"So how can we help you?" Archie asked after an awkward silence.

"Well…" Edgar pulled over a chair and sat between them. Three tables away Hilary De Lacey was craning her neck to see what was going on.

"I'm sorry," Edgar went on, "but I couldn't help overhearing what you were talking about. And I thought that perhaps there might be some connection between…your experience and mine." He was breathless with nerves and the words tumbled from him before he knew what he was saying.

"And the connection might be?" Kate asked, cagily.

Edgar dropped his voice. "Before I say anything, did I hear you correctly – something about missing *skulls*."

Archie and Kate exchanged glances.

"You are such a loud-mouth," Archie said, shaking his head.

"Actually," Edgar said, "it was you I overheard."

"Ha!" Kate began to warm to their new companion. For once that day it was Archie's turn to look crestfallen.

"We *thought* someone stole a skull," a humbled Archie

offered after a moment's pause. "A woman. She's a facial reconstruction expert, she rebuilds the faces of the dead from their skulls. And we had a suspicion she was involved in the theft of a skull...connected to...my work."

"That's right," Kate quickly added. "But we sort of... well...someone checked it out and perhaps we were wrong to think that she stole them."

"And she lives in Kings Cross?"

"Just around the corner," Archie said.

"Is everything all right Edgar?" Hilary De Lacey had come over to join them, looking from Edgar's eager expression to the confused Archie and Kate.

"This is Professor Hilary De Lacey," Edgar said. "I'm sorry – I don't know..."

"I'm Archie Cartwright. Dean of Winchester." Archie enjoyed their surprise as he shook their hands.

"Kate Grey. I work at a local newspaper in Hampshire."

"You're a journalist?" The effect of her words on Edgar and Hilary was marked.

"Oh don't worry. I'm nice press." Kate sought to pacify them. "The *Winchester Echo* never ruffles feathers. We're not allowed to."

"Tell us everything," urged Edgar, leaning in. Hilary pulled up another chair and Archie relayed what he knew, at the end of which the two Londoners were staring at him open-mouthed.

"So how do you think you fit into all this?" Kate asked.

Edgar looked to Hilary who nodded her permission.

"Three days ago someone stole Boudica's skull," Edgar said in a voice barely above a whisper.

Kate and Archie stared wordlessly at him. "I read about the Boudica dig in this morning's paper! And you think our woman got her too?" Kate said.

"Maybe." Hilary was looking round nervously; no-one appeared to be interested in their conversation.

"The paper I read had a picture of the body on the front with the head still in place." Kate said.

"It's the wrong one. The project leader ordered us to make a substitution at the last minute," Edgar muttered.

"To avoid embarrassment for the museum," Hilary added. "He thought it had been temporarily taken off for analysis. I don't think it ever crossed his mind that it might not come back."

"So someone has actually taken Boudica's skull? It's got to be connected to Canute. It has to be!" Kate gasped.

"And it's on her patch," Archie added. "Cora Montgomery is literally around the corner from you. Once the public started to know about the dig then the temptation must have been—"

"But it wasn't public knowledge," Edgar said in a hushed voice, hoping Archie would follow his lead. In his excitement the Dean was raising his voice and getting into full-blown sermon mode. "The skull was taken before even the press knew about it. It has to have been done by someone with insider knowledge of the dig."

"So who did know early on about the dig?" Archie asked.

"Selected senior Museum of London staff..." Edgar began.

"About thirty archaeologists, all of whom I could all

vouch for," Hilary added.

"The Prime Minister and a few members of the Government. Someone from English Heritage…"

"Two members from the Heritage Trust…"

"What about the police?" Kate asked. "Wouldn't they have been involved? If you're digging up bodies don't you need to have the go-ahead from them to check it's not a current crime scene? Cora's connected to the police through her day-job so maybe she heard about it that way? Christ – sorry Archie – she might even have been the one who was sent to confirm that the bodies they found on-site weren't recent."

Hilary was nodding, "Good thinking." Kate glowed with pride. "But no. A small team of officers were involved in the dig initially, but once it was determined that the bodies were *of historical interest* then the responsibility was handed over to the Home Office. And all they all knew it to be was a medieval plague pit. Just one man from the Home Office knew the full details of what we were uncovering and I have every faith in him that he didn't blab."

There was a silence around the table as everyone tried to work out a connection.

"Some of the finds were taken up to North East London University for cleaning," Edgar offered. "Does she have a connection there?"

"No," Archie said.

"Yes!" Kate grabbed Archie's arm. "The websites! Bob Gilroy!" Archie looked blankly at her so she added, "Cora lectures at North East London University. Isn't she part of the Biology Department? Biological Sciences?"

"There's your connection then." Hilary slapped the table excitedly. "Someone at the lab involved in handling the artefacts either talked to Cora or to someone connected with her, about who we'd really got here."

"And it proved to be too much of a draw for her to ignore," Edgar said.

"But what can we do?" Kate had her head in her hands. "We've called the police and they searched the place but didn't find anything suspicious."

"Maybe she works off-site," Edgar said, "on *special* cases…"

"*You* could ask the police to go into her studio again." Kate sat up, enthused by her sudden idea. "On behalf of the Museum of London. Then you could go in and get the skulls carbon dated or something. Prove that they're not recent unidentified persons' skulls."

"But that would mean owning up to the substitution of Boudica skull," Hilary said, "and we absolutely can't do that."

"Damn." Kate sank back down.

"You have an idea?" Edgar was looking at Archie who had been sitting quietly.

"*Exodus* 21:24." Archie grinned. "Eye for eye, tooth for tooth, hand for hand, foot for foot."

"He does this," Kate said to Edgar and Hilary, "and we're supposed to know what he means."

"It means—" Archie leant in "—that your *go in there all guns blazing* plan didn't work, Kate. So now we try my plan…which will appeal to her on the very level she works at."

Hilary looked excited. "I see where you're coming from – an eye for an eye!"

"Stop being so obscure," Kate whined. "Tell me what you mean without quoting from the Bible all the time!"

"We offer this woman access to a skull she hasn't been able to get to, in exchange for Boudica," Hilary said.

"We *loan* Cora Montgomery a skull," Archie said carefully, "just until she's made a cast of it or whatever she does. And then we take it back, along with Canute and Boudica."

"You're saying we do a deal with Cora Montgomery?" said Kate.

"Yes."

"But who on earth could we give her that would induce her to part with those two skulls?" Edgar asked. "Asking her to admit to what she does – if she does it – and then give up her work…"

"Ah but she would no longer need the skulls themselves," Archie said, alive with excitement about his plan. "She would have made plaster casts and worked off them. I agree coming clean about her activities is going to be a big deal – but parting with the actual skulls, once the casts are made, won't be."

"So who, Archie?" Kate asked. "Who would you give her?"

"Relax!" Archie grinned. "I have exactly the person she'd like to get her hands on."

Forty-Three

"You are doing one hundred and three!" Kate was clutching the sides of the leather bucket seat. The speed they were travelling made the rear lights of cars they overtook look as though they were stationary on the inside lane.

"No point hanging around." Archie nevertheless eased off to ninety-five. "If *you* were driving we wouldn't have even arrived in London yet."

"So funny." Kate turned to face her window and stared into the impenetrable blackness. She had been debating whether to say something for the last thirty nerve-racking, seat-gripping miles and she hated herself for having cracked – but reporting high-speed pile-ups for the past few years left her with no desire to be involved in one.

Archie had felt the change in Kate's mood since they'd left London. The freeze had developed the further they travelled from the capital. He'd made an intentionally ham-fisted attempt to coax her out of it, *you're not having a sulk because your plan bombed are you,* but it had failed to perk her up.

The silence continued.

Somewhere between Farnborough and Basingstoke, Kate cracked. "Why won't you tell me whose head you're going to bait Cora with?"

Archie stared straight ahead. "Because if I tell you, you're going to try and stop me." He was delighted to be the one with the clever plan for a change, instead of trailing Kate to Bristol and London, following up her leads and her ideas. Now, for once, it was his chance to take the reins.

Kate let go of the seat and turned to face him. She could barely make out his features in the gloom of an unlit stretch of motorway. The ruffled blonde hair was more tousled than ever, and he was frowning hard, having to concentrate on doing ninety-four miles an hour in the dark.

He glanced at her, watching him. "I'm not going to tell you, Kate."

"Fine. Fine." She turned away, angry at the fact that he was putting himself in a superior position to her, withholding information and wielding the power, just like Dr Evil with his patronising *little Jane Austen in the making* remarks. "Don't expect me to help you."

"I really want you to help me," Archie said simply.

"Tough."

Kate was glad of the sentiment but she threw it back at him, preferring instead to remark that he'd missed the exit for Winchester and sit back and enjoy the effect it had on him.

Yes, she *was* stung that her plan had failed.

Forty-Four

"We'll leave you to it then Dean." The Director of Music and the Senior Organist stood up.

"Of course. Thank you both. Richard it is then." Archie shuffled the papers in front of him and placed the CV of Richard Danbury on top of the pile.

Mildly vexed the two musicians buckled their satchels and left the room.

The afternoon had been spent interviewing for the new position of Assistant Director of Music, Winchester Cathedral. Archie had been tempted to instigate a *good cop, bad cop* routine during the interviews and have a bit of fun with it, but the desire quickly passed and he played his role straight, surprisingly enjoying the process of interviewing and then discussing the five shortlisted applicants. It was like being the celebrity panel in a glamour-free television talent show.

Now, alone once more, Archie sat back and felt pleasurably smug. To nick off with the Associate Director of Music from York Minster was a coup indeed. He'd taken their Marketing Manager six months ago and the Director of Communications eight months ago. The two colleagues who had just left him had favoured another candidate over Richard Danbury but Archie had convinced them to go for the York Minster chap and eventually they had relented.

His smug grin didn't last long, however. He checked his phone. There were still no messages.

He'd been trying Kate's mobile all morning, wanting to talk to her about Cora. He wanted to present Cora with the bait as soon as possible and collect Canute and Boudica. OK, he'd relented in the last message to Kate: *Perhaps I should have stopped gloating quite so much and told you my idea, so please forgive me for being such a dimwit. Call me. I want Canute back and I want you back.*

The process of leaving the messages for Kate had resurrected the ghost of Angela. All the furtive messages he had left Angela, the time he had spent thinking of her, lusting after her.

He stared out of the long window and into the sunlit gardens below seeing no detail but the overall shades of browns and golds and blues from a cloudless autumnal afternoon.

It had surprised him, his capacity to effortlessly turn off his desire for Angela. To have been thinking of her as *the one*, to conjure the sense of her up, night and day, and to suddenly stop without any feeling of remorse or sadness. Any why was that? Why had he moved on?

Because of Canute? It had to be. Just by being there, and then by not being there, his waking hours were plagued by the need to find the old king and return him. He'd stopped thinking about Angela because he had no time to think about Angela – there were more pressing matters that needed resolving.

And, of course, there was Kate, the enigmatic Kate, who saw right through him. Was she part of the reason too?

He picked up his phone and pressed redial. "Kate. Stop being an arse. Call me. Call me now. I'll tell you whose head I'm planning on borrowing. Just call me. I need you – I need *your* help – I mean I need your help. Not 'I *need* you'. Just bloody call me OK? Please."

He threw the phone down on the pile of CVs and swept out of the room. She'd got to him. She'd got under his skin. Was this – whatever it was – for real, or would this too pass in the blink of an eye?

Forty-Five

If the living room was in use, which it was as Mike was watching the football, then the only real alternative was to go to the kitchen. The spare bedroom was full of car junk, their bedroom was only big enough for the bed and wardrobe, and that only left the bathroom and miniature landing.

So Kate settled down on a hard metal seat in the strip lit, laminated glare of the kitchen with Radio 4 for company: Strong Woman no longer seemed very appropriate. She hadn't listened to it for days now, not since she'd come back from London.

Bored she flicked through the back sections of the newspaper, resolutely ignoring the limp efforts from her nemesis muddying up the first pages of the paper.

To rent in central Winchester, flat, 1 bedroom, lounge, own kitchen and bathroom. No bills, broadband, furnished basement within nice family home. Available from 16 November. £475 pcm. NS.

Kate lay the paper on the table and contemplated the advert.

How nice? And what was nice – the family or the home? Or both?

She rested her head in her hands and stared at the print until it swirled and melted into as meaningless a jumble of letters as one of Lynn Paget's articles. Was living with Mike worth the saving of nearly five hundred pounds a month? And what did that make her, if she stayed here just because it covered her bed and board?

When there was a knock at the front door she knew it would be Archie. Of course she didn't want to see him, hadn't known this visit was bound to happen tonight. The fact that she was shower-fresh and dressed in her skinniest jeans and softest low-cut jumper had nothing to do with anything, especially Archie. Her feelings were mixed: anger at his not involving her in his plans when she'd involved him in hers, anger at his arrogance and...

She stood in the doorway. "Yes?"

"Kate, I'm sorry. I didn't mean to upset you." Archie stood on the front step, wrapped in a long wool coat with a college-style scarf wound tightly around his neck.

"I'm not upset," she responded, as brightly as she could.

Archie looked at her pointedly. "Anyway, are you free tonight?"

"Tonight? You're not—"

"Absolutely. Tonight's the night. Didn't you get my messages?"

"I didn't listen to them all," she lied.

"To be honest—" he hopped from one foot to the other, patting his hands at his sides to keep warm "—I'm going off the whole idea, so we either do it now or by tomorrow I'll have lost my nerve."

"You don't need me," she said flatly.

"I do. I do need you. Please Kate – you're the only person I know who can help me."

"I'm busy."

"Doing what?"

Kate searched for what she might be doing. "Stuff."

"Yeah…you're not. Come on, grab your coat. Please Kate!" he pleaded, his hands together, shooting her his best doe-eyes.

"Tell me then. Whose head?"

"Jane Austen."

She stared at him. "Jane Austen?"

"Jane Austen."

"You can't do that!"

"Why not? It's only for a very brief time, and we'll put it back."

"But—"

"We have to think of the greater good, Kate. If borrowing one head means we get three back…"

"You *cannot* take Jane Austen's head," she hissed, looking down the darkened suburban street.

"It's not ideal, I know." He was hopping on the spot, as if eager to be away. "But it's a fair enough plan."

"A fair enough plan? Archie! Think it through! Apart from anything else you know how big her grave slab is – what if you lever it up from the cathedral floor and crack it in two? How will you explain that to the Bishop?"

"I could say one of the cleaning ladies broke it when they were going at it with a mop."

"Archie it's—"

"I won't break it Kate! I've been researching like billy-o how some chaps entered a neighbouring vault a century ago and I know how they did it safely. Come on Kate. Please help me."

"Archie this is *so* wrong!"

"I know. But to fight crime you've got to become crime." He assumed a mock-martial arts pose.

"What? That doesn't even make sense." But she couldn't completely suppress a smile.

"Coat. Now. Come on. Oh, and do you have a camera?"

"Yes..." Kate looked at him warily.

"Good. Bring it with you."

Kate reluctantly took her coat from the peg, scrabbled for her phone, keys, purse and camera, and called up to Mike, *"Just going out to steal Jane Austen's head..."* before slamming the front door and accompanying Archie into the night.

"I *am* really sorry. I'm not just saying it." Archie and Kate were sitting cross-legged on the floor of Winchester Cathedral, a single beam from a torch illuminating the two large crowbars that rested on top of the grave slab in front of them. "Being cocky was obviously not the right thing to do. As the Bishop of Wessex would happily testify. So...I am trying to change. And I do want to work on this with you. I suppose," he began, "I wanted to carve out a role for myself in our investigation. It's always been led by you... you're so damned clever you didn't need me..."

"Well, if it helps," Kate sighed, "I know what you're going through at work."

"Why's that?"

"I got my first verbal warning today."

"Oh Kate!" Archie looked over at her, seeing only her

vague outline in the dark cathedral. He took out a hip flask of whisky, unscrewed the top and passed it to her. She took a sip. "Dr Evil found out about the trip to London?" he asked, while she drank.

Kate passed the hipflask back. "Lynn told him that she'd seen me go off with you to London. And when he asked me what happened..." She paused. "Well, I was an idiot. I couldn't lie."

"You told him about us stalking our suspect?"

"And the fact that we involved the police."

"You didn't?"

In the silence that followed Kate shuffled closer to Archie, pressing against him in the hope that the warmth and solidity of him would be an antidote to the awful gothic gloom surrounding her. Watching motor-racing with Mike now seemed like a wonderfully fruitful use of a Friday night.

The whisky was helping, too.

"So what did Dr Evil say?" Archie asked. He desperately wanted to put his arm around her but sensed that, being on the cusp of grave robbing Jane Austen, it wasn't the most appropriate time to make such a move.

Kate shrugged. "He just said it pained him to do it, but my behaviour lately...said I was becoming unreliable. Didn't know what was wrong with me." She laughed unsteadily. "And said if I had anything I *wanted to talk about* then there were people I could go to!"

The words melted into the cathedral's fabric and they sat in silence again. She took a long drink from the hip flask and felt the whisky hot inside her.

"There is so much to lose," Kate said softly. "If this goes wrong… I know my plan wasn't the best. But this…"

"I know."

"Is this the only real alternative we have?" she said. "I cannot believe the only course of action left to us is to dig up Jane Austen." Thinking to herself, *how did that become our only option?*

"We could abandon our search. Let Canute go," Archie offered. "That's an option."

"What about if we tried the police again? Went to them personally? Gave ourselves up, as it were? We'd risk looking stupid if we got it wrong, but surely they'd have to investigate if the Dean of Winchester got involved."

"Kate we've been through all this before…"

Kate stared at the portentous crowbars. "We could follow Cora," she mused, "properly follow her I mean. We could trail her night and day and see where she keeps her other studio with all the stolen heads in."

"If she keeps the stolen heads," Archie corrected her. "Maybe there were only bona fide heads in her studio because that's all she's got. Maybe there aren't any more."

"I bet there are more."

They sat in pitch-black silence, draining the hip flask.

"Doing this," Kate began, "you know you're as bad as she is?"

Archie stowed the empty flask in his jacket pocket. "No. I'm not. I'm only borrowing Jane. It's a matter of how you choose to look at it. My predecessors carted bits of dead saints around as holy relics: the toe of St someone, the thumb of St someone else. Digging up and using our ancestors' remains has *always* been a part of our religion. And on top of this, it's for a good cause; the cathedral. In fact," he perked up momentarily, "I am living the motto am I not? *See it for yourself. Save it for the future.* I'm letting Cora Montgomery see Jane Austen for herself, but I'm saving Jane and Canute and Boudica for the future. Come on Kate, it's such a small risk..."

"*Is it?*"

"Yes. One head. One week. That's it. And if we've got it wrong and Cora Montgomery isn't the person who stole the heads, then we simply return Jane to her grave and forget the whole thing."

"I am never, ever going to forget tonight," Kate said.

Archie was grinning in the darkness. "You're not the first woman to have said that to me."

Kate conceded a smile. "OK. OK. If I am – was – a little *Jane Austen in the making* then I suppose it's only right that I meet her."

Archie stood up and walked over to the grave slab. "First things first, can I have your camera?" He quickly took a photograph of the untouched grave slab and handed it back. "Can you take photos of my progress?"

"For the papers?" Kate said lightly.

"I think not." Archie returned to the grave slab. "I imagine our head thief will want proof that we're offering her the genuine article. Now then—" he tapped a fist-sized stone beside the large grey ledger "—this is our way in. if I can just lever it up..."

In the light of her shaking lantern Kate watched as he set about prising up the grave slab. The rasp of metal crowbar against stone, and the crunch of stone breaking free from its mortar, cut through the heavy silence of Winchester Cathedral. Kate resolutely kept her focus on Archie and the task in hand, shutting out the impenetrable gloom around her.

With the cheery enthusiasm of a celebrity gardener attacking overgrown herbaceous borders Archie bent to his task, prising up the stones surrounding the ledger and then moving to the ledger itself.

He worked quickly, easing up the grave slab with two crowbars at each edge, the heavy stone grinding against the floor as it moved aside, inch by inch.

"Has the tomb collapsed in?" Kate asked when Archie had moved the thick slab full across leaving nothing but rubble underneath. She half expected to see a skeleton hand pushing through the gaps between the stones, in the manner of one of Mike's horror films, clawing its way to the surface to slap the face of the man who disturbed it. Kate took out her camera and photographed the rubble beside the ledger.

"Can you pass me the buckets?" Archie interrupted her thoughts.

She placed them beside the rubble and Archie began to fill them. Kate debated whether she should help him but, fearing the hand, she contented herself with holding the lantern.

"Is she mixed up in these stones?" she asked.

"Ha! No! We'd have treated her better than this: we don't make our residents part of the foundations. This is just infill. If it's the same set-up as another tomb excavated just east of here, there'll be a dome of a brick vault appearing soon."

As predicted within a few minutes the crown of a dome began to appear, small red bricks mortared close together. Archie moved the buckets aside and sat on the cathedral floor, his feet resting on the brick vault roof below.

"If you start to pick apart the brickwork of the vault roof," Kate began, taking a photograph of the newly exposed vault roof as she talked, "won't it collapse in on itself?"

"Ye-es," Archie said.

"What happened in the other grave they excavated?"

"It collapsed in on itself."

"Ah. So how are you going to repair it, once it's collapsed? You aren't going to be able to brick it up again?"

"Wooden planks," Archie said, leaning over and testing the key stone. His confidence took Kate by surprise.

"You can't plank up Jane Austen's tomb!"

"Why not? It'll hold fine, and it's not going to be excavated in my lifetime."

Kate conceded. "Do you want me to do anything?"

"You just keep the light shining on the vault here."

"Sure."

Archie took a deep breath and, with the corner of the smaller crow bar, he began to dislodge the key stone from the top of the vault roof. Kate watched with a mixture of fascination and horror as one by one the small red bricks loosened and carefully Archie lifted them away, stacking them on the cathedral floor.

From the space beneath came a damp, rotten tang that turned their stomachs. Kate put her hand to her mouth and focused on breathing smoothly. Throwing up over Jane Austen would be unforgivable.

After a quarter of an hour spent loosening and removing bricks, the vault opening was wide enough to allow Archie access, and the remaining bricks at a shallow enough angle to be stable. Only three bricks had fallen into the tomb itself, each time Archie shining his torch in, and each time giving Kate the thumbs up.

He eased himself up and, putting aside the crowbars, walked over to Kate.

"You OK?"

She nodded. "I want to help you," she said, "but I don't think I can."

"That's fine. You're helping just by being here." Kate couldn't see his expression but she heard a new tone in his voice.

"Do you want to see inside?" he said quietly.

She pursed her lips together, looking over at the open vault. So far she'd resisted looking inside, preferring to sit at the edge and pretend to herself that *this wasn't really happening*.

"Come on, it's not that bad down there," he said.

Kate knew that, in years to come, she would regret it if she didn't take this opportunity. But at that moment the thought of staring into a stinking hole of death in a gloomy cathedral didn't much qualify as an *opportunity*.

But to see where Jane Austen was buried. *Jane Austen.*

She stood up and smoothed herself down.

"OK."

He led her over to the edge of the vault and he sat with

her, shining the torch downwards.

"Ready?"

"Ready."

She looked inside.

In the light of the still-trembling lantern Kate could make out, six feet or so below, a long grey coffin-shaped mass resting on a floor of rough loose stone.

"Oh my God." She put her hand to her mouth. "Jane Austen is in there…"

"I bloody well hope so." Archie wiped the sweat from his brow.

Less horrified and more curious now Kate lay down with her stomach on the cold floor. Shuffling towards the hole she peered into the gaping vault, taking the torch off Archie and directing the beam onto the coffin.

"It's really hard to make out," she said, "the coffin looks kind of odd."

Archie lay beside her on the floor. "It's what you'd expect to see," he said, "she would have been buried in a wooden coffin with a lead casing. But the wood's nearly all rotted away, leaving just the lead, which has collapsed under its own weight. Can you see there?" He gently enclosed Kate's hand holding the torch with his own, directing the beam to the wider end of the coffin. "That's the impression of her skull showing through the lead."

"What?" Kate stared in horror.

"Lead flows over time, didn't they teach you that at school? Now that the wood's disintegrated the lead covering has dropped and moulded itself over her body like a thick blanket."

"Urgh! That's vile! So how are you going to do what you have to do if she's covered in a lead blanket?"

Archie reached across her and picked up a sharp-toothed saw.

Kate stared wordlessly at him.

He grinned.

"You still think we should do this?" Kate asked.

"Yes. Definitely. More than ever now."

"And you don't have any reservations? As a man of the cloth?"

"Yes. But not enough."

As he went to fetch the ladder Kate leant over the vault and took a photograph of its resident. "Sorry," she whispered.

Perhaps, Kate thought later, she should have gone with him down into the vault after all. Because the appalling noises coming up from the hole were made all the more terrible by her not knowing what they were. The thumping, sawing, and grating as Archie did what he had to do. A crack of what could be wood. Or bone. The scuff of trainers. A long drawn-out creak. And then, Archie's *Urgh! URGH! Oh dear God!* Followed by the stink of decay billowing up and assaulting her. It was a hundred times worse than the smell when the vault had been opened. Kate scrambled back. From below she could hear the echoey click of the camera capturing the dreadful scene. Thank goodness she hadn't brought her film camera along. Boots would have had a few things to say when they got round to developing the pictures.

The gasping and moaning continued. And then she could hear the rustle of plastic bags, *Right then...oh oooooooooh ewwwww*, and then finally the sound of his feet on the ladder.

"Don't tell me." She helped him out of the vault, gagging at the stink of decay on his clothes. "Don't ever tell me."

"Kate." He stood up and took a deep breath of putrid air. "That was the single worst experience of my life."

Kate laughed, despite the horror. "Would I be surprised at how many women say that to you?"

Half an hour on and the ledger slab had been ground back into place and the two small flagstones returned to their spaces beside the slab. Kate swept the mortar rubble into the gaps between the flags. Contemplating the scene in the dim light, neither could tell the grave had been tampered with.

"Ready?" Archie held up the lantern to look into Kate's eyes.

"I am so ready to get out of here." She couldn't take her eyes off the head-filled bag slung over his shoulder. "Here, let me." She took the dustpan and bucket, leaving him the crowbars and saw. They walked towards the staff entrance and Archie held open the door while she moved to go past him.

"Hello Archie."

Archie and Kate froze.

"Cedric!"

"Don't bother locking up." The Archdeacon bustled past them. "Forgot my Tupperware sandwich box would you believe! The Mrs wasn't best pleased because that means it stays in the cathedral all weekend and I'd have nothing to take my sandwiches in on Monday. Don't like using foil. And we don't have much in the house anyway. So I've come to get it now, before I forget. Again!" He chuckled to himself.

Archie stared at him, two crowbars and a saw held aloft, a skull-shaped lump in the bag over his shoulder. "Right-o," he managed.

"I'll lock up when I've left. Don't you worry about that!" the Archdeacon rattled on. "Good evening to you both. See you on Monday Archie, nice to see you again Miss. Oh, excuse me," he added, knocking in to Kate's bucket.

With a wave of his hand he bumbled through the narrow doorway and disappeared into the south transept oblivious to their accessories or the unusual smell about the place.

They stared after him. A moment later and Kate felt Archie tug her hand and she obediently followed him out into the Slype, over to the deanery, the icy cold drizzle lit up in the glow of the newly repaired cathedral lanterns. In silence they crunched across the gravel, glad to feel the cold mists of rain on their faces and the wind blowing away the stink of the tomb.

At the door Archie fished around in his pocket for the key.

"Do you think he suspected anything?" Kate whispered, looking back at the cathedral and seeing the glow of faint light from the high windows in the south transept.

"I have no idea." Archie opened the door and stood aside to let her in. "Let me put her safe and get these tools out of the way. And then can I get you a drink?"

"Yes." She followed him inside. "Two. No – wait – three."

Forty-Six

"Parmesan?"

"Yes, please." Edgar sat back and the waiter had some kind of fit over his dinner, covering it in a mound of cheese. "Lovely. Thanks."

"Sir? Madam?"

"Oh, no thanks." His parents grabbed their bowls.

"A toast to our beloved son!" Edgar's mother held up her glass of sparkling wine.

"So… Eddie, my boy—" his father tucked into the business of his dinner "—what's the mood down at the museum?"

Edgar was focused on snow-ploughing his way to the pasta layer. "It's good."

"Good? Hear that Brenda? They dig up Boudica and her army and the mood is 'good'!"

"I saw you on the news yesterday evening," his mother beamed, "I am – well, *we* are so proud of you! The BBC no less! And you looked so nice in your suit and tie. I recorded it too so you can watch it."

"I thought Hills De Lacey looked tired," his father added. "Are they working her hard Eddie?"

"I think it must be a strain on her," Edgar conceded.

"And how is the pressure on you dear? Are you able to cope?" his mother asked.

"Kind of. Fewer phone calls which is the main thing. And

I know what I'm talking about when they ask questions, so that's good. But there are other problems..." He bit his lip. Why did he have to go that far?

"Such as?" His father looked up, on the alert.

"Oh you know, Dad...the usual stuff I'm sure. You must have a whole list of the kind of things that can go wrong with archaeological dig sites..." The sentence hung in the air, Edgar looking expectantly at his father across the table.

"Oh God, yes! There was this one time..."

It worked! His father had been given free rein to launch into his favourite subject: *digs I have managed*, reeling off the same hackneyed tales Edgar had heard a hundred times before: *There was a terrible moment on the Sutton Hoo dig... I remember up in Shetland we'd just uncovered a hearth stone when it began to snow a blizzard... I remember once a dig we held in a field near Ely Cathedral...*

Happily, Edgar nodded along and ate from the lower food-layer in his bowl, feeling not unlike an archaeologist himself as he brushed back the more recent parmesan layers.

"Is that your phone dear?" His mother was looking at him.

"What, Mum?" Edgar hadn't even noticed it ringing. He'd been preoccupied with recalling the vision of Scandinavians in bikinis. "Oh. It's the work mobile. I didn't think I'd brought it. Sorry – do you mind if I answer it?"

"Go ahead son. It's late, so it's important business..." His father begrudgingly accepted his son's position.

"Hello? Yes? *What?* What? W-who? *Say that again!*"

His mother maintained an air of polite detachment and

focused on her meal while his father gripped his cutlery in a bid not to tear the phone out of his son's hands and insist on knowing what was happening.

"What do you think that's all about Brenda?" his father demanded the minute Edgar had left the table and briskly walked outside to take the rest of the call.

"You'd have a much better idea than me I'm sure dear."

"Sounds like trouble. Sounds like they found someone else on site. Maybe a Roman chappie. Who was the one that fought Boudica? Maybe they found him too?"

"Hadrian dear? Caesar?"

"Don't be daft woman. Eddie – everything all right? Do you need my help?"

Edgar returned to the table, as pale as his parmesan cheese. He sat down and stared at his bowl.

"I'm fine," he managed eventually.

"Who was it, love?" His mother laid a hand on his.

He looked her in the eye. "It was the Dean of Winchester."

"That's nice dear."

"What on earth did he want?"

"Just a chat…nothing really. You know…see how things are going."

"How nice." His mother dabbed her mouth with her napkin. "You have some very important friends my love. We're so proud of you."

"See him much, son?"

"I'll see him this weekend as a matter of fact," Edgar answered, pushing his plate away. The knowledge that he was going to be at a café with the remains of Jane Austen that weekend had stripped him of his appetite.

Forty-Seven

"He's on for next Saturday," Archie said, entering the drawing room with a spring in his step and flopping down on the deep arm chair opposite Kate's. He reached over to the side table and poured out a glass of wine. His blond hair was shining wet, dripping onto his fresh shirt.

In the fifteen minutes that he had been out of the room, having a shower and making the phone call, Kate had let herself gradually unknot, the awful remembrance of the tomb and the deathly dark cathedral burning away in the heat of the fire and the glow that came from a very large glass of wine after many fortifying sips of whisky. She was staring into the fire now, watching the flames lick the blackening glass of the wood burner.

Archie looked at Kate across the dimly lit room. She was beautiful tonight, thawed by the fire she had rosy cheeks and plump red lips, her usually neat hair haphazard around her face. She looked over to him to say something and he hastily looked away.

"Who's on for next Saturday?" she said. "The man from the Museum of London?"

Archie nodded, and when he spoke his voice was hoarse, "I just called him to check." He paused for a sip of wine. "And he's going to bring that professor with him, in case Cora Montgomery tries to fob us off with the wrong skulls when we do the swap."

"Good idea." Kate had drifted off to watch the flames again.

"He sounded pretty horrified by the whole thing, when I told him what I'd done," Archie continued, sipping more wine, watching Kate's stockinged foot as it unconsciously tapped up and down. "I thought he was right behind us with the use of a lure."

Kate looked up sharply, the spell broken. "Well it *is* really horrifying Archie." She couldn't believe he wasn't able to comprehend the situation.

He was momentarily taken aback. "But he said he agreed with the idea."

Kate gave a short laugh. "Agreeing in principle is one thing. Condoning the actual act is another. What we did tonight..." She paused and shivered at the recollection. "It was really dreadful."

"It wasn't that bad," Archie defended himself. "I'll put it back."

"It *was* really awful Archie."

"I thought you agreed with me," he said, a nagging doubt beginning to form now that the two people who were in on the secret had reacted in the same horrified manner.

"You never involved me in the idea. You excluded me, and I was unprepared when you asked me to take part earlier this evening. I should never have come with you. I don't know what I was thinking." Anxious bitterness at his behaviour was creeping up on her again.

"Admit it, you were bored," he said. "And I gave you some excitement."

Kate stood up, incensed at his self-belief. "I ought to get back."

Archie came back down to earth. This wasn't how it was supposed to end. "I'll walk you," he said.

"Really, there's no need," she muttered walking to the door.

"I want to," he said gently, taking her coat down from the peg and helping her on with it.

"I'm a big girl you know. I can look after myself." She mis-buttoned her coat and, looking down, laughed at her own incapacity. "Dammit!"

"Here." Archie buttoned her up and flung on his own coat, grabbing a large umbrella from the stand. "There are all sorts of strange people wandering the streets of Winchester late at night," he added, holding the door open for her.

"Exactly." She stepped out into the rain, accepting the offered arm around her waist, pulling her close to him underneath the umbrella. "And I don't think it's a good idea to be walking with one."

He squeezed her waist.

"I am sorry, Kate. I'm sorry that I didn't tell you about the plan. And I am sorry I gloated over it. I didn't think about how you would feel."

"It's OK. It's fine. I'm just tired."

They walked back to her boyfriend's house without another word, both enjoying the feel of the other's body pressed close to them, huddled against the rain.

Forty-Eight

"How about this?" Archie was saying, "*We have something you greatly desire. Meet us at Zita's Café, Pentonville Terrace on Sunday 11th at 3pm.*"

It was a Saturday morning and draped over a leather sofa in the cathedral's coffee shop Archie and Kate talked through their next course of action, the horror of the night before sufficiently dimmed for them to talk freely about it now.

Kate considered Archie's words for a moment. "I thought you told that chap from the Museum of London that we'd meet at two o'clock in the café."

"I did. We meet him first and Cora can come later. We have to make sure we're all in agreement about our plan. That will give us time to—"

"Fine. In that case, the information's OK but the note doesn't really do it for me."

"OK then. You're the journalist. What would do it for you?"

"What about that eye for an eye quotation you said the other day? *An eye for an eye, meet up at Zita's Café, Pentonville Terrace, on Sunday 11th at 3pm.*"

"It's vague though isn't it? It doesn't tell her who we have: seeing as we've gone to the trouble of getting who we've got then I think we should brag about it."

"How about, *We have Jane Austen. Come and get her?*"

"Yeah I really like that." Archie rolled his eyes. "We can just write it up on the postcard and when the Royal Mail read it we can all go to prison and live happily every after. We need more coffee."

He wandered over to the counter to join the queue and Kate bent down to her notepad and scribbled furiously, determined to be the one to come up with the winning ransom note. She was a journalist – so what that it was for a mediocre regional newspaper – this is what she did. She would not be literarily beaten by him: she would come up with the best note with which to lure their target. Writing, rewriting, scribbling out, staring into space and then hurriedly writing more, Kate didn't notice that Archie kept glancing in her direction, amused at the determination written across her face.

"Go on then, what have you got?" He came over with the drinks, seeing her eager *me sir, me sir* face.

She grinned and read out, quietly, "*It is a truth universally acknowledged that a single man in possession of a head must be in want of someone like you. How about a deal? Zita's café, Pentonville Terrace, on Sunday 11th at 3pm.*"

"That's it!" He laughed. "It's perfect." He leant over, cupped her face in his hands and kissed her full on the lips regardless of the cathedral café's watching staff. "You *are* a little Jane Austen in the making."

Kate forgot to be angry and, putting her forehead to his, whispered, "Does that mean we have it?"

"We have it," he said and pulled her to him once more.

Forty-Nine

"So, your boyfriend..." Archie looked over to Kate, sitting beside him in the car as they travelled up to London at a sedate 70mph. He'd wanted to bring up the subject before, but now she was a captive audience it seemed an opportune moment.

"Mike?"

"Yes. What's the story with Mike?" His lips were raw from kissing her and hers, he saw, were just as red.

He'd never been a big fan of kissing in the past because, really, when it boiled down to it, wasn't it just a means to an end. But here he was, wanting more than anything to pull over and then pull her over and kiss her like he had been doing all morning.

"I don't know," Kate said wistfully, "he's a nice guy and everything..." She found herself saying the words without thinking them through: it was more because that was what she was expected to say, rather than what she meant to say.

"Is he?" Archie briefly turned to face her.

"No," she admitted. "He's not that nice a guy."

"Would you leave him?" The words hung in the air.

"I've been looking at flats," she said. "House shares. That sort of thing. But there's so much going on with this story. And...you know." She tailed off.

Archie grinned and nodded.

"What about you? Anyone…you know…special?" Kate asked. Would there turn out to be a Lust-Red-nail-varnish-wearing beauty tucked away in some cathedral cupboard?

"No. There was. I thought so, anyway. But she turned out not to be. So she can't have been very special in the first place. To be perfectly honest with you," he said, "I don't think I've much experience of someone special. Anyway do we have an agenda for today? Do we have each hour planned and timetabled to perfection?"

"Actually there is no plan. Unless you can count *winging it* as a plan. In which case we are right on-plan."

"Jolly good. And how are you feeling about said lack of plan?"

"Pretty bad," she admitted. "But at least I resisted making one."

"Yes, well done you. Zita's café 3pm and then what will be will be."

"I hope it works," she said, checking that Jane Austen was still strapped in to the back seat.

"So do I! I'd be gutted if I'd gone through that wretched evening all for nothing."

"Well it wasn't *all* wretched was it?"

"No. Not all bad."

"Hey!" Kate snapped out of staring moonily out of the window. "Did that old man we saw at the cathedral say anything about seeing us?"

"Not one word. Cedric is completely harmless so I wouldn't expect him to report us to anyone, but the only risk is he might drop us in it unintentionally."

"Still – none of it will matter once we return victorious with Canute – and Jane," Kate said. But somehow the bright and confident words, once spoken, made their aspirations seem improbably unattainable.

Neither had considered the possibility of returning to Winchester empty-handed.

"Have you thought," Kate asked, "how we're going to explain how we came about finding Canute's head? We can't turn up and say *Tada! we found him*, without saying where and how."

"Not really. All I could come up with was to say we found him in a bush or something…" He caught Kate's expression. "OK, OK, I know it's lame. So what have you come up with then?" he said, steeling himself.

"Well…" Kate settled back in her seat, "I have been giving it some thought and there is somewhere we could explore. When the story of the break-in at the cathedral took place, it was at the same time as another story made the headlines in Winchester. An entire family were found dead in a remote farm."

"I did a sermon building that in! The Pit Close murders."

"Exactly! And while there were all sorts of stories of odd rituals with satanic elements, the real horror of the place was never made public."

"Satanists!" Archie spat the word out. They were a sect he would never be inviting onto the interfaith football pitch.

"I could go along to the site on the pretext of 'following up a hunch' and then I could 'find' the skull."

"In a bush?" Archie added, hopefully.

"Perfect."

"Sounds like a good plan Kate! I like it." He gave her a saucy smile and he would have attempted to kiss her had he not been travelling at about a hundred and negotiating his way past a stubborn Porsche.

Fifty

"What *is* that smell?" Edgar crinkled up his nose.

"It's Jane Austen," Archie whispered across the table.

Kate burst out laughing. "This is *not* a conversation I ever thought I would hear." Until that point the conversation around the table had been tense and formal, but the malodorous Jane Austen had broken down the barriers.

"I was going to ask you if I could take a look at her," said Hilary De Lacey, staring at the rucksack beside Archie's chair, "but I think I'll pass."

"Well I didn't want to clean her," Archie began. "So I put a couple of carriers around her, but I suppose it's not enough."

"Oooh." Kate wiped the tears away from her eyes. "I know I'm laughing, but it's so bizarre. To think we're in a café in Kings Cross, drinking coffee with the woman who wrote *Pride and Prejudice* on a chair at our table."

Despite joining in their laughter Edgar looked the least comfortable with the situation, unable to stop looking at the ominous head-filled bag.

"I tell you what," Archie said, finishing his coffee, "before I went down in the vault to get her, I thought that this head-stealing business was eccentric but I could understand the appeal. But having done the deed I couldn't do it again. There is no way that the opportunity to see a famous person from the past is worth the horror of manhandling what remains of them."

"I thought you said it wasn't so bad? And it was borrowing a relic. You made it sound like it wasn't a big deal," Kate retorted.

"Overall I'd say that. But the actual process of getting into the coffin and getting the object out," he said euphemistically, "*that* was bloody awful. And I don't understand how anyone, least of all a dainty little thing like Cora Montgomery appears to be, could choose to do such a thing."

"I can imagine it must have been unpleasant," said Hilary, with a great deal of knowledge, "but presumably you're going to have to go through it again to put her back."

"Yes," Archie sighed, "but at least I'll know what to expect. And it won't take as long. There won't be any sawing or wrenching."

Edgar turned pale and began to fiddle with the sugar bowl.

"She must be so sick to choose to do what she does," Kate said.

"I don't know," Hilary said wistfully. "It's just a job to her isn't it? I've been an archaeologist for thirty years, and to me, now, a body is just a specimen. Skulls and grave goods and weapons are no more than inanimate objects in my working day, like biros or calculators. I imagine your facial reconstruction expert has lived and breathed this kind of horror for years and is anaesthetised to it."

Kate looked doubtful, but Archie was nodding.

"I can certainly see the appeal," Hilary added. "To have

the skills to recreate the appearance of a lost person. I would love to know what Jane Austen looked like."

"Well at least we know what she smells like," Edgar said, eyeballing the bag.

"I wonder who else she's got hidden away," Kate was saying. "If we know she's got Canute and Boudica, then who's to say she hasn't amassed an enormous collection of the famous dead?" Kate and Hilary launched into a discussion on who else could have had their heads stolen, with Edgar making occasional half-hearted attempts to join in. Conspiring with criminals, however high up in the Church of England, was not something he felt comfortable with.

Archie, meanwhile, had dipped out of the conversation, choosing instead to stare out of the window and down the street. She should be here by now, he knew, and the possibility of failure was increasing minute by minute.

The café was situated on a busy side-street off the Euston Road, midway between the stations and Battlebridge Crescent. It must have been near to a university or college as groups of students were milling around: and a surprisingly high volume of them had bright red hair. Every time Archie saw a redhead his heart would leap, until they drew nearer and he realised it was just another pale undernourished student, and not Cora Montgomery.

As a rowdy group moved off from outside the front of the café Archie could see, in the distance, a figure approaching from the direction of Battlebridge Crescent. The person was slowly making their way in the direction of the café. A petite figure, dressed in a long, dark coat and with a shock of red hair rippling behind her.

Archie, with a calmness he did not feel, put his hand up to stop the others mid-conversation.

"She's coming," he said.

Kate, Edgar and Hilary stopped immediately and turned to follow Archie's line of sight.

Cora Montgomery was making her way to Zita's Café.

Archie stood up. "I should go out and meet her." His voice betrayed his nervousness.

"Why?" Kate asked.

"Because there's four of us and one of her..."

"Five actually. Don't forget Jane," Edgar said.

"I ought to go and explain who we are. Why we're here. That we're not the police."

"But she works with the police," Hilary said, "that wouldn't worry her."

"Are you going to tell her I'm a journalist?" Kate asked.

But Archie was walking away, past the tightly packed tables and out of the door. Hilary, Edgar and Kate watched from their table as Archie approached the woman. She recognised him, Kate could tell by the way she looked at him. And she wasn't surprised to see him either, she noted. She looked wary, Kate thought, which, given the circumstances, was understandable. Because, however it was presented, what they were attempting to do came down to blackmail and right now, outside Zita's Café, the Dean of Winchester was setting out what was at stake: what they knew, what they could do if they wished to, and what they wanted from her. Kate looked on as the inaudible conversation played out, trying to read the measure of its success or failure on the faces of Cora and Archie.

"She looks nervous," Edgar said.

"She looks interested," Kate added.

"I think we should leave them to it." Hilary turned from the window and toyed with the empty plate before her. "We don't want to unnerve her at this stage by staring at her."

"Someone who digs up the skulls of the dead is not going to be unnerved by three live people staring at her," Kate said, frowning as Cora laughed out loud and laid a hand on Archie's arm. But dutifully she turned away.

"Is he ever going to bring her in here?" Kate looked over at the laughing couple on the pavement. They looked like they were on a date, she thought, enjoying the first flush of love. They certainly did not look like the grave robbers that they were, striking a deal over the heads of the dead.

Edgar's phone went off and Hilary and Kate leapt in their seats, surprised at their own jitters.

"Sorry." He opened it up and read the text that had come in. *So proud darling. Just read* The Times. *Marvellous picture of you and others. Mum xx*

"Edgar..." Hilary motioned for him to put the phone away. Archie was bringing Cora inside.

They watched as he led her across the room. She walked sedately, picking her way through the maze of chairs and tables, unwinding a long pale scarf from around her neck. They stopped at the counter to order a drink, laughing, talking and then continued on to the table by the window where the other three were waiting. Edgar with a sense of dread, Hilary in eager anticipation and Kate entertaining the green-eyed monster.

"Hi," Cora smiled nervously at them. For the first time Kate had a good look at the woman who had occupied so much of her waking thoughts in recent weeks. Cora was older than she had first thought: maybe mid-forties, with faint lines around her mouth and eyes. But she was still beautiful, with those big doe eyes that looked to Archie for reassurance now. And she was impeccably dressed: smart but not staid.

"Here." Archie pulled out his chair for her. "Take my chair."

Kate gritted her teeth. He might have said *take me* given how it made her feel, she was shocked at the violence of her reaction to this woman flirting with the man who had not been able to stop kissing her just hours earlier.

Archie introduced them and, waiting while Zita delivered the drinks, began, "This is Kate, who's been working with me—" he winked at her "—and Edgar and Hilary from the Museum of London." Cora nodded at them, pausing momentarily at Kate who was glad to have been groomed and well-dressed, now that she was so obviously under inspection. The old Kate with her shapeless clothes and lanky hair would have withered in shame before her well-turned-out examiner.

"I've already taken Cora through how we came to be here," Archie continued. "Canute. Boudica. And I also explained," he added, quickly, "that we're not interested in the moral or legal implications of what's happened."

Cora stirred her tea, squeezing the bag against the side of the cup and placing it carefully in Archie's empty cup. Kate tried not to read anything in to the action, but having taken a degree in English Literature she'd come to understand that everything was portentous.

Cora looked up at their politely expectant faces and said, "I'm not proud of the fact I take what I do."

Nobody said anything to this, what – after all – could be said. Cora bent and took a sip of tea before replacing the cup on the saucer.

"It started," she said, in a voice barely above a whisper, "with Mary Ann Evans."

"Who?" asked Edgar.

"A colleague?" said Archie.

Kate, looking straight at Cora across the table said simply, "George Eliot." *So there* were *more heads*.

Cora nodded.

"Who?" Edgar struggled to keep up and Hilary whispered a quick explanation as Cora launched in to the story Kate and Archie were eager to hear.

"The body of a young man was found badly burnt in a cemetery a few years ago," Cora began, "and the Metropolitan Police Force called me in to do a reconstruction. There was no other way we could get an identity. I went to photograph the body in situ." She took a genteel sip of tea. "It was at Highgate Cemetary in North London. The man was lying next to a steep bank of trees covered in ivy, he'd been hidden there for months and no-one had noticed."

Kate winced.

"Well, anyway, I took my photographs, wrote up notes, and when I'd finished I saw that I was right next to the grave of George Eliot. And when I looked more closely I saw that there was a wide gap opening up between the slab of the grave marker and the earth. Anyway, she was, is, a heroine of mine. And I remember standing there and thinking, wouldn't it be wonderful to be able to see her for myself…"

"So you dug up her up?" Kate said with a trace of irony.

"I did. There area was so overgrown that it was easy to cover my tracks."

"And you modelled her?" Hilary asked.

"I did. And more than anything it shocked me."

"Why?" Archie asked.

"It wasn't so much her appearance that shocked me," Cora began, "I suppose it was my reaction to her appearance that shocked me. You build up a mental image of a person, an impression, based on in her case grainy photographs, paintings, descriptions. But to see her as she was, it moved me. It's like having a penpal for years and then all of a sudden meeting them and they look like Veronica Lake."

"And did George Eliot look like Veronica Lake?" asked Archie.

"Oh no! She was really quite unattractive."

"*Who*," said Edgar, "is Veronica Lake?"

"Oh Edgar!" Hilary lay a hand on his shoulder. "You need to brush up on your Arts and Literature if you ever want to be in with a chance at Trivial Pursuit."

"Anyway," Cora continued," I returned her skull. I always do. Nearly always." She looked at Archie. "But I couldn't in your case – you discovered King Canute was missing and there was a photofit of me. I could never go back. I knew when I bumped into you that night that my break-in would make the newspapers: I read about it online. I must say your photofit was very flattering."

"Well," Archie shrugged, "it was the best description I could come up with for the police artist. It was dark and you pushed me to the ground. How was I to get a picture of you?"

"I'm sorry." She bowed her head and went back to stirring her tea. "I'm sorry I pushed you. And I'm sorry that I caused you trouble. All of you." She looked at the others.

"You do still have him," Archie suddenly asked, "Canute?"

"Oh yes."

"And...you made him up?"

She smiled. "Yes."

Archie was speechless and sat, gripping the edges of the table.

Suddenly it was too much for the others: *what does he look like, why Canute, what about Boudica, who else do you have?*

"Perhaps," Cora said quietly, cutting into the questions, "you'd like to come over to the studio?"

"Can we?" Edgar gaped.

"And am I right in thinking—" Cora looked to Archie and then down at the bag on the chair beside his chair "—that is Jane Austen for me?" Her lips were pursed in a smile.

Archie nodded. "On loan," he said and fishing in to the front of the bag he pulled out a brown envelope and handed it to Cora. Frowning she opened it and flicked through the photographs that had been taken during the night they exhumed Jane Austen. Edgar, craning his neck to see, soon wished he hadn't. Hilary wisely didn't ask. Thirty years' experience had taken away her desire to know more than she already did.

Putting the photographs onto the table Cora carefully picked up the bag and tested its weight. "With jawbone?"

"Yes."

Cora looked around the table, taking in the anxious looks from her audience. "I understand what you're offering me, and I also understand the position I'm in, having been found out, so to speak. But that doesn't mean you can call all the shots. Yes I'll take you to my studio but I don't want to see anything about me or my work in the press." She looked at Kate.

"I know!" Kate said, "I know. You're asking a journalist to give up the most incredible career-making scoop." She laughed. "And I will. I'm in it with Archie anyway; I was seen leaving the cathedral with him the night we took Jane Austen. I'm as guilty as he is. There's too much to lose if I did shop you."

Cora considered her. "But you did shop me didn't you? I saw you, saw you both," she added, looking to Archie, "hiding in the park outside my house when the police came round to my house last week. I know what you did."

Kate looked to Archie.

"I agree with you though," Cora said. "Your involvement in the Jane Austen theft is probably my security that you're not going to the police again."

"I won't," Kate said simply.

"And if I give you back Canute—" she looked to Archie now "—and you announce that you've found him – what will you tell people? They'll want an explanation."

"We've already thought of that," Kate interrupted. "There

was a murder of a family in a placed called Pit Close Farm near Winchester and we could say we found the skull near the house. We'd pin the blame on people who are dead. The police have found all sorts of weird things happened in that farmhouse so this wouldn't be that incredible."

"I would say that I'd regularly seen the farmer at the cathedral leading up to the murders. And that he asked me about Canute a lot. See?" Archie grinned. "We've thought of everything."

Cora nodded. "And you?" She turned to Edgar and Hilary.

"We can't possibly own up to having lost Boudica's skull," Hilary added *sotto voce*. "The Museum of London would lose face and there would be a lot of painful questions to answer."

"And anyway, we all want an easy life," Edgar added, "so please can we go now?"

"My studio is in the garden. As you probably know..." Cora shot Archie a look as they walked through the hallway of 32 Battlebridge Crescent.

Archie grinned and looked to Kate who was walking close beside him. She looked away, turning red. She did not feel proud to have been caught snooping around Cora's property.

"This is not what I imagined," Edgar whispered to Hilary as they followed Kate and Archie through the house.

"What did you imagine?" she whispered back.

Edgar contemplated the luxurious furnishings. "Cobwebs and horror," he said.

"Well, we may yet find that." Hilary gestured before them. They had left the bright and airy conservatory and were out in a tumbledown garden, at the end of which, hidden behind rambling overgrown bushes and sheets of dark hanging ivy, was the derelict outhouse Kate and Archie had seen from the alley.

Edgar shot Hilary a *that's more like it* look.

Kate steeled herself for what lay behind the shabby wooden door. The unpublished photographs of the Pit Close murders back in Winchester had been circulated around the office. The true horror had come from the seemingly super-normal backdrop of a family home that had played host to the most gruesome horrors. She had the uncomfortable feeling that this could turn out to be the same. This neat and presentable woman, so well regarded in her professional field, returning each night to her gruesome secret life.

Carefully Cora unlocked the door to the shabby outbuilding with three keys, pushing it open and stepping inside. The others followed, fanning out into the room. In sharp contrast to the exterior, the interior was spotlessly clean and bright. The desk that blocked the alleyway door was neat and orderly with paperwork in a tray, a clay bust pegged out on the table and other completed heads on shelves around the room.

"Police work," she said, "and some university work too."

To Kate and Archie, who had already seen the work of a reconstruction artist, the sight before them was nothing new. But for Edgar and Hilary it was a vivid new horror and delight. They stared at the partially reconstructed head, marvelling at the disturbing sight of sockets filled with glass eyes and the grin of partially fleshed out jaws.

"So if these are all legitimate…" Kate said into the silence.

Cora smiled and, turning, unlocked a metal cabinet set in the shelves. It was no taller than five feet, very narrow and seeing it made Kate's heart drop: she had let her imagination run away with her, thinking that there would be hundreds of skulls of the famous dead, but a cabinet so small could only hold a handful. Still…

Cora opened it and the four, on tenterhooks, looked inside.

It was practically empty. All it contained were three metal shelves with two boxes and a few papers.

Cora reached up and pulled down a tambour front which clicked in to place at the bottom, sealing off the shelves. She then crouched down and gently took away a metal strip which disguised the bottom of the shelves, revealing that the cabinet was on casters and it was actually a separate piece of furniture to the metal shelving unit. Now that the cabinet and its contents were secured she reached in and pulled the unit towards her; it rolled effortlessly forward and behind it, the four saw a doorway into what must have been the outbuilding in the garden next door.

"I bought this studio off my neighbours," Cora said. "They moved to Boston about five years ago and they let the house out, so I'm never troubled. Come in."

Hilary and Edgar, morbidly curious, followed her through the narrow doorway, leaving Kate and Archie waiting behind. Archie took a step to her and kissed her.

"I haven't done that for a while, and I've missed it," he grinned, putting an arm around her.

"Well maybe I should have written up a timetable then." She pulled him towards her again. "And that way I could have ensured—"

"Are you two coming in?" Cora poked her head through the doorway.

"Yes. Sorry..."

Sheepishly they went to join the others.

There were heads. Everywhere.

There were heads on an old wooden table in the middle of the studio, on the floor, on the shelving beside them. Pale clay faces, watching them with their glass eyes which winked in the sun streaming in through the vast skylights.

Kate shuddered and stepped back. The scale of it was overwhelming. Archie was frozen, a hand to his mouth while Hilary and Edgar looked at each other, each hoping the other would say something, anything to somehow normalise the sight before them.

Slowly Kate made her way to the nearest bust on the table, its face full towards her. She reached out gingerly and touched the top of the head, feeling the cool rough hardness of the clay moulded into the shape and flow of hair. The bust was of a striking woman with a small snub nose, a full mouth and a high brow, her face framed by a mass of carefully ordered clay curls that fell down her pale clay neck in ringlets. Her glass eyes were a striking blue, almond-shaped with the hint of crows feet at the corners which, along with slightly sunken cheeks gave the impression of a woman just past the bloom of youth. Beautiful still, striking certainly, but not young.

"Nell Gwyn." Cora came over and ran a finger across its smooth clay cheek. "She was an early one. Taken from St Martins in the Field, Trafalgar Square."

"Why do you have her with such a glum expression?" Edgar contemplated the turn of the full mouth, plump lips that protruded a little too much to be conventionally attractive, turned down at the corners.

"I suppose," Cora said, "it's because I think she led a hard life. She was surrounded by fabulous wealth and beauty, but she had a struggle to get there and stay there. So I wanted to reflect that. She looks determined but also she knows how hard she's had to work to get there. Anyway," she added, "if I gave them all photograph-style grins then the collection would be rather bizarre."

"Yes, fortunately now it doesn't look at all bizarre," Kate whispered to Archie who winked at her.

"Here's one you might be interested in." Cora motioned to a head on shelves above Nell Gwyn. It was a man. His face was gaunt and weatherworn, the clay left rough and scored, the imprint of Cora's fingers visible and not smoothed away as they had been with Nell Gwyn. This was a strong looking man, broad-browed but not heavy and overly masculine: there was a sharpness to his face with its aquiline nose, a thin mouth turned up in a faint smile of amusement. Chocolate brown eyes set close together, turned up at the corners to echo his smile, a head of thick tousled hair and a rough goatee beard.

"Who do you think this is?" Cora asked, appearing to

enjoy the freedom that exhibiting her collection was giving her.

"OK," began Archie, "goatee beard. Old. Looks like a sailor. Impossible to determine a time period. Timeless. I don't know. Bluebeard? What other pirates are there? Long John Silver?"

"Idiot. Long John Silver's fictional. I think he's Guy Fawkes," Kate said.

"Of course! Fantastic." Hilary came over for a closer look. "Where did you get Guy Fawkes from?"

"It's not Guy Fawkes," Cora said, turning the bust around so they could see the back. Below the hairline was a carved tablet. The four leant in to read the words scratched lightly into the clay.

Canute. Winchester. 995-1035.

Kate looked to Archie who was standing, speechless, staring at the face of the old king who had so nearly cost him his job.

"Can I?" he motioned to Cora. She nodded.

Slowly he lifted the bust from the shelf, tilting Canute's head left and right, looking at the features of the man come alive as the light caught him full in the face, on the brow, to the side, eyes shining. *The reuniting* thought Kate, enjoying the spectacle of seeing Archie so delighted. Finally, after such a tortuous journey they had found him. She wished more than ever now that she could tell the story as it was, to be able to expose *all this* to the world. But Cora had been right – the threat of being exposed as an accomplice to a grave-robber would forever hold her in check (at least until she penned her memoirs).

341

Edgar, so far left speechless by the collection, craned his neck, looking across the shelves, searching for Boudica.

"Ha!" He pointed up to a top shelf. "I know him." After suffering his ignorance over George Eliot and Veronica Lake he was glad there was one face that he recognised.

"Of course." Cora smiled and took down Shakespeare. "Quite similar to his portraits it turns out. And I have him with a cheeky smile because I think he was a lively minded man. There are too many formal portraits of him."

"This is just so incredible." Kate dumped her bag on the floor and explored further into the room.

"This—" Cora pointed to a dour woman with a stern expression looking down at them, her plain flat face partially hidden behind thick wings of hair "—is Charlotte Bronte."

"Amazing…" Kate bent down to take a better look. "I've seen watercolours of her, line drawings, and this bust does look a bit like them. But I thought she would have been—" she searched for the right words "—more *delicate* than this?"

"No, she was quite the broad Yorkshire lass it seems," said Cora. "Although her father was Irish, of course."

"Who's he?" Edgar pointed to a handsome face looking down haughtily from its shelf.

"Byron," Cora said.

"But how did you get into Westminster Abbey?" Hilary was aghast.

"Ah they wouldn't have him." Cora picked up the bust on the shelf and passed it to Hilary. "He didn't live morally did he, naughty boy. He was buried in Hucknall, in Nottinghamshire."

"Handy," Kate quipped. Cora ignored her.

"Where is she?" Hilary could wait no longer.

Cora reached down below the table and withdrew a bust. Hilary instantly walked up and took it from her hands. A woman in her mid-thirties, proud but not haughty. A long narrow face with small lips pressed tight together. A broad nose and brow ridge. "Masculine, look!" Hilary turned the bust to Edgar. "See, so many markers of a male skull, but all together it's a woman."

"I had trouble with her," Cora said, "you're right, she does share many characteristics of a male but the jaw, you see, is slightly less pronounced, and there is a delicateness to the face around the cheeks."

Edgar stared agog at the warrior queen, running a finger on the rough and ragged clay around her head, like wiry hair.

"I'm just amazed at what you've done." Hilary looked up at Cora. "It's been two days and you've created this."

"If need be I can turn a reconstruction around in a couple of days."

"So how long would you usually take?" asked Kate.

"Two weeks? Maybe more. I'd take my time researching the person's lifestyle, trends that were current at the time, looking at surviving portraits, accounts, that sort of thing. By the time I'd arranged my access to the dig site I'd already done my research, so once I had her it was just a matter of applying what I already knew and working late into the night."

"And the skull. Is it damaged or covered in wax? Is it under here?" Edgar made to turn it upside-down and Cora

343

quickly intervened and took it off him.

"No. I make casts of the skulls. I never use the actual skulls within the recreations. Like I told you in the café, I return them when I've finished with them. Except Canute, of course."

"It's a good point, though," said Archie. "When you make the cast, doesn't the material you use to make it get left on the skull? How can you be sure every bit is removed from those tiny pit marks and cracks?"

Replacing the bust of Boudica on the shelf Cora reached into a drawer and pulled out a long cardboard box. "Foil," she said, opening the lid and pulling a length off the roll, "like kitchen foil but finer. I push it in sections onto the skull before making the cast. It keeps the contours, even the suture marks are retained. And when I remove it, it comes away completely clean. Every one of these—" she gestured to the heads in the room "—was foiled, with the skulls returned in an almost untouched condition. It would be difficult to tell they had ever been modelled."

"The others…" Kate looked up from the bust of Boudica and into the room again. "Who are they? Who did you choose?"

"Josiah Wedgwood." Cora pointed to a portly face on a lower shelf. "From St Peter's Church in Stoke on Trent. Beside him Owain Glyndŵr, from a rustic church in deepest Herefordshire. Dante Gabriel Rosetti, All Saints Church, Birchington-on-Sea. I was nearly caught there too…by the vicar. Sir Walter Raleigh from Beddington Church in Surrey…"

"The reason you were caught recently," Kate interrupted

her flow, "is that you've upped your game haven't you? These are all buried in parish churches across the UK. Small out of the way places. And then you moved up a level to Winchester Cathedral."

"Yes, the draw of the bigger churches, the cathedrals…I must admit …it is growing."

"Have you ever taken from Westminster Abbey?" Hilary asked.

"No. It would be impossible."

"St Paul's Cathedral?"

"Again, impossible."

"But how do you do it? How do you physically manage to carry out the actual act of breaking in?" Kate asked. "When we got Jane Austen it was hard enough for Archie. Physically as well as mentally. Tombs are heavy."

"I usually have help," Cora said. "Two friends from the East End who don't ask questions about what I do. I hire them. I didn't need to at Winchester, I could do it on my own, and it's better that way. It was a good job too. If they'd have been with me that night when Archie burst into the Cathedral, well, he'd have been in trouble."

"Ha! I can handle myself," Archie quipped, privately recalling the agony the female student had dealt him during the television re-enactment.

"When I need help, I know I can count on them to do a good job and quickly," Cora said. "I'm always there with them," she added, "so I can be confident I get the right person and they're handled in the right way with the right level of care."

"God forbid you treat the bodies of the dead improperly,"

Kate muttered under her breath.

Cora had walked over to the furthest end of the room and retrieved two cardboard boxes, each faced with a handwritten sticker. She gave one to Archie and the other to Hilary.

"These are what you're looking for," she said.

Archie and Hilary lifted the lids of their boxes.

Inside were the skulls of their respective missing persons, placed in tissue paper. In Archie's box Canute's skull was grey and brittle, in Hilary's box Boudica's skull was brown and mottled. Neither gave any indication of having being tampered with, let alone moulded. "I am sorry I caused you so much trouble. That was never my intention," Cora repeated as the four bent over their boxes and enjoyed mutual sighs of relief.

While they looked on, Cora placed the bag Archie had given her on the table, loosening the ties and drawing out the carrier bags. The stench leapt out and everyone around the table recoiled.

"OK!" Cora said, hastily tying up the top of the bag and thrusting it under the table. "I'll trust you on this."

"So what will you do with her?" Edgar asked, recovering from the shock of the stink by stepping towards the exit and taking deep breaths of the clear air. "You're not going to use her as she is are you?"

"Heavens, no!" Cora gave a laugh. "There would be no tissue left on her but I need to remove the substances that remain in the bone itself. She's not like the dried-out specimens you hold in your boxes. I didn't need to prepare them in that way."

"How are you going to clean her?" Archie asked, despite the look on Kate's face that clearly meant *don't tell me any more*.

"I boil them. In water and chemicals…"

"Eye of toad…" Kate laughed.

"Formaldehyde, things you won't have heard of," Cora retorted. And then turning back to Edgar said, "It takes a couple of hours for everything to come out and leave me with a clean skull to work from."

Kate pictured Cora dressed up as a glamorous Nigella Lawson-type frilly apron on, boiling her vat of skulls with carrots and potatoes in a gory kitchen of horrors.

"You do that here? Or in the house?" It was Hilary's turn to look disturbed.

"Oh no. I'll take her up to my studio at the university. It's got all the facilities there as well as a stock of chemicals."

"I thought it was just a matter of hosing her down and starting to push clay onto her," Archie said. "I was going to ask if we could stay and watch."

Cora shook her head. "It's a long process and not very interesting. But I take it you want her back this weekend?"

"Yes. Please."

"Well I'll go into university this evening. Clean her up, then bring her home to make the cast. I can give the skull back to you tomorrow, say midday? I should have what I need by then."

"And how long will you take to make her up?" Edgar asked. "Two days like Boudica?"

"Oh no, not with the preparation as well. A week? Maybe less. I'm in court next week giving evidence from a forensic point of view, so I may have to wait to start on her until after then."

"So...if you're going to be boiling her," Kate began, "won't it then be obvious that something has happened to the skull?"

"It will," Cora said.

"That's fine!" Archie hurriedly stepped in. "No-one is going to be digging up Jane Austen any time soon. I'm going to put her back in the vault and no-one will be any the wiser."

"Will you send me a photograph of her?" Archie asked. "When she's done?"

"Of course," Cora said, and then, gesturing to the narrow doorway behind them, "if you've seen enough then..."

Reluctantly Kate, Archie, Edgar and Hilary filed out of the room, leaving the array of famous faces behind them, watching them go with their shining glass eyes.

Fifty-One

The hidden studio already seemed a thing of the past. Down on the Euston Road, amid the comfort of filth and bustle and traffic, the spectacle of the room filled with the heads seemed very far away: as if it could never possibly exist alongside this stark normality.

They had reached Kings Cross station and stopped.

"I don't know what to say." Hilary De Lacey looked to Archie, the box with Boudica's head clasped close to her. "Thank you. Thank you both very much. And well done Edgar, of course."

"Yes, my powers of overhearing will go down in history," he scoffed. But privately he was rather pleased with himself.

"So what will you guys do now?" Kate asked.

"Put her back. What time is it?" Hilary checked her watch. "In two hours the dig will be closed to visitors. So I'll have a word with Security, and while backs are turned we'll return her to where she belongs."

"I know it's a bit late to ask." Kate peered at the box. "But you are sure she gave you the right one?"

Hilary nodded. "Yes, and thanks to her use of the foil it's impossible to tell anything has been done to her. Thank the Lord the woman didn't need to boil the bones! Will you be putting Jane and Canute back tomorrow night?"

"Jane, yes," Archie said, "but Canute will have to go for analysis. The Winchester archaeology unit will need to verify him. And I'll need to parade him around too. I'm going to milk this for all it's worth."

"Of course you are." Kate grinned. Archie grabbed her by the waist, planting a kiss on her lips.

"And what about you?" Archie turned to Edgar. "What will you get out of all this?"

"A lesson well learnt?" Edgar said humbly and then grinned. "It's been fun. Of a sort. And what else could they throw at me that's worse than this — I am a man empowered."

"All's well that ends well, eh?" said Hilary, patting him on the shoulder.

They shook hands, and after wishes of good luck and *if you're ever in town drop by* they went their separate ways.

"I'd better call Aubrey." Hilary fished her mobile from her jacket pocket. "He'll want to see her returned."

Edgar waited beside her, taking out his own work mobile and, scrolling down the menu, he came to Erika's number. And then he hit *call*.

Kate and Archie stood before the Dorchester: neither aware of how they had arrived at the hotel from the other side of the capital. Not that the Dorchester had been their intended destination: there had been no such thing. They had simply started walking at Kings Cross and come to a standstill where they now stood. The route they had taken and what they talked about, when they talked, were only half-remembered things.

"So…" Archie began, looking to Kate as a guide to see how he should play it.

"So… We should probably stay over in London shouldn't we?"

"It *would* be a waste of time to go back tonight and come in to London tomorrow just to pick up Jane. And the car will be fine where it's parked."

"Absolutely."

"And we could use the time to plan the set-up at Pit Close Farm. And you could run through the article you have to write up."

"That would be very useful."

"It would. So would you like to…?" He gestured to the hotel.

"I would." She was smiling now. "But there's just one thing." She pulled Archie back as he made to enter the building. "What do we do about *him*?" She pointed to his rucksack.

"Oh I'm sure Canute would have wanted to stay in the Dorchester given half the chance. And I'm equally sure a closed wardrobe would more than meet his needs."

Fifty-Two

De Lacey and Edgar stood at the barrier of the viewing platform, alone in the empty old station, looking down at Boudica's body. A lone security guard leant against the defunct cigarette vending machine and eyed them suspiciously.

"What time did he say he'd be here?" Edgar asked.

Hilary, still clutching Boudica's box, said, "He promised he'd be here ten minutes ago."

The doors behind them slammed open.

"Tell me it's good news!" The Head of Marcoms strode into the station, making straight for them.

He saw the box, registered their expressions and then, laying a hand lightly on the lid he barked, "You can leave us!" at the security guard. Taking the pass from around his neck he held it out to the man who had made his way over to them. "Aubrey Tomsin-Bowen, Head of Marketing and Communications. I'll take responsibility. Wait at the entrance by the ticket office and we'll be with you in five minutes."

The security guard nodded and slunk off. His boss had radioed him a few minutes earlier to tell him as much would be happening. Something was going on. He took a last look back at the group assembled above the Boudica grave as he pushed through the doors. *What was in that box?*

"So." The Head of Marcoms slapped Edgar on the back when the three were alone. "Tell me all!"

Hilary stared at Edgar.

"Well, we owe you an apology," Edgar began, seeing that Hilary was about to launch into a lengthy explanation.

"Beg pardon?" The smile froze on the Head of Marcoms' face.

"Well, Professor De Lacey forgot that Boudica's head was in fact stored with the Finds unit because it was undergoing some...tests." He squirmed under the stern gaze of his boss's boss.

"That's right," Hilary joined in, "Edgar's absolutely right. Clean forgot we wanted to run some test on the old girl. Still, she's here now. Sorry about that."

"*Sorry about that?* You're telling me—" the Head of Marcoms looked from one to the other "—that all this stress was down to you *forgetting* that you moved Boudica's head?"

The two nodded.

The Head of Marcoms gave a guffaw which echoed around the vast hangar. He lifted the box out of Hilary's hands. "Professor you must think I was born yesterday. Still, I don't care where it was or how you found it. Just so long as it doesn't happen again..." He looked pointedly from one to the other.

"Oh, no."

"Absolutely not," Hilary added. "And Edgar here has come up with a cracking idea to generate some more publicity."

"And?" He looked expectantly at Edgar.

"Facial reconstruction, sir." Edgar said.

"Good stuff my boy." It earned him another slap on the back, pushing him close to the edge of the platform. "We'll talk about it later. Now then, Hilary, if you will." He took the lid off the box and peered inside, grimacing.

"Ugly bloody things aren't they?"

"Edgar, you hold her while I get down the ladder." Hilary passed him the box and began to descend, down the ladder through the layers of time to the first century. She was near the bottom when she held up her hand to Edgar for the box.

Gingerly Edgar passed it down. The corner touched her hand, she closed in on it and in a horrible gradual action the lid flew off and the skull and jawbone seemed to slowly roll free from the tissue paper, out over the lip of the box, pausing on the very edge, and in a slow motion it arced through the air and fell into the jumbled pit of bones at Hilary's feet, the jawbone slipping out of view.

The Head of Marcoms' face moved up the spectrum of pasty pinks to vivid purples.

"Jesus CHRIST!" he barked. "Can we not have an end to these sodding ACCIDENTS and underhand dealings? CHRIST it's worse than a bloody Shakespeare play. Hilary – SORT IT OUT." And he marched out of the station.

An hour and a half later a young man and an older woman sat in the bar at St Pancras station, working their way along a long line of stiff drinks, toasting one another as they went.

Fifty-Three

"Hey babe." Mike was pounding down the stairs as Kate tentatively let herself into the house. He dropped her a kiss on the forehead as he jogged passed her, making his way into the kitchen. "Stay at your mum's last night?"

"Not as such." Still holding fast to the front door Kate searched for what would be the best way to let him know the altered state of play.

"I was out myself. Dan called. We had a late one at the Bell. Mental!"

"Actually I stayed over in London with the Dean," Kate plunged in with full honesty. Shutting the front door she joined him in the kitchen. "We stayed at the Dorchester."

"What, that weird vicar bloke? Have you seen my football shorts anywhere? Did you wash them from last week? Oh hold on – here they are dammit they're still filthy! Did you forget them babe? Christ I'll be a bloody laughing stock in these, look at the state of them!"

"And I've just had a journey back from the capital in the Dean's car with Jane Austen and Canute strapped in the back seats."

Mike lowered his claggy shorts. "Is this about that head stuff?" he said eventually.

Kate was momentarily taken aback that he even knew about the missing head story, let along remembered it.

"Yes!"

"The Dorchester, eh? Hope the Church of England footed the bill." He shoved the muddy shorts back into his kit bag and zipped it up. "Well, if you can't trust a Dean with your woman, then who can you trust?"

Images from last night flooded back and Kate found herself grinning, and turning red at the remembrance of an evening, night and morning well spent.

"I'm off out to footy practice. See you later."

Alone in the house Kate picked up the local paper and turned to the property section. The nice basement in the nice family house was about to be tenanted.

Fifty-Four

Edgar felt as though nothing could touch him now: he had come through his trial by fire as fresh as an unstruck match. He had survived. Clasped to the bosom of proud parents, swept briskly up a career ladder to Senior Press Officer... there was no stopping him: which was why he had taken his opportunity and plucked up the courage to ask Erika out on a date.

He went to pour out the wine but the bottle was already empty. Looking up he caught the eye of a waiter.

"Can we have another bottle of this, please?"

"Right away, sir."

Erika leant back and looked at her handsome dinner partner. "Oh Ed-gar you are very good at taking control. I am hopeless in restaurants. I never get served and they never seem to notice me. You – you just have to move and they run over to serve you."

Edgar shrugged. "I guess you've either got it or you haven't," he said, without quite knowing what he was talking about, but not able to think any more deeply as Erika's foot had come to rest somewhere quite, quite distracting.

The Office of
The Right Reverend The Bishop of Wessex
Cloisters Lane
Dorchester
SO12 4ZZ

Dean of Winchester
The Cathedral Office
No 1, The Close
Winchester
Hampshire SO23 9LS

To The Very Reverend Archibald Cartwright

It is with deepest regret that The Right Reverend The Bishop of Wessex seeks to inform you that he will be unable to attend your celebration evening *Welcome Back Great Dane!* at Winchester Cathedral on the evening of 12th December. He sends his warmest congratulations on your recent success in reclaiming the Church property you were unfortunate enough to lose. He also thanks you for your kind concern over the recent marked deterioration of his health, which he is happy to inform you is improving, slowly.

Most sincerely yours

The Right Reverend The Bishop of Wessex

Other titles by Claire Peate

Big Cats and Kitten Heels

"Claire Peate writes with wit, affectionate humour and insight" –
www.gwales.com

Rachel's staring a Dull Life Crisis in the face... With a lifestyle that owes more to *TV Quick* than *Tatler* or *Wanderlust*, it's time to get up off the sofa and out into the wide open spaces before she loses any more of her best mates to the bony-bottomed, manipulative, but 'marvellous', Marcia and her dazzlingly awful zest for life.

Luckily, the very next weekend offers her best chance of excitement in months: she's booked on a hen weekend in the Brecon Beacons packed with horse-riding, hiking and lots, lots more.

And what with sheep torn in two, perma-tanned South African big game hunters and a devastatingly attractive Welsh farmer in waxed jacket and wellies, it turns out to be a much bigger adventure than even marvellous Marcia could have wished for.

ISBN 9781870206884
£6.99

The Floristry Commission

"Vivid descriptions, at times dry humour and sarcasm make this an enjoyable read with more substance than your average chick lit." – Big Issue

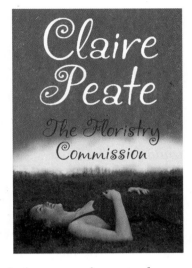

There are some things in life you'll never forget – or forgive – that mean flinging your lime green kitten heels into a bag and leaving without a backward glance...and most of your wardrobe. For Rosamund it was the sight of her erstwhile boyfriend making love to her swine of a sister in front of the fridge.

She's nowhere to go but the Welsh Marches and her old schoolfriend Gloria – after all, she could hardly run home to mum.

But if Ros thought the City was full of intrigue and betrayal, it's got nothing on *Kings Newton*. Before she knows it, she's up to her eyes in trouble with the testily pre-nuptial Gloria, planning floral subterfuge with a camp and gossipy colleague, and covering for all and sundry in a desperate attempt to survive the battle between the swoon-inducing lord of the manor and his unruly townsfolk.

ISBN 9781870206747
£6.99

Other titles from Honno

Chocolate Mousse and Two Spoons, by Lorraine Jenkin

"Witty, clever, fun and sad – couldn't put it down!" – Miranda Krestovnikoff (BBC's *Coast*)

Lettie Howells has hit a new low. This is the last, the very last, time her soon to be ex is going to leave her counting the bruises. Her housemates and super-sorted sister persuade her that she's not going to find the man of her dreams among the tourist traffic in Lyme Regis and she duly sends off her ad to the Lonely Hearts columns. From a motley crew of respondents she selects Doug – a jolly but 'once-bitten' hunk of a Welsh forester.

But the path of true love does not run smooth: there are two whole communities of friends and relations to muddy things up. Though her day job sees her serving tea and cake, Lettie yearns to paint. A trip to Doug's home town provides a new canvas and a surprising brush with fame...

ISBN 9781870206952
£6.99

About Honno

Honno Welsh Women's Press was set up in 1986 by a group of women who felt strongly that women in Wales needed wider opportunities to see their writing in print and to become involved in the publishing process. Our aim is to develop the writing talents of women in Wales, give them new and exciting opportunities to see their work published and often to give them their first 'break' as a writer.

Honno is registered as a community co-operative. Any profit that Honno makes is invested in the publishing programme. Women from Wales and around the world have expressed their support for Honno by buying shares in the co-operative. Shareholders' liability is limited to the amount invested and each shareholder has a vote at the Annual General Meeting.

To buy shares or to receive further information about forthcoming publications, please write to Honno at the address below, or visit our website: **www.honno.co.uk**

Honno
Unit 14
Creative Business Units
Aberystwyth Arts Centre
Penglais Campus
Aberystwyth
SY23 3GL

All Honno titles can be ordered online at
www.honno.co.uk *or* by sending a cheque to **Honno**.
Free p&p to all UK addresses

More than Just a Hairdresser,
by Nia Pritchard

"Enjoyed it loads. A good juicy read!" – Margi Clarke

Shirley runs a mobile hairdressing service from her Liverpool home, ably assisted by her camp-as-a-row-of-pink-frillies sidekick, Oli. When she catches Oli's boyfriend Gus red-handed, arms around devious two-timing Matt, and gets the evidence to prove it, a couple of her clients are keen for a repeat performance. Within weeks she's on the case of Dave 'n Mave, looking for clues among the curlers and clinches behind the counter... With her mobile hairdressing business taking off in a new direction, Shirley's little pink diary is the keeper of surprising secrets...

Sit back and relax, while Shirley and Oli take you on a hilarious journey round Liverpool's finest, from the girls on the production line to the perky pensioners looking for more than just a blue rinse.

ISBN 9781870206853
£6.99